THE
CELLIST
OF DACHAU

THE
CELLIST
OF DACHAU

MARTIN
GOODMAN

BARB
ICAN
PRESS

Published by Barbican Press:
London, Lowestoft & Los Angeles

Copyright © Martin Goodman, 2023

An earlier version was published in the UK as *JSS Bach* by
Wrecking Ball Press, 2019

Registered office: 1 Ashenden Road, London E5 0DP

www.barbicanpress.com

@barbicanpress1

Cover by Rawshock Design

A CIP catalogue for this book is available from the British Library

ISBN: 978-1-909954-88-5

Typeset in Adobe Garamond

Typeset by Imprint Digital Ltd

Martin Goodman's debut novel *On Bended Knees*, shortlisted for the Whitbread First Novel Award, heralded a major theme of his writing: the aftermath of wars. His nonfiction picked up the theme when his biography of the scientist who worked to counter WW1 gas attacks, *Suffer & Survive*, won 1st Prize, Basis of Medicine in the BMA Book Awards. In *Client Earth*, which won the Jury's Choice Business Book of the Year Award 2018, and the Green Book Award from Santa Monica Libraries, he told the story of ecolawyers who battle to rescue the planet from human destruction. He is Emeritus Professor of Creative Writing at the University of Hull.

www.martingoodman.com

Twitter: @MartinGoodman2

Instagram: @martinjgoodman

For

*The adults who made music in the ghetto, and
Honza Treichlinger and the child cast of Brundibár,
Terezín 1943–1944*

We create hell and paradise here,
Where love and hate blossom together,
Animating life.

> – Luis Cernuda, 'The Lover Digresses'
> trs. Rick Lipinski

Time is the *element* of narration . . . It is also the element of music, which itself measures and divides time, making it suddenly diverting and precious.

> – Thomas Mann, *The Magic Mountain*,
> trs. John E. Woods

Music is mankind's greatest miracle.

> – Alice Herz Sommer

1
Vienna, 1938

We need what the words miss out.

From his cello Otto Schalmik drew notes that went up through the ceiling and into the apartment above, and down through the floorboards to the apartment below. Otto was nineteen and stuck in his bedroom at home. He might have been quieter, but was not in the mood. His manner of playing his cello was to attack it.

Otto's head was bowed and his large ears were close to the belly of the cello, yet what he heard most acutely was not the notes he played but the tread of soft leather shoes on parquet flooring. Though stout, Frau Schalmik walked in a crisp rhythm. That rhythm had nothing to do with the rhythm Otto was playing. Why not? It was deliberate, he decided.

He speeded up a little and played still louder. His mother's footsteps stopped. She opened his door and watched him.

'What?' he said.

He sliced the bow free of the strings and sighed.

'It's a gigue,' she said.

'So?'

'A gigue is a dance. Try making it dance.'

'I am making it dance.'

'You're making it stomp about. Do you think Bach was angry when he wrote it?'

He looked at her, one of those glares that said *go away*. She wore an apron, its pattern of flowers washed and faded to whiteness. Beneath it was a skirt and blouse of dark crimson. Her hair was pulled back beneath an ebony headband. She was dressed for cooking and yet ready for a party.

'Come, set the table,' she said. 'Your sister will be here soon.'

The cloth was spread over the table. His mother had starched it so its white was brighter than ever. A grandmother he never knew had stitched clusters of tiny daisies around its hem, white on white. Two candles were lit and in glass holders.

'Oh no,' Otto said. 'Hugo's coming.'

'Would Erna come without Hugo?'

Frau Schalmik bundled cutlery onto the table for Otto to set in place. Otto's father brought the wine glasses from the cabinet, one at a time, and polished each with a soft cloth. His mother headed to the kitchen. Otto set down the last knife and followed her.

Frau Schalmik backed away from the oven and even Otto felt the blast of heat as she reached inside and pulled out a blackened tray. She handled it so the spits of fat fell back on the chicken and not into her face, and set the tray down on the hob. She turned the potatoes and spooned fat on the chicken's flesh that already showed signs of gold. Asparagus spears were aligned in an earthenware dish on the counter.

'Erna comes, and we find food suddenly?'

His mother heaved the bird back into the oven and slammed shut the door and then took a moment to set her fists against her hips and face him.

'A boy who won't stop growing resents that we feed his sister.'

'I grow on potato soup.'

'You grow on air. You grow on anything. You just grow. But today you can grow on chicken and be thankful like the rest of us. Go put on your kippah.'

'Let Hugo wear what he wants. I'll wear what I want.'

'You'll wear what I say. You'll put on a clean shirt too.'

She out-stared him. He turned and left the kitchen.

Herr Schalmik stood by the dining table, folding his own kippah down across his skull. He lifted one eyebrow at his son, and then smiled. 'Your playing was good,' he said.

'It was terrible.'

'The boy knows best. Me, I am not so musical. I have ears for music like a mole has eyes for the world. Still, when my boy plays my heart sings.'

Otto almost smiled, and went to fetch his headgear.

A clean starched shirt hung in his wardrobe, its buttons done up so he could slip it over his head. His head was emerging from the cotton when he heard the knock on their front door. Erna had her own key, but nowadays the door was bolted when they were all at home. This was Erna's knock, a light and rhythmic frapping with her knuckles. It announced her presence without yelling it out.

The bolts, both top and bottom, were pulled back, the door opened, and the bolts shot back into place. The four adults let themselves murmur as they moved along the corridor. Once inside the dining room their laughter and greetings swelled out.

Otto heard all this, and then went to join them.

'See,' his mother said. 'Look at the smile on the boy. See how happy Otto is to see you. We thought that smile was packed away somewhere, but he gives it to his sister without asking.'

Otto tried to turn the smile off, but he couldn't. His sister held out her arms and he grinned and hurried into a hug.

'Look at me,' Erna said over his shoulder to the others. 'I used to be the tall one and now I have to go up on my toes to hug him.'

She stepped back, her hands on his shoulders to link them.

'You look good, Otto. When you don't find time to come and see me, I imagine you living a wild kind of life. But you look well.'

'He looks pale,' his mother said. 'And thin. He does little but practise. We have to invite you here, Erna, to entice him from his room.'

'Well hooray for the cellist's long arms, I say. You give great hugs, Otto,' and his sister closed him into her arms again.

'All my children round one table!' Herr Schalmik opened his arms wide and grinned. He was pleased yet he was also hungry. He had done without lunch, and the smell of bread and chicken was a trial.

The mother laughed and pulled out her chair. The family gathered into their places. Hugo slid his kippah from his pocket and set it on his head while the father poured red wine into his glass.

'You'll do us the honour of reciting Kiddush?' the father suggested.

Hugo nodded, his face solemn. See such a face and you don't expect much. It was pinched and sour. Otto still could not believe his sister loved such a face, and so he closed his eyes. Hugo raised his glass and gave voice. This alone was an excuse for love. The voice came from a musical soul.

The prayer of thanks for the Sabbath settled into Hugo's soft high tones. Then it dipped and rose between major and minor keys, like a magpie at flight in a storm.

The prayer was sung. Otto opened his eyes. He raised his glass with the others and sipped. The wine was safer that way. It fired up the tongue and then bit at your throat as you swallowed, but second tastes were kinder. In one movement, the family's glasses went down and their freed hands reached for bread. They chewed, and their heads turned slowly as they looked each other in the eyes.

Otto was the first to swallow the food.

'Shalom!' he said, so loud he surprised himself.

The others jumped a little, and then laughed.

'Shalom,' they joined in, and raised their glasses. They didn't chink them, the glasses were too delicate for that, so thin with a dainty pattern of vines etched around their rims. Each person reached their glass across the table in a silent pressing of air.

And then Erna touched her glass to her lips in a token gesture as the others gulped the wine down.

The chicken was small, but even so it was a chicken.

Otto checked around. Most of the precious objects were in the china cabinet, but he could see no gaps on the shelves. What had his mother bartered for the bird? Jewellery maybe. She seldom wore it so that was something he would not miss if it were gone.

Herr Schalmik carved, though really all it took was steering the blade as it slid through the meat. Frau Schalmik served: a leg each for her husband and Hugo, a token wing and two slices for her two children, and a slither for herself. The best piece of a chicken was its carcase, she always said. That's where the goodness lies. She could do so much with a carcase.

The potatoes were lush with chicken juice. The family pulled the asparagus between their teeth. Their mouths were too busy for talk.

'You have work still?' Herr Schalmik asked Hugo when his plate was clean.

Hugo was trained as an engineer. A friend had lent him the rear of an old carriage house where he now worked repairing bicycles.

'You know, some days bad and some days good.'

'Some days good!' Herr Schalmik nodded, and licked his lips like he could taste the good news.

A silence hung for a moment. Otto wanted to fill it but he could not find the words. Herr Schalmik had returned early from work that day. He carried a small cardboard box that contained the contents of his desk. The civil service had dismissed its Jews. Otto had watched his father's shoulders shake as he sat in his armchair and tears ran down the man's cheeks. Frau Schalmik stood behind her husband and stroked his hair. All was so quiet. Otto had returned to his bedroom and played a Bach Suite, gently at first.

Herr Schalmik had asked Hugo about his work. Now Hugo should ask a question back.

'Erna,' Frau Schalmik said, to draw her daughter's attention.

Good. His mother had moved the conversation sideways.

Erna looked up. Her face flushed red. Otto noticed, but did not know why. His sister had a calm way of viewing the world. She never blushed. What had he missed?

'You have some news for us?' Frau Schalmik asked.

Erna's face turned a still deeper shade of pink. She looked at her mother, then at Hugo, then down at the table, and then up at her mother again.

'A baby,' she said. 'We are going to have a baby.'

'Anaiah.' Frau Schalmik raised her arms out in front of her, like the news was a dove she had released from her heart. Her chair slid back as she stood up and she hurried round the table to her daughter. The women wrapped arms around each other and held close, as though frozen in dance. And then the men and the women all took turns to hug each other.

'May I touch?' Otto asked.

'There's nothing to feel,' Erna said, but let her brother lay the palm of his hand on her stomach in any case. Otto felt the slight curve of her belly, and its heat.

He drew his hand away slowly.

'It's a girl,' he said.

'Don't be silly,' she said. 'You don't know that.'

'The world needs more girls,' he answered. 'God is good.'

The family laughed together. Even Hugo joined in. God was always a joke for Otto, and this was a good joke.

And so they were all standing and laughing when the butt of a pistol rapped against their front door.

2

A Front Room, Vienna

The family went silent. This noise at the front door meant instant calculations. The noise was hostile. Whoever was outside was hostile.

You don't arrive at a door and bang on it straight away, you stand a moment and listen. Whoever was outside, what had they heard?

A family laughing, that was for sure. They had all let themselves loose for a moment. They could not pretend that nobody was home.

Who had laughed loudest? It was hard to say. It was a mix, for sure, soprano to baritone, men and women both. What did they want, these people at their door? Most likely they wanted men. They were rounding up male Jews, so rumour said.

The pistol smashed into the door once again.

'Polizei!'

At the shout, Frau Schalmik jumped from thought to action. She piled her son's cutlery on top of his plate and thrust them at him, his wineglass too.

'Go,' she said. 'Take these away. Hide. Go to your room. Get in the wardrobe.'

Her hands reached toward Hugo's plate, just a fraction, and pulled back. Hugo would be the provider for her grandson. He should be saved. But the police outside had heard men laughing. They needed to find two men. Hugo must stay or they would look for Otto. They didn't know Hugo was here. They wouldn't be looking for him. They did not want Hugo. He would be safe.

Herr Schalmik moved toward the corridor.

'Stall them,' Frau Schalmik said.

She reached out and plucked the kippah from her husband's head. It would only goad them. It disappeared into a pocket in her skirt. She made her own clothes. Her family made fun of her for all the deep pockets sewn into their folds, but hands can't be holding things all the time.

Erna watched her mother and made calculations of her own. She tipped the chewed bone from Hugo's plate on top of the carcase and pushed his plate, cutlery and glass into his hand. He had to hide all evidence of his presence at the table.

'To my room,' she said. 'Under the bed.'

'Coming,' Herr Schalmik called out as the pistol thundered against the door once again.

What was wrong with knocking? Otto wondered. A heavy brass doorknocker was fixed to the door, in the shape of a hand emerging from a laced sleeve. His mother kept it polished to brightness.

Then he guessed. It was gone. He bet it was gone. Bartered for a chicken.

'You say you're the police,' Herr Schalmik called through the door. 'How do I know? You could be anybody. Show me your papers.'

A man on the far side cursed him, but papers slid under the door. Otto saw them appear and hurried away down the corridor, Hugo right behind him. The front door had two bolts and a lock. Herr Schalmik rattled the top one, as though finding it difficult.

The man on the far side cursed him again. The father looked back to watch his son disappear, and jerked the bolt free.

Otto closed himself into his wardrobe but still he could hear. The second bolt slid back, and the lock on the door turned clear. There was a scuffle, the bang of the door against the wall, the gruff voices of loud men. How many, two? No, three.

He heard his father complain. They were pushing him in front of them.

'You're Jakob Schalmik,' one man declared. It was an identification, not a question. 'Where is Otto? Where is your son?'

'He's not here,' Frau Schalmik answered.

'Where is he?'

'He's nineteen. It's a Friday night. There are things a mother does not want to know. He is where he is.'

'He is here.' The voice of the third man from the corridor. Herr Els, the superintendent of the building. 'I heard him. He's been playing that cello all day. He's here. He must be hiding.'

Two voices responded at once.

'That was the gramophone,' said Frau Schalmik.

'That was me,' said Erna.

'Two answers,' the officer said. 'How many lies?'

'It was me,' Erna said, 'and the gramophone. We have new recordings, Pablo Casals playing the Bach Suites. I'm learning. I listen to a disc and then I play it myself.'

'She's lying.' The superintendent again. 'She plays the violin. Frau Schalmik the piano. It's the son who plays the cello. They play together sometimes. It's endless. And so loud.'

'I fear Herr Els is not very musical,' the officer said and laughed. The second officer followed the laughter with his own. No one else joined in. 'Me, I like Bach. Let me judge if it was you who was playing. Fetch your cello. Play for me.'

Otto heard Erna walk down the corridor. His wardrobe door was not firmly closed. She pushed it to. Still he could hear. She picked up the cello, the bow, the music and music stand, and carried them from the room.

'Herr Els is right,' she explained to the officer. 'I'm only a beginner. This is Otto's cello. I only get to play when he is out of the house. My parents have the patience of saints, to put up with the noise I make. Herr Els too.'

She had played the Bach before. It was like a dare when Otto was beginning to fathom the music, before he bought

Casals' recordings. She had picked up her violin and instantly transcribed the cello music to suit it. The result was so alive, so sweet, that Otto's eyes burned with tears as he listened.

But she had never, so far as he knew, played the cello. It didn't interest her. As the first-born child she had her pick of instruments and chose the violin. You can't practise too much, she told him. For her, every note not played on the violin was a note wasted.

Now her first ever note on the cello would be in concert.

It wasn't bad. Not so bad. She played with confidence if too lightly. The note was recognizable, and the ones that followed fitted into a tune. It was hard to adapt a violinist's technique to the cello. For a first attempt, this was brilliant.

Hands clapped loudly, three times. It wasn't applause. It was an order for her to be silent. Erna stopped playing.

'Is this what you heard, Herr Els?' the officer asked.

'I heard Otto. He's a student at the Academy. He practises all the time. He's good. I know what I hear. It wasn't a gramophone. Like she said, that is Otto's cello. Otto must be hiding somewhere.'

'I think you're right, Herr Els. Under this table, maybe? Haussmann, perhaps you can look for us?'

The other policeman in the room made his move. The china and the plates smashed on the floor first, and then the table crashed down. Otto heard his mother's cry, and her gasp as she tried to hold the cry in check.

'So where is he? You have a clever son, Frau Schalmik. Hiding under the table is too obvious for him. Perhaps the

china cabinet has a hollow back? Haussmann, is this Otto
hiding behind the china cabinet? Check for us, please?'

The joinery on the cabinet was delicate. The wood
splintered as it landed, the glass in its doors shattered, the
contents smashed.

'Not there? I'm running out of ideas. This boy could
be anywhere. Over to you, Haussmann. Search the whole
apartment.'

Otto thought it through. Would they find him in the
wardrobe? Surely they would. Might they find Hugo first?
Most likely they would. Hugo was under Erna's bed. They
would look there first. Erna's bedroom was closer to them
than his own.

Would they mistake Hugo for Otto? Possibly. Hugo might
even allow them to.

And then Herr Els would correct their mistake.

Otto pushed at the wardrobe door and climbed out. He
could not save himself. If he was quick, he might save Hugo.

The front door was open. Otto considered running.
It looked like freedom, but it wasn't. The officer called
Haussmann stepped into the corridor and pointed a revolver
in his direction.

'Otto Schalmik,' he said.

It was all quick. Herr Schalmik was pushed into the
corridor ahead of Otto. Frau Schalmik followed, asking
questions, firing demands. Where were they taking them?
Should she pack? She must pack. Her men needed changes

of clothes, food for the journey. It would take her only a minute. They must wait.

They would not wait.

'This is for their own good,' the officer explained. 'The streets of Vienna are not safe for Jews. We are taking them into protective custody.'

Otto turned toward his mother and sister as he passed the door in which they were standing. Haussmann pushed at the boy's cheek with his revolver, to keep Otto looking forward. He was at the bottom of the stairs when he heard the loud wail of his mother's cry.

3
Vienna to Dachau

Otto stood among six hundred men snatched from all districts of Vienna, arranged in lines across a school gymnasium. His father was over to his right, he thought, though he did not dare turn his head to look. Young Nazi guards were teaching the terrors of the human voice. One guard stood at an end of each row and yelled abuse. Officers stamped in to inspect and flash swastika-banded salutes. These young guards were being judged. Their abuse had to be vile and loud and on point.

This wasn't a gymnasium of a school Otto knew. Its bars and high beams were on a roller system that let them be stacked along the side walls. Its ropes were strung in the ceiling. The yells of the guards echoed against the gymnasium's wooden surfaces. Occasionally a soft thud showed a man had crumpled to the ground.

The captive men stood and they stood. In the morning the guards moved them. The process was ordered and alphabetical. Both Schalmiks, father and son, were locked in the same barred wagon. They were sat on a bench and pressed their knees to touch each other and felt the other's warmth. They were told they were heading for the police headquarters in Elizabeth Promenade but through the bars they could make out a different route. Westbahnhof, where passengers board trains, went by on their right. The wagon drove them around to the Gueterbahnhof, the freight-loading area. Father and son climbed down and the press of the crowd forced them apart.

'Schnell schnell!' Otto watched an old man whose legs moved fast but his steps were small. Quick quick, the old man was being as quick as he could, no one wanted to obey as much as he. An SS guard raised his rifle, lined up the barrel, and shot. The old man fell.

'What are you looking at?' A rifle butt slammed into Otto's face. A tooth broke off and impaled the inside of his cheek. 'You want to be shot too? Why should we bother to drag you to Dachau to die there? You want to die here, now?'

The young officer wore the death's head skull in his cap. Otto glimpsed two men being pulled side by side, both their beards gripped in one young officer's hand. Now this one wrapped his fingers in Otto's hair and yanked him away from his father and to an open carriage. His rifle butt rammed Otto's backside and sped him through its door.

Ten men sat in the compartment, five facing five. They did as told and stared at the lamps in the ceiling. Doors slammed, whistles blew, the engine heaved and belched, the men in their seats shook against each other and they started to move. Otto was shunted from his city.

The windows were shut. The curtains of the carriage were faded brown and drawn closed. Shadows of buildings blanked out the glare of sun and then shadows of trees, and then no shadows for they were speeding through open country. Summer heat baked the carriage. Otto tuned in to the rhythm of the wheels on the tracks.

Dachau was a small town in Bavaria. One man had known this fact and the word had spread around. That destination meant they would have to cross the state border between Austria and Germany. Would the train stop? Would they be inspected? Was there hope in that thought?

Otto kept waiting. And waiting. The train's rhythm thrummed on and on. Otto let that particular hope fade.

Each compartment had its SS guard. Some guards had both a pistol and a baton. In Otto's compartment the guard had a rifle with its bayonet. He was uniformed in grey. Sweat streamed from under his steel helmet. The compartment's ten captured men went through their forced exercises while the young guard shouted: Kneel down, stand up, kneel, stand, forty times fast. One man lurched with the swaying of the train. He lost balance and fell. The rifle butt slammed into his chest.

The guards changed every half hour. A different man, same uniform, stood in the doorway and screamed the slogans he had been taught. 'You degenerate Jewish pigs. All your life you lust after Aryan girls.' The same words came from the other compartments along the corridor, at the same volume, at the same pitch and in the same jagged rhythm: 'Jewish scum. All your life you've robbed us blind.' The guards screamed and their faces reddened.

Otto's seat was in the corner of the carriage from where he could look out through the glass and into the corridor. Whenever Otto spotted an officer he must shout: 'Attention!'

Otto sprang to his feet, set his eyes to stare up at the lights. 'Attention,' he shouted.

The door opened. The officer stood there.

'Reporting obediently!' Otto spoke to be loud and clear but without shouting. Don't shout at an officer, he was told. He did as told, how a young guard had trained him. 'Ten Jewpigs in the compartment,' he reported.

It was a role, he decided. Singers don't only have good parts to sing. Operas, even oratorios, contain evil parts that also need to be sung.

Otto's compartment was in the centre of the carriage, with three more compartments to the right and four to the left. Eight compartments and so eighty Jewish men, and he listened for the staggered chorus of their shouts and hoped to distinguish his father's voice within them. He couldn't.

He pitched his own shouts a little higher, in case his father was listening for him, in case he could give him that comfort.

Night came. Were they now in Germany? Beyond the curtains the world went dark and then the sun glimmered and flared and heated them up again. There was no bedtime nor lunchtime just time. Not hunger or tiredness just fear. Their compartment was dank with sweat and a faecal stench and piss.

The train slowed, the engine died, doors were flung open. Munich, one man said, and the news spread. Men climbed down and stumbled over gravel. Rifle butts prodded and jabbed and slammed and pushed at them. A new train awaited. This had no carriages but only black windowless cattle cars. Two carriage-loads, one hundred and sixty men, were assigned to each. Otto looked for his father but saw just a surge of men. He was stuffed into a cattle car and locked into blackness. Sounds were muffled by the pack of bodies but still bounced off the steel roof and walls.

Would a song help? Otto thought about singing but his throat was dry.

He sat silent among the howls and yells and curses and whimpers and the rattle of the cattle freight train over sleepers as it rolled from Munich to Dachau.

They say it's not far from Munich to Dachau. You can go there for a picnic. For those who say that, time is measurable. Those who say that have order in their world. In their world there is such a thing as 'up' which is different to 'down'. There is light and dark, cleanliness and filth. Shit does not coat their ceiling. They walk on nobody's head and nobody walks on theirs. Screams don't pierce their skulls. Their skeletons don't vibrate with the banging of metal.

They arrived. In the blinding light outside the freight cars an officer stood with a clipboard. He was of average height but he was broad, with a buzz of ginger hair above a square face. He was tallying the men from each boxcar; some passed him by on foot, some on stretchers and living, some stretchered and dead, and it was when these stretchers passed him that his pencil slashed a mark on his paper. The surrounding guards were frantic and herded the men with yells and screams and dogs on chains, while this senior officer quietly watched and made notes.

The phrase *Arbeit Macht Frei*, 'Work Makes you Free', was wrought in iron on the gates of this Dachau camp. The newcomers walked through, onto the gravel expanse of the camp's *Appelplatz,* the parade ground where they would stand in lines and be counted at the start and end of each day. They filed into those lines for the first time now.

Ahead of Otto a guard gripped hold of a young man by the tassel of his thin black beard. This man stumbled, fell, hurried along on his knees and tried to keep pace with the progress of his chin till the guard took a hold of his hair and simply dragged him. Man and guard reached a trestle. Other guards joined in, stripped the young man naked, bound his hands and feet and then dopped him so his stomach pressed onto the trestle and his hands and feet hung either side. Count out loud, the guard ordered. Shout out one number with every lash, one to twenty-five. Make a mistake and the whipping begins again.

The guard beat him with a strip of ox tendon. The man counted out loud, a shout of pain at first till his voice vanished into a croak.

Otto hung his clothes on a hook above a bench. He tied his shoes by their laces and hung them too. Remember the number that is written above the hook, they told him. 7236.

He would remember it forever. He was becoming a good Jewpig.

They would take his clothes and disinfect them. That at least was good. After days without toilets what could men do? Otto's clothes were filthy.

Naked was odd. Otto didn't do naked, but he filed naked behind others and into the showers. The room was large. Pipes dotted with showerheads snaked around its ceiling. The men moved till they each found a space. Head back, eyes shut, mouth open. Pipes shook and tepid water spurted out. Otto caught some in his mouth and swallowed. His first drink since home.

A thin cake of soap did the rounds. The grit in it scratched Otto's skin. Men's piss splashed down with the shower water. Otto smelled it, and pissed too. Better here than in his pants. It was just a trickle. His bladder was dry. He scraped his fingers across his scalp and gulped more water down.

The showers stopped. There were no towels. The wet and naked men walked off. The next room buzzed with electric razors. Inmates wielded them, shearers not barbers. Men yelped as skin was clipped. Otto's hair fell across his shoulders and down his back. 'Up up!' The shearer gripped one arm and lifted it. Otto raised both. The shears snatched the hair from his armpits. The shearer's left hand grabbed

Otto's penis while the shears sliced through his pubic hair. All done.

In one more line, disinfectant was wiped on Otto's head, his armpits and his groin. It stung. Later it only itched.

At first Otto had thought the inmates pitiful things, with their shaved heads and hollow cheeks and blank eyes. They herded, shaved and doused him. Now he stood in a line of men and picked up some sandals with wooden soles and canvas tops, a collarless shirt, and a set of drawstring pants and jacket. The jacket was large on his shoulders yet short on the sleeves. The pants rode high above his ankles. They were made of hessian, rough against his skin, striped grey and blue. Otto looked at the other men in their new outfits and noted their frightened eyes. They were all inmates now.

'Not me,' Otto told himself. 'I don't want dead eyes. My hair, my clothes, my freedom, they've taken that, but something's left. I will be the Otto that's left. I've got to find out what it is.'

The newcomers lined up across the parade ground. A loudspeaker system delivered the Kommandant's welcome address.

'Everything is forbidden!' The Kommandant's voice was amplified to yell at them from every direction. 'Even life itself. Do not ask permission for anything because nothing is permitted.'

4
Dachau Concentration Camp

Months passed and Otto had a new work assignment. For two days now he had been digging sand. His spade had a broken handle, and splinters cut into his hands. His job was to shovel a load onto his spade, ferry it to a point eighty metres away and drop it down, then return for another spadeful.

Other men had a different job, moving boulders from one site to another. Guards yelled to hurry them all. Their paths crossed, Otto with his sand and men with their boulders. His sand pile grew into a mound. To drop his load on top he had to climb. He kept on shifting the sand from one place to another till there was none left to move and he was forced to dig at the ground instead, creating a hole. Shovelling dirt.

Was there a point?

The point was to force the men into an utterly pointless and backbreaking task, repeat it again and again, to break their spirits.

On the second day the men with boulders were ordered to lift them and carry them back to where they had hauled them from the day before. And Otto was ordered to shift his mountain of sand back to its starting point, to fill up the hole he had dug and replace it with a sand mountain, spade by spade.

The sun blazed. Headaches pierced Otto's skull. So they were out to break his spirit with this utterly useless heavy labouring task? He couldn't let that happen. He was a musician; that's what he had to remember. He had to rekindle his musicianship. He had to bring the best of himself into play.

He could hardly whistle while he worked; any such sign of freedom would see him floored to the ground by the blow of a baton. And honestly he was too weary to conjure music to play in his brain. This was such monotonous work. But it had rhythm. At the moment it was nothing but a loose, shambolic rhythm but he could take control of that. His head throbbed. That gave him one line of rhythm. Call that pulse in his head 2/4 time, a heavy, intense and regular beat. Be grateful for it; it could keep the whole work steady. And then set his other actions against it. The movement of his spade, the flex of muscles in his right arm, a pattern of fingers and thumbs pressed against the shaft of the spade, the slow tread of ferrying the spade of sand from one spot to another, the faster tread of the forced run back to pick up a fresh load, it could all be brought into a contrapuntal whole.

He could try different rhythms to set against that 2/4 time beating in his temples. What about moving his arms in waltz time, a little 3/4? That worked. His heel, his toes, he could assert different degrees of pressure on each part of each foot to bring in some syncopation. Would 7/8 work for that? He stumbled. Be careful, Otto. Don't rush. You're a musician. This will take practice. And you have a lot of sand to shift. You have all the rhythmic practice you can ever want.

Now it was to be the third day. While Otto waited in line for his breakfast, the Capo approached. The Capo was a fellow inmate, selected to give orders. He was delivering that day's detail.

'Back to the sand?' Otto asked.

'Not today. You're to stay behind,' the Capo said. 'Attend the roll call. And then remain in place.'

'What?' This was hard to understand. 'Do you mean just stand there, on the *Appelplatz*? Others go and I stay? Why?'

'I've done my job,' the Capo said. 'You've been told.'

Don't stand out. That was the motto for life in the camp. Shaved head, striped outfit, squeeze in line among the thousands on the parade ground. Martial music blares and off you all stride. Dig sand, hammer rocks, haul carts, do whatever crazed task they assign you and don't fall over. Simple as that.

So what's gone wrong?

All the thousands marched off and Otto remained; one man alone in acres of pressed dirt. The sun blazed and a migraine bit into the sides of his head.

Don't move. That's all Otto could think. The watchtower guards had only him to stare at. Keep his head erect, stare ahead. A piece of dogma was painted in white across the roof of the kitchen and laundry block.

There is one road to freedom.

That's what Otto needed. He read on.

Its milestones are called obedience, industriousness, honesty, orderliness, cleanliness, sobriety, truthfulness, a willingness for sacrifice and love of the Fatherland.

It was language as lie. A hateful lie.

A note started jabbing in Otto's head. E flat. On a bassoon. The sun rose, his head ached, and that single staccato note struck inside his head again and again. The note matched his pulse and flamed ever louder. It's like it wanted to be music but it came out as noise.

Otto stared at the words on the roof and took them out of context. He stared at LOVE till it spoke to him in the voice of a clarinet.

Then he looked at TRUTHFULNESS. It came with the smash of chords on a piano.

FREEDOM soared in the lines of a French horn.

HONESTY came as an oboe, low slow lapping waves.

Otto weaved the sounds together. And so a lone man stood on the *Appelplatz* at Dachau and a quintet for oboe, piano, horn, clarinet and bassoon assembled in his head.

Two guards came for him. Their boots crossed the square in unison and crunched the dirt but still he jumped when they reached him. 'The Adjutant will see you now,' one said.

The instruments of Otto's quintet scattered. They weren't gone. Surely they weren't gone. They were hiding.

Left, right, left, right, Otto managed to move.

Did it matter, the loss of his quintet? Ultimately no, everything goes, but right now yes. More than his life. The quintet's five elements made a whole: savage yet beautiful. He had created it. He mastered it. It wasn't a dream that could scatter on waking.

Otto in his clogs and they in their boots marched toward the main gate. He looked for his pulse. It beat much faster than they were marching. That was it: E flat, the jagged beat of the bassoon, his bass line.

Out through the main gate and the guards turned him right, toward the military barracks. Every third step Otto turned into a stamp and hit the ground extra hard. That's where the piano comes in. Come on piano. Crash. There it is. Welcome piano. Crash. And with the piano and bassoon in place the clarinet knew where to go. It had just two main themes and he recalled them. Otto pulled at the oboe and threaded it back around the bass line. You do this, you go there, you do that, he told it, and at last it obeyed; he could hear it.

Here they were, marching along, the wall now on their right. They were beyond the wall. Freedom? His horn resounded. Freed from the camp it came so loud and clear he almost stumbled.

That was it. He had his quintet back.

They might shoot him, he knew. Any moment they might shoot him. And when they do, he'll have his quintet playing.

It was a reason to live.

The barracks cast shade across the road and the guards chose to walk within it. They made a sharp right to enter an office building and left the sun outside.

The Adjutant's name was Dieter Birchendorf. It was written on a nameplate outside a closed door. The guards knocked and a barked response made them enter. The man was sat behind his desk. His ginger hair was cropped close to his head. The SS insignia was slashed on his right lapel. His desk held an in-tray and an out-tray and a sheet of paper filled with tiny figures in neat columns. He gripped a pen. Otto recognized him. This was the same man who had stood with a clipboard and tallied the bodies stretchered from the train on which Otto had arrived at the camp.

'Leave,' Birchendorf said to the guards.

They did so and closed the door. Otto needed to concentrate, but perhaps it was enough that he stayed on his feet.

5
A Dachau Villa

'We sent word around seeking musicians.' The Adjutant's voice was now soft yet gruff. The effect of his having being gassed perhaps. 'You, 7236, were asked directly. You stayed silent. Why is this?'

'Reporting obediently, the question was from a fellow inmate, sir. In the camp I am not a musician. I am a prisoner.'

'You are what we say you are. You are nothing. And yet you seem to have big ideas about yourself. You tell no one about your musical abilities, and yet you are a member of an illegal orchestra.'

The Adjutant had asked no question so Otto said nothing. He had learned not to presume to speak.

'You think we don't know about your musical sideshow? You can hide nothing from us. What we want to know, we know. If we want to know your guts, we will slice you open and stare inside. You understand this?'

'Yes, sir.'

'I doubt it. You're a pompous young Jew. You're tied to your secrets. I have little hope of correcting you, but it is good that we try. You are a cellist. Are you competent?'

'It's not for me to say, sir.'

'Another secret you're keeping from us?'

'No, sir. I am a competent cellist, sir.'

'I've received mixed reports on the matter. From mixed informants. When is your next secret concert?'

'I don't know, sir.'

'You lie. It's no surprise that a Jew lies, but it wearies me. Never mind. We have our non-Jew informants. You'll come with me.'

Birchendorf shouted a command and the two guards reappeared in his office. From the desk he picked up his peaked cap, with its death's head skull and crossbones, and spoke to the guards in passing. They shouted at Otto to step ahead of them and off they all marched, Adjutant in front, Otto in the middle, guards behind.

Where was Otto heading?

He knew of three possibilities: Execution by rifle on the north side of the crematorium was one.

Or they could wheel back into the prison camp and he could be locked in isolation in the prison block behind the kitchens. They would leave him with a belt to loop around his neck, after teaching him the advantages of suicide. Perhaps, if his hands were shaky, they would help, tie the belt to the window boards for him and kick his feet away.

And then there was poling. They would tie his hands behind his back and string them from a pole, leaving him to hang till his arms were wrenched from their sockets.

His brain reminded him of these things. Clever men have died from a brain better than Otto's. Take information, spin it around, and you've died several different ways while moving one foot in front of the other. That's how you get dead eyes. You turn them inwards and stare at death. A brain's got better things to do than that.

Otto switched focus. He checked on his quintet. It was there, a background sound in the rear of his head, but he needed more than that right now. He needed to earth himself in his body.

An abrasion on the top of his right foot had been rubbed to bleeding. Blisters had burst on his left big toe. What might a dead man give to feel such things? Otto tuned his mind to these pains in his feet. He made sure to feel the weight of his body on every footstep.

The Adjutant wheeled right and the guards and Otto duly followed. That took them away from the crematorium but not to safety. Stories told of a fourth possibility, a rifle range used for executions to the west of the camp.

Don't think of that, Otto. Back to your feet.

Right foot, left foot, each with a different quality of pain.

They passed the main gate to their right so they were not going to step through it. That meant two more possibilities for death were gone. Otto was running out of options.

Left foot right foot. Out through the gates of the service compound, and they were leaving the camp completely. Birchendorf set a rigorous pace. His breeches ballooned above the tight leather of his knee-length jackboots.

They walked out past factory units to their right and down a tree-lined avenue. A residential neighbourhood of white apartment blocks gave way to white-painted stone villas. Their steep red pantile roofs shone in sunlight. Birchendorf moved toward a villa's front door.

'Halt!' the guards shouted.

Otto stood at attention as the Adjutant took out his key. A white plaster relief of an urn, with grapes and vine leaves draped from its sides, decorated the wall above the doorway. Look up, Otto, look up, don't find yourself in eye contact and upset them, look up the way they like.

Above the urn a window box of red flowers was hooked on a trellised railing and behind that was the dark space of a balcony. Some pale figure ghosted into its darkness for a moment, and looked out. Then it withdrew.

With the door open, Birchendorf turned to the guards and accepted formal custody of the prisoner. They were to return at six o'clock to escort him back to camp.

'Go in, go in,' he said, and flapped Otto forward with the back of his hand.

Birchendorf followed, closed and locked the door, and dropped the key into his pocket.

The air inside the house washed against the young man. From the rear of the hallway a staircase swept up to the second floor. The cool breeze seemed to be coming from there, till Otto noticed it not only touched his face but stroked the back of his head too, and his cheeks. All the internal doors were open for maximum ventilation. The switch from the parade ground's hot dazzle to the spacious halls of this home was radical. All he could take in at first was this absence of sun, this refreshing movement of air.

'*Komm mit!*'

Birchendorf had moved across the hallway to a door in the far right corner. Otto's clogs clacked against the wooden floor as he stepped forward. He stooped to take them from his feet and carried them, barefoot.

Birchendorf led Otto straight across the kitchen, through another open door and into the scullery. A glass panelled door led out into a garden. He turned its key and pocketed it with the other.

'If you so much as look from a window,' the Adjutant said, 'I will take it as an attempt to escape, lead you outdoors and shoot you. If you break free and run when I am not here, I will send my troops out on a pig hunt. Is that clear?'

'Yes, sir.'

'When you are in this house, you will focus your attention on the floor. Is that understood?'

'Yes, sir.'

'Then look at it. Look at the floor.'

Otto stared down.

'Well, what do you see?'

'The floor, sir.'

'And?'

He felt the surface under his bare feet.

'Wooden, sir. Parquet.'

'That's all?'

'Reporting obediently, sir, my vision's none too clear at the moment. Large dots are floating in front of my eyes. It's hard to focus.'

'Here, bend your head.' Birchendorf pulled a lever and water hammered down into the white porcelain basin. 'Quick, quick. Put your head under the spigot.'

The shock of the cold blasted a new level of pain that eased away the migraine's throbs for a while. Otto parted his lips so water could run down into his mouth and moisten his tongue from its cracked dryness.

The water stopped. Otto wiped his face with his hands and stood back to attention.

Birchendorf lifted a metal pail into the sink and turned the faucet back on for the water to roar into it. When it was half filled he turned off the water and took up an earthenware jar. As he pulled out the cork Otto caught the smell of vinegar. It poured, clear like the water, into the pail.

'Now bend down. See if you have anything sensible to say about the floor now.'

'Reporting obediently, parquet made of oak, suffering water damage.'

'The damn fool woman we had here before you blocked the sink and left it to overflow. The floor needs sanding and waxing. That's your job. I want no wax elsewhere in the house though, where my wife might slip. You'll clean those areas with this vinegar solution. Wet the cloth and squeeze. Damp is good, water dropping between the cracks is a killer.

Scrub and repeat till each section is clean. We'll start you off in the drawing room.'

The drawing room joined on to the kitchen, and the dining room lay beyond that. Otto followed him through.

Light filtered into the room through the leaves of shrubs that grew tight against the window. The walls were papered an olive green, lined with framed etchings of mountain scenery. Cues were lined up in a rack, for the room was filled with a full-size billiard table, but a hardwood board covered the baize top.

'You're not interested in trains?'

'Reporting obediently, I'm keeping my attention on the floor, sir.'

'Do that in a moment. For now, put the pail and the clogs down. Look at this, new out of the box last weekend. Isn't she beautiful?'

The Adjutant showed him a miniature locomotive, complete with its tender carrying a shiny load of coal. The locomotive was matt black, its nose streamlined, its wheels red, about twenty centimetres long in total. It stood on rails, part of a twin track network that looped and curved around the entire tabletop. Small houses and a signalling box decorated the sidings, a lamp stood above a level-crossing pole where a road intersected with the railway, and the trees of a pine forest marked a mound of green hillside in the centre. A clock on the red-tiled roof of the station house said it was ten to six.

'It's a Märklin SLR700. And see?' Birchendorf walked off to the control box and flicked a switch. The light at the front of the engine came on. 'Its headlamp works. Anybody walking the tracks at night would see the train coming and have time to step to safety.'

He picked up a tiny guard carrying a lamp of his own and waddled him so he stood to the side of the tracks.

'This is the finest H0 set-up in all of Bavaria I believe. Better than anything you will find outside of this nation. Even in this small level of engineering Germany is a world leader. That is a secret to our greatness. No detail is too small to be perfected. Our trains are the finest in the world, and this 1/87th sized model is so too. The manufacturers came down from Stuttgart to help me install it. The trains can run in reverse as well as forward. Watch.'

He moved back to the control box. With a whirr of electricity the engine shifted forward, and then paused. Birchendorf hurried to pick up carriages from the twin track and place them appropriately.

'Two 1780 sleeper cars. Come, look here, I'll take off the roof a moment. See? They have real bunks, and these perfect little washbasins. And now the 1750 Rheingold baggage car. There, all linked. Now I'll reverse the SLR700 to connect it.'

The electricity hummed again, the locomotive began to shift backward, and then with a loud click the whole operation stopped. The air smelled scorched.

'Damn!' Birchendorf span on his heel and yelled again, at the control box. 'Damn! I've telephoned and told them. Sent telegrams. The damn thing keeps shorting. They should have insulated the wheels.'

He turned to glare at his prisoner.

'What are you staring at? Have you seen the state of this floor? Clean it, man. Start under the table. Section it into fifty-centimetre squares. Go with the grain of each tile.'

The light in the room was filtered and gentle, but beneath the billiard table it was darker. Otto put the cloth in the bucket and swirled it around, lapping the water and vinegar into his mouth with his right hand, disguising the sound of his swallowing. He had stood in the sun since breakfast, left alone on the parade ground without a drop to drink. Vinegar's not so bad. The raw blisters on his hands stung, the mixture seared his throat and the acid began to scour his stomach lining, but at least vinegar is a familiar taste. Foul though it was, it was good to have a taste be recognizable. It cleansed him and reminded him of home. It only lacked gherkins or pickled walnuts. The water rushed through him like balm. He let his head hang over the bucket, appreciating the deep shade, breathing in the vinegar vapours as his headache eased.

One set of rhythms he squeezed out of the cloth, water splashing down in thuds and droplets, and he built a counter rhythm from rubbing small circles over each tile.

After some murmured swearing, the flow of electricity resumed and toy trains ran around the table above him. Jackboots clicked on the flooring as Birchendorf headed for new vantage points across his track.

'Enough,' he said.

Otto had worked his way out from the centre till now only his head was beneath the shelter of the table, rubbing clean the tiles along the edge.

'Stand up.'

Otto stopped, but didn't want to. The work was curiously companionable. In the rhythm and the silence of his task, his quintet came back to him in all its fullness. Hiding under the table, wiping the floor, kept him absorbed and safe like a child.

Birchendorf was concentrating. He flicked a lever as a locomotive appeared. It switched from the outer to the inner track. One more flick and a second locomotive branched from the inner to the outer.

'You see?' he said, standing up. 'Everything is in order. That's what I need, this period of everything working in order. It is fine that it is trains, it is appropriate, but it is not essential. I simply find ease in proper functioning. My eyes watch the trains, and my mind finds space to expand to cover the complexities of a railway network covering the entire Reich. You came from Vienna. Do you imagine that was easy? Do you think it simple to double the capacity of the network without disrupting the regular pattern of departures and arrivals? Management of transport to Dachau provides a model for the whole Reich. It's a severe responsibility. I credit my time in this room with my remarkable success to date.'

Birchendorf watched the run of the locomotives in silence for a while. For want of anywhere else to stare Otto watched the locomotives too. Birchendorf seemed in need of such company.

'That will do,' he decided, and turned off the power. 'Show me your hands.'

Otto held them out palm upwards.

'Turn.'

Birchendorf leaned closer to examine the inmate's nails.

'That's better. Your nails were black, man. Your hands looked like they might start bleeding any moment. Do you have no respect for yourself? I thought we'd have to send you back. There's no point our taking care of the damn thing if you're going to come in and grub it up. Take the pail back to the scullery, dry your hands, and come straight back here.'

He leant forward to decouple the sleeping car. When Otto came back Birchendorf had closed the door on the billiard room and his train set and was standing by an open door on the other side of the hall.

'It's in here,' he said.

6

A Front Room, Dachau

For Otto, the room was a glare of brightness. Light streamed through three high windows edged by white drapes. All walls were white, lined in a paper embossed with the imprint of leaves. Twin cream sofas commanded the central area, flanked by white side tables and white ironwork lamps with frosted glass globes. A rosewood *Blüthner* baby grand afforded a break in the whiteness. Its closed lid was a platform for a photograph of Hitler in a silver frame.

Was this it? Was this what the Adjutant had to show him?

'Over there.'

Otto followed Birchendorf some steps into the room and saw where he was nodding to. A cello stood in the far corner, erect in a box stand.

'I'm getting a case made, at my own expense. I swear the thing was damp when they brought it in. It seems you Jews are great at hoarding things but piss poor at taking care. We're keeping direct light off it, letting it have some air. Go, take a look. Tell us if it's salvageable.'

Otto walked barefoot across the parquet to stand beside the cello.

'You can tune such things?'

Otto nodded.

'Don't nod at me, man.'

'Reporting obediently, yes, sir, I can tune a cello.'

'Then do so. The whole thing's slack. Work on it. Let me hear it.'

Otto crouched in front of the instrument. He straightened the bridge first of all, and then lifted the cello free of the stand.

'Seeking permission to sit down, sir.'

'Yes, sit sit sit. I'll tune you from the piano when you're ready. My wife's the player, but I know what note's what.'

Birchendorf moved to the piano stool and sat at an angle to watch his prisoner. Otto plucked the thickest string, which resounded several notes short of a C, and then ran his fingers round the curved wave of the scroll down to the tuning pegs. String by string, so as to balance the pressure, he brought the sound higher till he was ready for the fine tuning.

'Now?' Birchendorf asked. 'I will give you a C.'

He struck his index finger down hard on the key, and kept repeating it while watching his cellist turn the fine tuners on the tail piece.

'You're grimacing. What's wrong? You can't do it? The thing's broken?'

'Begging your pardon, sir, it's the piano. It's out of tune.'

Birchendorf looked down at the keys, as though ready to spot a fault there and demand an immediate cure.

'I suppose so. We had it tuned every quarter, but last quarter we missed. Maybe the ones before that too. There seems little point.'

He struck the middle C again. Otto winced.

'This hurts you?' Birchendorf struck the note again, then bounced his finger along different notes on the keyboard, watching Otto all the while. 'So, you are a sensitive Jew. False tones hurt you. Here, let me play you something. A little song from your home city of Vienna to make you feel better.'

Birchendorf arched his fingers and bent low over the keyboard. The tune to 'Ach du lieber Augustin' was jolted out, more or less. The left hand crashed through broken chords in 3/4 time.

'A song of the plague of 1679,' he explained. 'The drunken street musician Augustin is chucked into the pit with the corpses. He wakes, and starts playing on his bagpipe. Some who hear him run in fear but others pull him out. That plague killed a third of Vienna, but Augustin climbed free. Do you think he would have pulled faces at notes out of tune? You are feeble. You have no chance.'

Birchendorf smashed his hands down on the keys, and then slammed the lid down over the keyboard.

'You would do well to take my help even when you don't think you need it.' He kept to the stool. 'You have perfect pitch?'

'Yes, sir.'

'My wife too. It did her little good. Go on, finish.'

Otto brought the notes C, G, D and A, into place.

'So that's it? Your job is done? You don't wish to play it?'

Otto picked up the bow. It was perfection, light but weighted for balance.

'You need Kolophon?' Birchendorf asked. 'It's on the floor, behind the stand.'

Otto applied the rosin to the strings, and bowed the first note. He then moved up the C major scale, came back down two octaves, and then up again.

'Ha!' Birchendorf slapped his hands against his thighs. 'You are funny to watch. Your eyes are watering. Your soul is gulping in your throat. Yet you play steady notes as though nothing is happening. Look, man. Examine the thing. What do you see?'

Otto spun the cello around and looked through the F hole. Black ink was scripted onto a yellow label inside. He read it aloud. 'Cremona, 1717.'

'And what does that suggest to you?'

'A Stradivarius?'

'Ha. Listen to him. His voice goes thin and whiny. "A Stradivarius?" Yes, indeed it does seem to be a Stradivarius. A part of a Jew collection held in a squalid basement in Vienna. Now the cello is like you. We've taken it into protective custody. It needs exercise. Play it. Play something.'

Birchendorf stood and fetched a music stand from out of the corner where the cello had been standing. A manuscript was open upon it.

'Play Bach.'

Otto recognized the notes before reading the title. Bach's first suite for solo cello.

'You don't know it? You must know it. Play.'

The Suite in G was Otto's admission piece for the Academy. To overcome his nerves in front of the examining committee he had learned the opening prelude by heart.

A glance at the manuscript registered the pattern in his mind, and he closed his eyes. It was good to hear the opening bars of a piece before committing his bow. The prelude calls for lightness. It needs the spirit of dance. He knew that much, even if he did not always apply the knowledge.

I'm young, he told himself. I can still dance.

He pictured the parade ground in the camp at Dachau, the *Appelplatz*, and peopled it with a fantasy. In this fantasy of his, men broke rank and women broke rank, and magically there were enough of each for couples to form and for no one to be left out. They all knew the steps of the gavotte. That first G that Otto played was like the earth rumbling to life. It energized every dancer. He played and they span, their heels kicking up dust.

The cello was dancing the way a cello can, turning around the sweep of the bow.

And then it stopped. Otto opened his eyes. Birchendorf knelt before him, his right hand set flat on the cello's body.

Otto finished the Prelude, and stopped.

'*Weiter!*' Birchendorf's shout bounced off the cello and made the strings hum. 'Play! Stop when I say stop.'

Otto resumed with the last note of the Prelude, the piece's first chord, played fortissimo. It was his version of yelling back. He broke into the Allemande with its own opening chord, and suddenly the situation did not matter. A Nazi officer pressed a hand on the cello and ordered him to play, but he was a boy and this was Bach. He played. How he played! Now he was staring at the notes, for he did not know the Allemande by heart, but still his dancers whirled around the *Appelplatz*.

'Stop!' Birchendorf pulled back his hand. 'You don't know this piece? You played the opening with your eyes closed. Now you lean forward and press your Jew snout into the paper. Who wants to see you bending forward like that? You look deformed.'

Birchendorf picked up the music stand and stood it back in its corner.

'Now play. Play again. Close your eyes and sit up straight. Play whatever's stuck in your memory.'

Otto struck the G and recommenced the Prelude. He played for a few bars. It was automatic at first and then he found the rhythm. The cello started to sway in time with the music. And then it stopped; there was no movement in it, it turned rigid somehow. Otto kept playing, but opened his eyes. Birchendorf was sitting in front of him. The Adjutant's legs were opened wide and he had cupped his hands either side of the cello's body.

'Stop,' Birchendorf ordered, and withdrew his hands. 'Did I say open your eyes? Did I say stare at me? When you play, play with your eyes shut. That is the only way. So go on. Play.'

Otto's playing became mechanical. Birchendorf's hands shifted all over the belly of the instrument. They affected its tones and constricted Otto's movements.

'Stop,' Birchendorf said. 'Now open your eyes. Open your eyes when I'm talking to you.'

Otto looked. Birchendorf had risen to his feet.

'Stand man, stand.'

Otto did so.

'I'll be gone a while. Every moment I'm gone, I'll be listening. Practise. Use the sheet music if you have to. Bring in some discipline. Do you think Bach is a romantic? Do you think he gushed emotion into his work like Mahler? You have two ways of playing, like a fairground organ or like a blushing bride. That is so sick. Do you think the world wants to hear you playing? Of course it doesn't. It has no interest in you. Wipe yourself out. Get out of the way. Let me hear Bach. What is Bach?'

'Bach, sir, he is the summit of contrapuntal technique in composition . . .'

'This is your verdict? You think you are qualified to speak in this way about Bach? Did they not instruct you in humility in Vienna? Of course, you will be spiritually deaf to the Aryan qualities of Bach, his syncopation, that fast patterning of his accents, the strong and the weak, but you are a Jew. You can pretend. Stop your mawkishness and try, at least try, for the rhythm. *Fortspinnung*, that's what I must hear, this drive, this forward pushing, this constant endeavour to achieve what is greater and defy what is lesser. You give me that or you give me nothing. You think I want to hear you? You think I want a young Jew to fill my house with the strains of his lamenting? Exterminate yourself. That is your one hope. You play that cello like it's your spine, so desperate to make it shiver. That is such sick playing. This music has nothing to do with you. Strip yourself away. The scrap that remains will be a hint of Bach. You have technique. Apply yourself to that. Allow my ears to do the rest. Before I come back, let me hear Bach for a moment.'

Birchendorf brought back the music, and then his boots clicked their way across the room. They tripped a light series of steps up the staircase, and the steps crossed the ceiling above Otto before a carpet muffled them.

Make a noise. That's all Otto had to do, make a noise. Pull the bow across the strings and finger the notes. Out of the Prelude and on to the Allemande, across the Courante, through the Sarabande and the Minuets, sprint through the Gigue, play every repeat and whip from the closing G to the opening G. It was raw playing. Haul rocks as they made him do in the camp, dig ditches, play cello. Each was a work task.

That Stradivarius was a brute to play. It was a work task.

'Better.'

Birchendorf had re-entered the room.

'Now it is better. Your playing is mechanical, but that is not wrong. Bach was an organist. An organ is a sublime machine. The organist doesn't pump volume so his instrument wails or whimpers like a child. He doesn't slide the notes he plays one into another. He doesn't race his fingers through excitement or set the notes dragging because he is sad. He plays the instrument, not his moods. Show the cello some respect. Treat it like Bach would treat an organ.'

He stepped across the room and moved the music stand to one side.

'Now play again. Close your eyes, keep them shut tight, and play, only play.'

Otto began. Birchendorf's boots clicked their way over to the door where they paused a moment and then returned. He stopped and stood a little way to Otto's right. The air still smelt of the vinegared water Otto used to wipe the flooring, but inside that was the Adjutant's own scent of carbolic soap, and it was still.

Yet within that was a new scent; lavender, rosewater, lemon, maybe freesia, he didn't know. Some chemical concoction of summer infused by skin. Otto opened his mouth to take it in and kept on playing. His eyes were shut against the brightness and he screwed them tighter. The man wanted the playing to be mechanical, then he could have mechanical. Otto sawed through to the end of the Prelude. He needed to read the music to play further so instead of playing the Allemande he went *da capo* and started again.

The cello rocked and twisted as he played. It would have stamped out the rhythm if it had legs.

'Closer. Come come.'

Birchendorf spoke loud but he made no sense. How could Otto come closer? He opened his eyes to see what he should do. Birchendorf was beckoning with his left hand. He was looking toward the door. Otto looked toward the door too, even while he played.

A woman. That was the first flash of recognition. He saw no women in the camp. Look away, Otto. This woman is not a sight for you.

His brain worked at the speed of light as details filled his vision. He was in trouble. He knew that. The woman stood barefoot in the doorway. Her hair was russet brown and buffed into curls around the top of her head. More curls hung to her shoulders. Her neck was bare beneath a lace collar. She wore a cream frock that was marked with dark blue dots and had no belt so the frock was loose around the bulge of her stomach.

The Adjutant stormed across the room and the back of his hand swiped Otto's face.

'Shut your eyes! Shut them!' he yelled.

Otto held on to the neck of the Stradivarius so it did not fall.

Birchendorf gripped both of the boy's ears and he pushed close with his face so his breath warmed Otto's skin. His voice squeaked high with the pressure. 'Eyes shut!'

Birchendorf let go his hold. Otto screwed his eyes extra tight.

'Come, *mein Schatz*.' Birchendorf spoke loud, almost shouted.

Otto heard the click of the man's boots, and imagined the tread of the woman's bare feet as she was led away.

The door closed.

After a few minutes Otto opened his eyes. The room was empty.

His hand was clenching the bow. The bow's screw was tarnished but of beautifully modelled sterling silver and with a full moon mother of pearl inset in the frog. The bow itself was made of the finest grade of pernambuco. Such a bow was in the collection of the Academy. The authorities allowed him to handle it once and to play with it for a supervised ten minutes. This bow had the same lightness yet heft as that one, and the same supreme balance. It had to be a Francois Tourte.

Otto was in the living room of the Adjutant of Dachau. He had caused grave offence and would be punished. By the evening he would be in the prison block. That much was inevitable. By nightfall his hands would likely be strapped behind his back and hooked high to leave him hanging. The guards would leave him there till his arms were paralysed. He would never play the cello again. Such was his train of thought.

In the camps, doing nothing is never an option.

Otto had been left in charge of one of the world's premier cellos, and he was holding a bow by the most illustrious bow maker in history. His mind span with terrors of the future but his hands began to play. His shaved head turned to the music. His nineteen-year-old body was lanky and turning scrawny, and his limbs and neck ranged out of the striped uniform. The Stradivarius was held between his knees and his left hand pressed into the strings.

He held himself straight and looked up, for even though he often forgot to do so that was how he was trained. Do not hunch over the cello as though the sound comes from there but look up, hear the sound that plays back at you from the highest corners of the room.

Otto didn't hear Birchendorf return. It seemed he knew this first suite after all. It was not so hard. At some point his eyes closed to the pages of music and the music continued. It began to play him.

'You do not look at my wife,' Birchendorf said.

Otto was at the close of the piece. His eyes had remained shut. He opened them.

'It soils her to have you look at her. Do you understand that?'

'Yes, sir.'

'She is vulnerable. You see her situation. She is expecting our first child. A woman does not need a man staring at her in that condition. So you have learned this piece?'

'Yes, sir.'

'Good. You will come tomorrow. You will clean the floors, and then you will play. With your eyes shut. This is not strange, it is normal. My wife is a musician. She and I share a love of music. One day last year she woke and could hear nothing. She has idiopathic deafness. It is hard to console her. Sitting in front of you, feeling the vibrations through her hands and in her body, it will be something. And for the baby . . .'

Birchendorf turned his head to the side. His eyes were moistening. The Adam's apple wobbled in his throat.

'A baby is important in these times. The world is sick but we can make it clean again. Our baby needs music, good music, to be born into. Bach structured a proper world through sound. From inside the womb our baby can know this. You will play Bach. Play it, not pollute it. I'm sorry it is a Jew who has to give us Bach but that is the way it is. Jews can be good imitators. Take this music with you.' He took the manuscript off the music stand and held it out to his young cellist. 'You will memorize it.'

'Reporting obediently, sir,' Otto said, 'I have no access to a cello outside of our concerts. How can I memorize all this?'

'You ask me?' Birchendorf said. 'My life doesn't depend on it. How should I know?'

7
Dachau – The Camp

Thursday evening

Otto sat in the dust, his back against the wooden wall. In minutes they would close him into the hut for the night. He shut his eyes, ran the music in his head, and then stared at the line on the paper. Mistakes. He had made mistakes. His head shook fast and then grew still. He must do better. His eyes scanned quickly, left to right, left to right.

'You see the problem.' His father had gone off to find a musician. Now he was back with Herr Zipper. 'Tonight my son can read from the book of music. Tomorrow he must work. In the afternoon he has a test. He must play every note perfectly without the book. Otto, sing for Herr Zipper that line you are reading now.'

Otto looked up. Otto had known Herr Zipper in Vienna. They met in the basement of the Café Drobner, next door to the *Theater an der Wien*. Zipper led a five-piece band from a battered upright. He was in his late thirties. His hair was long then and swept back from his forehead. Locks flopped over his brow when he bent to the keyboard. Now, of course, his head was shaved.

'Do it,' his father repeated. 'Sing.'

Otto looked down at the paper. The music came out through his mouth, softly. Just the line, and then he stopped.

'Thank you, Otto. Herr Zipper, do you know this music?'

'It's the Sarabande. From Bach's first Cello Suite.'

'Very good. Now please sing on from where Otto stopped.'

Herr Zipper smiled.

'You can't? You don't know it?'

'Not so well. I have heard it only twice.'

'Please do what you can.' He spun his right hand in encouragement. 'Improvise.'

Herr Zipper repeated the line as Otto had delivered it. And then he sang on. It was not a singing voice, it came from his throat more than his chest, but it kept a tune.

'More,' Herr Schalmik prompted, and crouched by his son's side. 'Keep on, keep on.'

The father's hands closed around the boy's head and pulled it back. 'Don't read, Otto. Herr Zipper is singing for you. Listen. Just listen.'

He kept a hand on the back of his son's head. Herr Zipper sang, while Herr Schalmik caressed his son's scalp with his fingers. He felt the bones beneath the buzz of the boy's hair. The sung music rose and sank and levelled out in a long phrase, and then the singing stopped.

'Was that right, Otto?' Otto looked back down at the music but Herr Schalmik took hold of his chin and pulled it up. 'Don't look. Just tell me. What Herr Zipper sang, was it musical? Might it have been right?'

The boy was silent.

'So I will speak for you. It was not right and it was not wrong. I think the Adjutant does not know Bach. Tomorrow he will simply listen for when you hesitate and then pounce. So do not hesitate. Herr Zipper sang without knowledge and without hesitation. Remember that. Play whatever you remember tomorrow. When your memory falters? Improvise.'

The door of a distant hut slammed shut. Herr Schalmik got to his feet.

'We must go, Herr Zipper.' He looked down at his son. 'My boy can't bring himself to thank you, so I thank you.'

Another door slammed shut. Herr Schalmik rubbed the top of his son's head.

'Play, make it up, whatever you need, Otto. And then come back to us. Tomorrow, I will come and find you.'

Friday evening

Otto sat with his legs bent and his back against the wall of the hut. His fingers shielded the notes of Bach's second suite on the pages in front of him and shifted left to right. In his mind he was playing three bars ahead and checking, always checking.

His father hadn't come. Otto worried for him, but not so much. It does no good to imagine the worst. Imagination is too valuable for that. Survive the worst when it happens. That's what you try for.

Then he heard the quick shuffle of clogs against dirt. This was the new sound in his life; his father hurrying across the dirt ground to see him.

'Come,' Herr Schalmik said. 'You have work to do.'

'It's bedtime, Father. They are closing us in.'

'You're young. The young shouldn't want to go early to bed. Come. Bring your music and come.'

Father and son walked the avenue that ran between the ranks of huts. The sun had dropped to softness and cast long shadows. The father shuffled two steps for each of his son's strides. It was hard to raise feet off the ground and not leave the clogs behind.

'You made it,' the father said.

'The Adjutant wasn't there. It was just his wife. She shouted orders at me. Clean this patch of floor, she said, and then play the cello till the guards come and collect you. She's deaf. She came into the room when I was playing and opened all the windows but she could hear nothing. She walked back and forth in the bedroom and then I heard the springs on the bed. I guess she lay down.'

'You played well.'

'You don't know how I played. It was a mess.'

'Your eyes have light in them. That's how I know. You played well.'

'It was a farce. I'm not Bach. I'm not even Herr Zipper. I improvise and it's like I am playing for children's skipping games.'

'Then work. Learn as much of your Bach as you can.' Herr Schalmik turned left. 'I have a job for you. They were asking for volunteers. I put your name forward. You will be very good at it.'

'I have jobs.'

'Not at night. At night you lay in the dark. Now you have a whole block to yourself and it's fully lit. You are the new cleaner of the latrines.'

Herr Schalmik looked up at his son as they walked along, and smiled.

'You gave me one of your mother's looks,' he said. 'I keep my head down, but that doesn't mean my brain is not working. Give the job to my son, I told the Capo. Why should he get to spend every afternoon in the Adjutant's house? He says he is cleaning floors. OK, then he's your expert. Give him some real shitty floors to clean. Ask the Capo for a kindness, it won't work. So ask him for help with a grievance.'

'The Capo just did what you asked?'

'Maybe it took a little bread as well. What do I need with bread? Since Vienna bread has never tasted good.'

They reached the latrine. Herr Schalmik opened the door.

'The smell is not so bad. You can breathe. Clean it first. Clean it fast and clean it well so you keep the job. And then sit under the lights and learn your music. You will have hours and no one to disturb you. Go on, get in.'

He put his hand on his son's back to urge him through the door.

'Tomorrow evening,' he said as he walked away. 'I will come and find you.'

Yes, father was right and the light was good. It was so bright that Otto could even see how shit smeared the walls.

Already the book of music was grimy from his touch. His hands sweated. His body sweated. And now he was supposed to protect the paper from stains in this room of shit and piss.

He pushed the music back into the band of his pants.

A bucket and a scrubbing brush stood beside a spigot. That was all. No broom, no mop, no cloth. He filled the bucket and carried it to the far end of the room.

He had guessed right. The brown tiles contained no drains. The only exit for water on the floor was beneath the door. He crouched in the far corner, brushed it clean and swept the water away with his hands. He took off his clogs. They made a platform. He took off his jacket. Folded up, it made a neat surface on top of the clogs. He took off his pants and folded them. They made the surface higher. That would have to do. He placed the book of music on top of the clogs and clothes.

Now he was naked. And set to work.

He gagged over the first brown bowl, and threw up into the third. That felt better.

At first he walked on his arches to fill his bucket, and then he walked flat-footed. The floor became patterned with his imprints in the mess. When the last lavatory pan was done, he returned to the corner with his clothes and the music. With both hands on the brush he pushed forward at the footprints and washed them away.

Here I am, he thought, on my hands and knees, stretched naked in shit.

It was its own kind of freedom.

The film of water gathered and surged above the tiles with each push of the brush.

A memory sprang upon him. He thought of a river. It was not the Danube of Vienna and not even the Traun where it ran beside the esplanade on a family holiday in Bad Ischl. The water in those rivers was heavy and grey and serious.

What came to him was the Ischl, where it flowed out of Bad Ischl. The river carried scents of mountains and forests. It tumbled from high and gathered real momentum. He had walked on his own beyond the town and sat on the river's grass banks and listened. The river pushed forward but that wasn't the point. Its sound was not one sound from rock to rock, from source to sea. It wasn't a melodic line. It held sideways patterns where waters swirl round rocks and flow collides with flow.

Often when he played his cello his mind opened out in memory. It was usually a memory of summer; the swift banking of a tern in flight and then its white dive into a dark river; a young girl in a light blue frock running, running up a grass hillside. Music took him to such moments, and he kept on playing inside the space until his bow began to fail and the music asked effort of him once again.

Now he had no bow in his hand, just the scrubbing brush. He pushed water across the tiles, he remembered the river, and then he heard the music. Notes grew clear in his mind, as though now the latrine was clean they were ready to be heard.

It was Bach. A cello suite. He could not name it and listen to it so he simply listened and pushed the water across the floor. The memory of the Ischl remained. The Bach and the river's sound were as one. Each note that was played span off one that was not played, for absent notes were like rocks on which music resounded.

He brushed his way toward the end of the room, the water brown and thickening, and then he pushed the flow out beneath the door. He filled the bucket, dipped his feet into the water and rubbed them clean with his hands. He brought up scoopfuls to clean his groin and beneath his arms. That bucket he threw into a toilet bowl and filled another. This he poured over his head and into a toilet, the water curling round his face and chin to stream down across the porcelain.

Still the music played inside his head. He stood and closed his eyes while his body dripped dry. Dry hands were all he needed, the rest could wait. He shook them, and crossed the room and reached beneath the book of music to wipe his fingers on his jacket. That would do. He pinched hold of the music and lifted it so he could dry all his hands. Now he could turn the pages.

He turned fast and it took time. Here it was, the music in his head as an image on the page. Bach's fourth Suite had reached the Sarabande as it played in his mind and here it was on the page. He followed it through to its close where it fell silent.

His body was still wet. He would dress in a while.

The rim of the toilet bowl was hard but clean. He sat. With his left hand he masked the staves and revealed each bar once it had played in his head. Most times he was right. Sometimes Bach sprung a variant to surprise him.

Soon each note was inevitable and yet also a surprise. He read at the suggested tempo and then read again, sounding the music ahead of himself.

Finally he dressed.

Daylight was soft when he stepped from the latrine and walked back to his hut. He timed his pace to the rhythm of Bach's fourth Suite as it sang inside his body.

Sunday afternoon

The camp guards were off duty for the Sunday afternoon. Otto studied his Bach beneath the shade of the tree, till it was almost too late, and then hurried to a different latrine. This one was unused, just the plumbing in place but no fittings. Otto nodded apologies for his lateness to the thirteen other members of the orchestra as he walked to his cello.

'We were wondering,' Herr Zipper said. 'Is our latrine not up to your standards? Do you play nothing less than a Stradivarius nowadays? Or is it our music that is substandard? If so, then my apologies. This is not Bach, but it is what I can do.'

He held out a sheet of music. It was handwritten, on paper pasted together from strips cut from a Nazi propaganda broadsheet. The sheet contained just the cello part; numbered bars of silence and then his notes.

The cello was slim, all spruce with no varnish as yet, about ninety centimetres tall. Before they made him a bow he spent three weeks simply plucking it. The bow's wood was still green. It flexed with each note. Otto tightened the strings, and tuned his cello to the orchestra as closely as he could.

The music Zipper used to write for the Café Drobner in Vienna had a bite and attack which was good for satire. For this concentration camp occasion he had produced a lament in F-minor. Notes elided across the bars. Zipper raised a pencil to conduct, and the first rehearsal began.

As the last note ended the players sat in silence. Tears smarted their eyes.

Zipper rushed between them and dashed alterations into the score. 'Wipe your eyes,' he said. 'You weren't that bad. Let's try again.'

The world premiere immediately followed this rehearsal. It was a royal gala. Inmates crowded into the room and sat on the floor. Zipper made his way through the crowd and welcomed two men at the latrine's door. They were brothers, broad chested and with square heads.

'*Kaiserliche Hoheit*,' Zipper addressed them, with a nod of his head to each. 'Your imperial Highness.'

The older man was Maximilian Hohenberg, and the younger his brother Ernst. They were the sons of Archduke Franz Ferdinand who had been assassinated in Sarajevo in 1914. Now they were in Dachau accused of imperialist tendencies. To teach them their place they were assigned to latrine duties and made to shovel shit with their bare hands. To do that, you suppress your feelings.

The men in the orchestra played. The concert ended. Otto looked across at the princes. Ernst Hohenberg's face was wet with tears. That's what these concerts could do. They gave space for men's feelings.

The orchestra played their short concert several times to accommodate a number of audiences that shuffled in and out, packing the latrine. Herr Schalmik came to the last of that Sunday's performances. Otto knew the score by then. He looked up from his manuscript page, found his father's eyes, and father and son took the chance to look at each other while Otto played.

Zipper held his pencil in the air as that last audience filed out.

'Stay a while,' he said to his orchestra. 'Herr Schalmik, you please stay too. Your son has been practising. Otto would like to play us something.'

Otto looked back at Herr Zipper in surprise. He had been watching his father and not the conductor. Now he was stood to go and resume his studying.

'What?' he said. 'What shall I play?'

'Some Bach, I imagine. Play us the music you have put in your head.'

Otto did not even think. He took his bow to his cello and struck the opening notes of the Prelude to the fourth Suite, segueing into the Allemande. He left its last note to fade to nothing.

Men murmured their appreciation. Otto nodded his head, stood, and walked away.

8
Katja's Day Out

From the doorway Katja watched her husband walk to work. He did that normal thing, almost a saunter at first before he clicked into briskness and raced away. He never looked back.

She retreated into the house but left the front door open. She opened the windows too, all of them. A summer breeze passed through the rooms.

It barely helped. The taste of the air was still there when she tested for it. It was a smear on her palate, and soon it invaded her body. For a moment she thought she would throw up.

It's only vinegar, Dieter had said. She was extra-sensitive, that's all. Vinegar was the best thing for oak flooring. It was volatile. The smell would soon pass.

Well soon was not soon enough. The boy would be back again today. Day after day he was back, his tall frame tucked into a kneeling crouch as he swabbed each centimetre of the floor. Every shift of his cloth gusted stench from his armpits. It was unbearable.

She went upstairs, checking for the vinegar taint along the way. It was everywhere, even in the tiled bathroom where it had nothing to stick to. A fear set in. Maybe the stink had been around so long that it was inside her now; she carried it with her.

She stepped out to the balcony that arched above the front door. Air moved across her face and she breathed some in. Yes, this was better. Her mouth felt besmirched still, the vinegar taste still there, but maybe it was bearable.

She stayed there. Once she had to have a break to take a pee but she held her breath as much as she could and hurried back. She stood and looked down the road. The height of the sun gave her a sense of the time of day, but she couldn't be sure. It was about now that the boy should appear, surely? After his morning shifting sand around the pit. She had watched his approach to the house before. Three men marched in line, a guard in the front and another at the rear with the boy in between them. They all walked in step but somehow his pace was different, more languid perhaps, or just clumsy. Maybe it was the clogs that caused it.

There, was that them? The figures were still distant, specks of men, so she screwed up her eyes to be sure. Yes, that was the boy, that shaved head of his bobbing along above his ludicrous gait.

She didn't think. She just decided she couldn't bear it and hurried down the stairs as fast as she dared. She grabbed herself a broad-brimmed straw hat, squeezed her feet inside the hard leather of proper shoes, and fetched a basket from the kitchen. The kitchen door was still open the way she had left it so she simply walked outside. It was less obvious than leaving from the front door.

The boy was coming with two guards. One could close all the windows and doors and stay behind on guard. That was his job after all, not hers. Or they could march the boy straight back to the camp.

She really didn't care.

Turn right out of the Birchendorf residence and the town of Dachau was not far at all. Katja preferred the bustle of cities rather than small-town Germany, but Munich though nearby was no longer practicable for an independent outing. Dachau still had the feel of an art colony about it, with a ramble of streets around its medieval hillside. Dachau wasn't a city, but it could break her isolation for a while. It was better than nothing.

Katja wore a yellow smock that matched the ribbon on her hat. Her feet, though swollen, fit into cream leather shoes with raised heels that reminded her to keep her back straight despite the stabs of pain that shot through it now and again. Her basket was covered in a white linen cloth. An artist might have chosen her for a portrait of a woman in bloom, one who was contented. Such were the lies of art.

Walking was an experiment; the weight in her womb repositioned itself with every step she took. She came to the signpost that marked alternative ways to the camp. Three soldiers, uniformed and running, were carved on one of the spurs of the wooden sign. Go that way and you would reach the SS drill ground and military barracks. For the other way, a carving showed three jolly peasant types; one of them sported a cello, another a brolley, and the third played a violin, all in the company of a horned goat. It was an absurd sign that angled right and directed newcomers to the concentration camp, as though it were a place people would choose to go rather than be sent as punishment. Every step from here and away from the camp made this more of a proper day out.

An Adjutant's wife has no comfortable space inside her husband's male domain. Of course, the internment camp never did hold any interest for her. People are locked away for a reason. It was somewhat sordid to be curious about the details. And the administrative section simply made her feel sullied. Female support staff clicked around with their busy heels, almost shouldering her aside to deposit bundles of paper on desks. Their lipstick-lined mouths turned down at the sight of her. She dampened their spirits. These female functionaries saw women out of uniform as soft and silly things.

Katja paused by the bridge to rest and stared down into the river. The water was dark and dense. The sight of it chilled her. That wasn't so bad in such heat.

She walked on, her hat casting thin shade.

In truth, the path from home to town made for too long a walk. She veered left at the railway station and paused to stare after a girl who zipped past her on a bicycle, her hair tied in plaits and tucked behind her ears. Katja was such a girl once, only yesterday it seemed, the wind whistling around her as she rode her bicycle.

Still, best plod on. There's only sour juice in envy. She might as well envy her baby for being as yet unborn. Nothing lasts. Everything is stripped away.

The town's hill was so steep as to seem improbable. Her progress was through a slowly counted thirty steps at a time, unless a shop window gave her reason to rest sooner.

Her larder back home was well stocked, for supplies were brought regularly from the camp, so she had no true need to shop. The basket was a version of a game she had played as a child, when she headed out with a matchbox to fill with precious things. She would buy something pretty to lay in the basket's white linen. Duck eggs were set out in straw in a grocer's window, their whiteness almost blue and translucent. She bought four, each wrapped in paper, and placed the bag of them in her basket. Her collection was begun.

The baker was busy. Four people were already waiting in his shop. The baker was a chatty man. While her deafness meant she couldn't eavesdrop on the conversation, she was happy to be kept waiting. It gave her the chance to idle among the baking smells. When her turn came she watched the baker's lips move. He finished speaking and she smiled, and then pointed to a rye loaf with a latticed top. It joined the eggs in her basket.

Next came the butcher's. A sausage, dark and stippled with fat, hung by a string above the butcher's counter. To save her basket becoming overly pretty, she bought it.

The air outside the butcher's tasted clean. Maybe the effect was simply the escape from the meat and the blood inside his store. On jaunts to the nearby Alps she enjoyed the clean snap of the air, and could almost taste it again now. It was so unlike the current smell of home.

The thought brought back the taint of vinegar on her palate. From there her mind moved on to that peculiar smell of the boy, all his pumped-out sweat of late adolescence, really quite nauseating. The camp's inmates all showered on admission, she knew that much for she had toured the premises. The shower room was huge. She saw no reason why prisoners couldn't be marched through on a regular basis, whether they liked it or not. It was inhumane to smell as bad as that.

Her husband often headed straight for the shower on return from the camp, as though the smell of it had tainted him too. He stood there, often till the hot water tank drained dry, the water gushing.

Shouldn't the boy be cleaned before entering private homes? He needed fattening too; he was so gaunt. A sausage or two would do him no harm, only his teeth might not withstand all that gnawing. His breath gusted of poor dental hygiene.

How old was he? He was tall, but then she had a brother who reached full adult height aged only twelve. The hair on the boy's upper lip was pale and downy. His angularity looked so out of place in her living room, like a teenager pulled from bed and still in his striped pyjamas.

Others like him had amused her at the Conservatory. She spent her time with pianists mostly. Even the plump ones grew spiky and intense when they sat down at a keyboard. One in particular had excited her. His head dipped, and then his fingers arched and flashed over the keys like an army of dancing puppets. His cheeks flushed in orgasmic rapture that was possibly associated with genius. Certainly with oddity.

Her brother had kept a rat in a cage. It rattled through the night in an exercise wheel he had made for it. The exercise wheel was a dynamo with wires attached to a miniature lamp. Her brother would giggle when the rat ran and made the light glow. The first thing Katja smelled on coming downstairs in the morning was its filth. Rats don't belong in houses, and it was the same with that boy swabbing their floors. She shivered at the memory of him flailing at the cello. The visual stuck in her head. Without sound for her to hear, that wild marriage of boy and cello was grotesque.

She entered a café at the summit of the hill. The chair at her table was spindly and painted white. Her cushion was of satin and striped in gold and cream. The comfort and support it gave her as she sat down was blazingly good. When the waitress came she ordered tea and a slice of cheesecake. The order seemed not to disturb those at other tables. What a relief. So often she found she had shouted. This was a good outing.

She drank a whole cup of tea before pressing a fork into the cake. She paused the fork, for she had sensed a change. Small groups around the tea tables had grown still. Their eyes beamed her way. Women were looking between her and someone else.

She turned left. A young man in uniform stood there. He nodded his head and spoke. Her lipreading was guesswork, but the words seemed to fit.

'Your car is outside, my lady.'

So she had been sent for.

She lay some coins down on the table. With a spasm of annoyance she rammed her fork into an extra-large piece of cheesecake, chewed, and swallowed. The soldier picked up her basket and she followed him outdoors.

The smell of leather in the rear of the car was sickening, but the comfort of the car was welcome. She wound down the window and let the wind of the return journey blow across her face.

A guard stood on the front step. He clicked his heels and nodded, and then reached back to open the door for her. She stepped inside and he closed the door while staying on the outside.

That boy was in the hallway. A steel bucket filled with his vinegar water was by his side, and he was bent over and working the grain of wood with a cloth. The sole of his right foot was blistered and raw at the heel. Why clean the floor if such feet were to walk across it?

'Filthy filthy filthy.'

The boy looked up from the parquet floor so she guessed she must have spoken out loud. His eyes were so wide. They were a shockingly dark brown, almost like a black mirror. In the camp they shaved his head but left his eyelashes. How thick and long they were. She looked at the clean bridge of his nose next and the high bones of his cheeks. He kept still, like he was waiting for her to speak.

She thought back for the word she must have said out loud. Filthy. She had spoken her mind. Well so be it. She could say what she wanted to in her own home.

'You think this is cleaning but it's not it's filth and you're filth and this whole place stinks you make the whole place stink and I just hate it.'

She had come in quietly but now she stamped across to the kitchen and her heels made more of the pitted dents the boy found as he worked the floor.

Birchendorf had returned home when told his wife was gone.

Katja did not know. He was closed into his billiard room. The train set and all its landscape of grass hills and mini stations and signals and little people was cleared from the billiard table and stacked beneath it. Now the table top was spread with charts and timetables. Winds from all the open windows had scattered them. He had shouted to a guard to close the windows and then set to replacing his papers in their proper order. At the sound of his wife's return he left his work and came out of the room and closed the door again.

Katja sensed him there and slammed the basket down on the kitchen counter so she could turn and face him. Normally he bothered to speak slowly, so she could learn to read his lips. Now he just barked at her, his mouth producing a series of black flashes. She knew his anger sprang from his worries for her but even so this was intolerable.

'This isn't the camp,' she yelled at him. It wasn't meant to be a yell but she saw his face flinch. 'This is home. You don't run it. I'm free to come and go. You bring me a Jew to clean the floors and play the cello like it's company for me but it's not. It's hateful.'

She moved around him and out into the hall. There was that boy, head bent, rub rub rub, sweat gusting with every movement. Sweat and vinegar.

Her steps were tiny and rapid as she hurried past. She took hold of the rail to help pull her upstairs. It was no good. The smell of the vinegar and sweat and breath was like acid poured down her throat. She swallowed the bile but it kept rising. A lump of cheesecake clogged her throat a moment and then out it popped, surfing a yellow stream.

She turned her head just enough to avoid the Turkish runner on the stairs. The warm vomit hit the boy's hand and splashed around it onto the floor even as he rubbed.

Birchendorf sat at the desk in the front room and wrote his wife a letter on cream notepaper. Each letter was etched in place by a thin steel nib. For all the intensity, the handwriting was controlled and careful.

My dearest Katja

I want to say these words softly to you, but you cannot hear them. This is me speaking softly. Breathing against your neck.

You are living for our child. It is a duty. I know it is hard, that you want to break free, but we are not free, we are tied to this world. All that we do we do for our children. Their world will be better than ours, because we are making it so.

You made music, Katja. Now you are making life. It seems smaller to you, but you know it is so much bigger. Bach gives us life in its sublimest order, but he fathered children too, many children. He wrote his music for his children, to keep them in clothes and alive.

Music has not died, Katja. For now, you have lost your ability to hear it, but you must not kill yourself to it. It will find you again. Let it surround you. Let yourself feel it.

The young Jew disgusts you. Of course he does. I am pleased for it. But he can disappear when he plays, he is good enough to do that. I know this. I have watched him. In those moments it is safe for you and he to be together. It is not a boy, not a Jew, but a cello, a Stradivarius, and music. We are human and our progress is messy, but in that music is the order of our world. That is where we are heading, Katja. You know this, you must remember it. I want you to feel that music. I need you to head into this brave new future with me.

You are the music of my world. Life is a prison, but together we are free. Our baby will inherit a fresh new world. You will see this, Katja. It is something to live for.

You have the whole of my heart.
D

9
A Private Recital

Was Otto permitted to clean up the wife's mess? He could not know. At least he could stop himself gagging and throwing up at the smell. He cleaned the vomit with his cloth, took his pail to the kitchen where he refreshed its water, and came back. He squeezed the cloth so it was just damp and wiped at the wood again.

He heard the rests being slid back into the maplewood desk and the lid closed. Birchendorf stood and repositioned his chair. He had finished his letter to his wife. The click of his boots was muffled by a stretch of carpet and then he was back on the wooden flooring, standing beside the boy.

'That will do,' he said.

Otto pulled back his cloth.

'Stand up when I'm talking to you.'

Otto dropped the cloth in the bucket and stood straight, his arms loose by his sides. He was tall but in his boots Birchendorf was at his level.

'My wife is right. The house stinks. Your breath's bad. Are you sick?'

'No, sir.'

'Then we can hope for no improvement. You'd best rinse that bucket, put it away, and open all the windows.'

Otto held still, not fast enough at recognizing an order.

'At once! Hurry!'

Otto picked up the bucket and ran as fast as he could without spilling any water. He rinsed the bucket, lay the cloth over its rim, and stacked it on its shelf in the scullery. Pushing open the scullery window allowed the first breeze to blow through.

Birchendorf remained at the bottom of the stairs. 'The door too. Open the door,' he called.

Otto did as told, turned the key and pushed the door wide. Outside was a stretch of lawn; the full-leafed burst of an apple tree and clear sky shocked him with colour.

'Now the kitchen,' Birchendorf called, urging the boy back.

Otto pushed up the kitchen window then moved round through the hall to the billiard room.

'Not there. Who said to go in there? The papers will blow everywhere. Just shut the door.'

He did as told.

'And now the living room. Open the windows in the living room. Do I have to repeat my orders every time?'

Otto moved round the piano to push a sash window high, and then the one in the corner by the desk. Birchendorf entered the room and sat down on the piano stool.

'Come. Help me. Take off my boots.'

Otto knelt in front of him, eased the boots back from his heels, and pulled.

'My feet stink like you do. We've both been working. Good.'

Birchendorf bent, pulled off his socks and stuffed them inside his boots.

'Now stand, and close your eyes.' Otto did so. 'Face the room so I can see you when I move. I will look to see that you have kept your eyes closed.'

Otto turned around.

'You're a listener. I've noticed you. You're listening all the time. So listen for me now. Count for ten seconds in your head and tell me where I am.'

Otto started, drawing out the seconds in his head so he did not call out too soon.

'You're by the piano, sir.'

'Of course I'm by the piano. Did I say start? Now, start.'

Otto heard the click of cartilage in the man's ankle, and then nothing. He finished counting to ten.

'I don't know, sir. I don't know where you are.'

'Then guess.'

'By the door.'

'You didn't know. You heard my voice. Try again.'

He counted.

'In the corner, sir. By the cello.'

'Wrong.' The Adjutant's voice came from the corner window. 'Again.'

Otto counted. He heard nothing.

'By the door, sir.'

'No!' Birchendorf shouted the word. The breath of it gusted into Otto's face. 'Ha. You didn't hear me move. I am right in front of your face and you didn't know it. If I stand this side of the light I cast no shadow on you. The breeze from the window carries my scent away. Remember this. When you close your eyes, know that I may well be as close to you as I am now. I will see you. If you ever open your eyes, will I know it?'

'Yes, sir.'

'So remember that. Now open your eyes.'

Otto did so.

'You will now play that cello. If the sound stops even for a moment I will know you have stood up to escape through the back door and will chase you down. If you are still in this room, if you are still holding the cello, I will know you are thinking of jumping through the open window and will shoot you. Do you understand?'

'Yes, sir.'

'And if I come upon you with your eyes open my face in front of you like this will be the last sight you ever see. Do you understand that?'

'Yes, sir.'

'Very good. Then play, 7236. Play that cello as though you'll never get to play the cello again.'

Otto walked across the room and took the cello from its stand and picked up the bow.

'Please, sir, may I tune it, sir?'

'You can tune it with your eyes shut?'

'Yes, sir.'

'So long as you are making a sound with that thing I will consider it playing.'

Otto sat and he began. After some time he heard the creak of stairs under the tread of feet ascending. He kept his eyes closed. The tuning was done. He was playing.

The floorboards above him thundered as Birchendorf stamped his presence across his wife's room. Otto sensed the steady tread of the woman too. A male rumbled angry bass commands, while a contrapuntal female voiced shriller defiance.

Then silence, no more speaking. The sound of Otto's cello masked other sounds. Then air rushed against his face. The living room door slammed shut. Was somebody inside? Keep your eyes shut, Otto. Keep your eyes shut.

Katja headed first for the piano, taking hold of the ornate silver frame that stood on the closed piano lid. The frame had once held a portrait of her brother. Dieter had inserted a photo of the Führer to cover it. Such display was statutory in all homes of rank, he told her. Well not today, not in her own front room. She flipped the photo to crash Hitler flat, face down.

The crack of metal on wood jarred Otto's body and jolted his right arm. He rushed at a note but kept on playing, eyes closed.

The woman was in the room. He recognized her sounds. Her physical movements around the house – the shift of an ornament, the closing of a drawer, the placement of a teacup in its saucer – were all abrupt and loud. Otto put it down to deafness. Her world was silenced so she poured noise into it. As the baby kicked in her womb, she kicked out against the world.

From as far away as the piano, the boy still smelt animal to Katja. His hands were clean, Dieter had explained that much. The hours of swabbing the floors had wiped away the grime of the prisoner's morning work. He would not be fouling the Stradivarius. But her sense of smell, always fastidious, became acute with her pregnancy. From this distance she might tolerate it. Step closer, as close as she would need to, and his stink would consume all breathable air.

The boy's brow was moist. He was playing up still more sweat. Dieter had told her what he had ordered the boy to do. He was learning Bach so as to play with shut eyes. Which meant that Bach would be the sound winding through the air all around her.

The striped pants short on his legs, the cuffs of his jacket high above his wrists, the boy's body was stretched thin like it had been through a growth spurt. His eyes were shut but his head kept tilting and turning in continual movement, as though watching the course of the music.

She studied his bow arm and followed its sweeps and its dashes. Some people played with their arms and their hands, their brains transmitting appropriate instruction. This boy was not one of those. She watched his shoulders, broad yet as thin as cuttlebones, and the sinews in his neck. She looked down to his feet. Waves of tension flexed and relaxed his long naked toes. His fingers pressed firm on the strings. The pressure moved up the tendons and into his arm, but his touch danced fingertip nimble as required. This boy had the look of the rare ones, with mastery of technique alongside full-body commitment.

That was one view of him.

Another showed a gaunt youth flailing. There was no contract with music. It saved nobody. Yet here he was, wrapped in a soundless mania, as though lines of music could spin him to a place of safety.

Her shoes pinched at her swollen feet. She eased them away to stand barefoot, and began a gradual approach.

To Dieter on the far side of the door, the scene could be nothing but its sound. Katja had insisted on this. She refused to allow her husband into the room so he could stand and gawk, and watch his deaf wife and his pet Jew.

That was her deal.

She would enter the room if he stayed outside. He could track the Bach suite through its movements, listen out for any faltering, and stay alert for any emotional charge that might insinuate itself into the boy's playing.

Any prolonged silence was his invitation to barge into the room. The boy could allow his wife the touch of music. Nothing else.

For his wife, the soundtrack was mute. She had the visuals and the smell, the barefoot boy and the Stradivarius that made for a wild mismatch of guests in the corner of her room. The boy held the cello, of course he did, but the bow was the clear connecting force. On one end the boy, on the other the cello, like the conjoined hands of a boy and girl swing dancing.

Eyes shut, the Bach suite playing itself like an automatic music box, Otto's senses reached around the room like a blind man's. Was that the brief shade of the wife passing by a window? Was that the click of her ankle? Was she alone?

Birchendorf had the habit of coughing to himself before moving. Otto stayed alert for that cough.

None came.

Her first touch was light, the fingertips of her left hand laid against the belly of the cello. Otto felt the slight dampening of the sound, the restraint of the cello's free movement. Then he reached for her through smell. Today she wore no perfume; her smell was nothing reckless, just the clean sweet scent of woman's skin.

And then the rattling. He played on, wary of crescendos for the rattling intensified with the volume. Birchendorf would hear the noise. He would investigate. Otto guessed what it must be. The picture came through clearly, the gold wedding band on the woman's finger. She couldn't hear it vibrating off the wood. Of course she couldn't.

In time she felt it. In time enough to keep her husband from charging in? Otto hoped so. He played on as her hands withdrew. The slight tap of the ring sounded as she laid it down on the parquet and then the hands were back, left and right, the fingers sliding flat and then the palms laying themselves against the wood.

And now this woman shifted forward on her knees so that her swollen belly was set against the belly of the cello. One hand, her left, touched the cello's flank. The other rested on the swollen skin of her belly, and felt the vibrations that played there.

And then the cello was free, there was no touch. The muting removed, Otto worked to keep his playing in a restrained mode. Birchendorf was listening on the other side of the wall, alert to any tempering, or any excitement in his play.

And then came her touch. The softness of her hands pressed against his forehead. They wiped clear his sweat and then reconnected, to feel for the vibrations that arose there.

And then she reached for his head. Air breathed between his scalp and her fingers as she brushed above the soft growth of his hair.

And then her fingers moved back across his temples, and settled lightly against the lids of his eyes. Her fingers pressed in and then up so as to raise his eyelids. His eyes were made to open and look back at her.

Her eyes were grey. Some might call them blue on outdoor days of reflective summer skies, but they were grey. Her hands shifted around his face to hold his cheeks as she gazed into him and then she let go her hold and kept on looking. Their eye contact stayed true even as she settled back on her heels.

Her hands withdrew. Her left hand patted her chest just below her throat.

'Katja,' she mouthed, but a whisper came too because he heard it even as he played. 'Katja.'

'Otto,' he mouthed, with no voicing. She looked blank. Perhaps he should give her his camp number: 7236. 'Otto.'

She nodded. Only then did she smile, a light smile.

She slid the wedding ring back onto her finger. She shifted her legs to the side and raised herself to her feet to balance the weight of the baby inside her. Her feet found her shoes and squeezed their way inside them. He kept playing and watched her walk away, and closed his eyes as she opened the door. She was gone, and still he played.

Katja left the door open. She was gone no more than a minute and her ankles clicked as she hurried back. Otto played as she drew near and played on when she stood in front of him. Katja gripped the cello by its neck so all the strings were stilled and Otto kept his eyes shut and still he played. He fingered the strings below her grip and swept up a sound with the bow. She tugged the cello beyond his reach.

'Enough.' Her voice was loud and the words were separate and clear, like she was speaking for Otto but also for her husband in another room. 'That is enough. Your breath stinks. You are not well. Take this sausage to the kitchen.

You need food. There is fruit there, and milk. Eat, and rest till it is time for you to go.'

She held out the sausage till he took it. Its skin was dry.

'Go!' she said.

Birchendorf's boots clicked in through the doorway.

'I told him to go,' Katja shouted across. 'This is crazy playing. You think a deaf woman needs this? You think our baby needs this? We need a boy to play Bach till he collapses? You want music? I'll give you music.'

She plucked the individual strings of the cello, string after string so they sounded at once. There was rhythm to it. She was a musician. Each note came sooner than the last. She pinched and pulled at the strings like you would feathers from a dead hen, faster and faster to keep them all vibrating. Then she picked up the bow and scraped it back and forth, back and forth. Her hair flew wild as she shook her head.

Birchendorf rushed forward and yanked the cello from her hold.

Otto left. He didn't look back. He had learned that in the camp. Never look back.

He took his bucket to the kitchen. Its door was still open. He stepped outdoors and looked up at the blue sky. Was this freedom? Not really. It was a moment. He took a bite of his sausage and chewed till his mouth was coated in fat. Back indoors, he swallowed and knelt on the floor. He had not yet sanded the bleached wood. He would do so now. He placed the rest of the sausage inside the band of his pants. And then he took it out and ate it all.

10
Buchenwald,
November 1938

Birchendorf had men cover the billiard table with sheets of plywood and then he layered these with printed papers. Here's why, in his home at the edge of Dachau, he had packed away his train set. Dachau was to be emptied and its prisoners transferred to Buchenwald, a new camp near Weimar. Well, near enough but for a ten-kilometre straggle of roads and hillsides.

Those pages spread across his boards grouped the prisoners in batches. He had to match them with guards, with rolling stock, with the timetables of the state railway, and with a whole stack of other criteria on pages that he began to lay out on the floor.

Weimar was a small town. The citizens would not relish the sight of thousands of social undesirables in a loose shamble of a march through their streets. Birchendorf could schedule a process of human cargo in the cover of night, but that would give prisoners the opportunity to slip off into darkness. He dismissed the option.

What if he loaded the prisoners on the backs of trucks? He could have them sit with heads between their knees and out of sight.

It seemed a good idea. He spread aerial photos on top of the papers. The photos showed a small lane which wound up the final stretch of hillside to the camp. One breakdown on that narrow climb and the whole operation would snarl. All those little engines chugging away, their maintenance records haphazard at best, their tyres worn to balding, the trucks prone to mindless drivers hitting potholes. How he hated road freight. Ah well. Let that be someone else's problem.

He would use carriages for the trains from Dachau to Weimar. That much at least was clear. It was possible to equate the arrival of carriages, so many men to a compartment, with the departure of trucks. Stand men in cattle cars, pile them atop each other, and such calculations go to pot.

Besides, if his reckoning of the efficiencies of road freight had any value, likely as not there would be no trucks at all and men would be required to march. To march, men must at least be able to stay upright. How likely was that after transport in cattle cars?

No, carriages it must be.

The prisoners gathered outside Weimar station, where they were marshalled into ranks and set to march. German Shepherds strained at their leashes. The dogs kept the file of men tight enough to allow traffic to pass.

The iron-shod boots of the guards accompanied the wooden soles of the inmates and slapped a rhythm on the road. A breeze gave life to the freshness of early autumn and the sun radiated an open blue sky. Flowers grew in some of the verges. For a while there were no buildings, just men and dogs and countryside and sky. The hemp of the prisoners' clothes gave a roughness that stimulated skin. Bodies felt loose inside their striped uniforms. Heads sweated inside their caps.

Otto was near the front of the line. Somewhere back, way back, walked his father. Father and son were out walking country lanes on an early autumn day.

Goethe, it was said, stepped out this way on his strolls from Weimar to climb Ettersberg Hill. Here the great man would rest in the shade of an oak. The new camp of Buchenwald was built around this oak and the prisoners were on the same route as Goethe. The leaves of Goethe's oak tree would be shifting colour now, turning brown before they fell. With that oak tree Buchenwald held roots, quite literally, in the finest civilization Germany had to offer. Such a place could only be a transit station out of horror to freedom. Surely.

The men sang a marching song. Otto let go of the music in his head for a while and opened his throat and joined in, full voice. The song was 'Märkische Heide'. Otto did not know the heathland of Brandenburg which the song recalled, but Bach would have walked through that land. '*Rise high, you red eagle,*' the men sang, and Otto imagined the flight and the flash of red in tail feathers that turned against the blue.

'*High over swamp and sand. High over dark pine forest. All hail to you, my Brandenburg land.*'

Wooden soles clacked against asphalt and then slowed to march up a hill. The songs stopped. Blisters became open sores. *Es macht nichts.* Skin closes, wounds heal.

Heads pulsed through dehydration, and from marching waterless through the glare of sun. *It doesn't matter.* Without thirst there could be no quenching.

Otto's head ached for water. It meant his body was functioning. It knew how to correct itself.

The road entered a forest; beech, oak and birch bunched the men into a narrowing strip. It meant no more horizons. The world was closing in. *Es macht nichts.* He was not free to turn his head in any case.

The men marched toward the gatehouse. The first sight of it startled. For a moment the country march seemed like an infernal loop of a dream, for the gatehouse was a duplicate of the one at Dachau. Low administrative blocks stretched to the sides, and on top was a tower from which guards surveilled the camp on one side and the approach road on the other. Iron gates sealed the entrance.

Otto was close enough to view the gates as they were opened. A message was forged into the iron, and this at least was different. The slogan was no longer the *Arbeit Macht Frei* of Dachau. The lettering was elegant, in a Bauhaus-inspired font, and the message read *Jedem Das Seine*. To Each His Own. That had to be more than a racist slogan. It couldn't mean Jew will be locked up with Jew. It had to go deeper.

The iron inscription stood in recognition of the flame of individual existence.

That at least is what Otto hoped as he stripped naked, entered the showers, and was shaved and disinfected. Buchenwald was a new beginning.

Most men worked in the quarries. They broke and hauled stone. After work they jostled toward the twenty-five feet long lips of the four latrines. The camp had no direct provision of water. Rations were halved. One bowl of grey soup and two grey coffees was all men had to drink. You would think they would sweat it out. Yet these open pits of shit, twelve feet wide and twelve feet deep, soon filled to overflowing.

This gave Otto his job. He and his team lowered buckets on ropes to haul the shit away, five gallons at a time. They carried the buckets downhill and emptied them at the bottom of the camp. When the men were at the quarries, the level of shit in the pits grew lower. They returned each night and the pits were filled. That was the cycle of a day.

The men with the buckets had a board by the rim. It was slippery, just one black and sodden plank, but it gave their clogs purchase on the mud. Otto focused on his task while the bared and bony backsides of inmates jutted out above the pit and let loose. Some things you don't need to watch. Arms flailed though, there was a squawk of terror, and Otto looked sideways. A skeletal man, head shaved, white flesh pressed to the cheekbones of his skull, shrivelled arse, striped pants lowered to the ankles, his feet slipped on the mud and shot into the air and the man plunged backward.

They were slow in their progress with their buckets that day. The pool of shit was thick enough to break the man's fall.

Otto did not think. He took the rope from his bucket and tied it around his chest. Two colleagues lowered him. The shit passed his kneecaps till his feet found ground firm enough to hold him. Guards looked down and jeered. Others yelled at the inmates around the pit to hurry. Quick, quick, shit till you drown them both. Ashes to ashes and shit to shit.

The fallen man sat in the pool of shit, his mouth gaping. Otto took the rope from his chest and tied it beneath the man's arms. The men on top pulled. The shit pool squelched as the man was pulled free and dragged to the top. Otto waded back to the side wall. The rope came back down to him, its end tied into a large noose which he slipped over his shoulders. They pulled him up. Once on top, he untied the knot of the noose and reattached the rope to his bucket and resumed his hauling.

There had been no water to wash with since his arrival in camp. There would be none now.

'You Jewpigs,' a guard laughed at him. 'Show you shit and you just have to jump in it.'

Otto's father came to find him.

'News of Hugo,' he said. He carried a letter. Otto recognized his mother's handwriting and reached out for it.

'Your mother cannot be as clear as she likes,' Herr Schalmik said, and handed over the letter. 'She knows our mail is censored.'

Otto read. 'She's clear,' he said. 'She asks us to say Kaddish. Hugo is dead.'

Hugo had taken to living in the back of his friend's garage, where he repaired his bicycles. He had no papers for such a business. They came for him. He tried to fight and run but he was never a good fighter, never a good runner.

'She does not say he is dead. We should keep an eye out for him. They might send him here.'

'And that would be good news?' Otto asked.

He found his way to his father's hut before bed that night. Men sat in the door and began the prayer. 'Yitgaddal veyitqaddash shemei rabba.' They were the opening words of the Kaddish, the Jewish prayer for the dead. Otto's lips moved, and a murmur came out. 'Be'alma di vra khiruteh.'

And then silence took over. How could he praise God's name? What was this God whose people were herded to oblivion?

The rabbi noticed. He stepped up to Otto's side as the men walked into the cold.

'Your father is a good man,' the rabbi told him. 'And I am sure your mother is a good woman. They brought you up well. I know this. When someone dies, you speak to God. They told you this. It is a big step, to leave this life and be with God. When you say Kaddish, out loud and strong, you build a bridge to God. The dead hear the living, and know which way to go.'

'If the dead can hear the living, why can't they just come back?' Otto asked.

'You would come back? Even to this?' the rabbi said. 'Then why do I worry about you? You have your God.'

Erna had her baby. Another letter told them this. It was a baby girl who was beautiful and heavy although the birth was long and hard. One thing was lucky. The baby was born in the Jewish Women's Hospital, where Frau Schalmik had found a job. She heard Erna scream and left her mop and bucket in the corridor and went right to her. They called the baby Greta. Mother and daughter were healthy and would go home soon. Frau Schalmik would give up the apartment and go join them. It was for the best.

'Why?' Otto asked his father. 'Erna's place is tiny. There's only one bed. Will Mother sleep on the sofa?'

Herr Schalmik blinked. The letter was all he knew.

'Erna's is near the hospital,' he tried. 'It will make your mother's new job easier. And she can rent our place out. The extra money will be good, till we can both go home.'

Ah yes, home. They would both go back one day. Otto would pick up his cello and play his records and resume his education. His mother would bake chicken and his father find a new job with a kinder government. Erna and Hugo . . . Well, Erna and now Greta . . . would visit every

Friday and stay over. His father still felt the past contained the future.

Once Otto was a son who argued back all the time. Now he just smiled at his father and handed back the letter.

The night was clear. Stars glitzed like ice. Two men had escaped. All the inmates stood outdoors, in their thin uniforms. They must stay there until the escapees were captured and returned.

Breath misted from noses as the temperature sank. The cold bit at Otto's throat. Fingers grew blue and numb as they hung by men's sides. The freeze was coating Otto's hands. It crept in beneath the skin to settle into his bones.

He alerted his brain to the lively presence of his heart, and to the blood that flowed from its surface. Go, blood, go to the hands, to the feet. Hold your nerve. Maintain your flow. Beat back the cold.

He sensed the cold on his scalp, and the ice that grated around his ears, and to his scalp and his ears he sent the blood. His mind had no place for Bach now, but this was also Bach, this unifying flow of warm blood around the extremities of his body.

Night endured and still the prisoners stood, motionless.

Otto shifted weight between his feet, and flexed and relaxed his muscles in a regular sequence. Toes to head and back again, he exercised each part of his body in tiny, undetectable movements.

Men fell. He heard them, and the beatings from officers who forced the fallen to rise. Some men would not stir however hard they were prodded. They were dead. Their corpses were stretchered away.

Flow, blood, flow.

Frostbite was eating at men nearby. Otto stayed alert, and directed the coursing of his blood.

The sun rose low and smeared colour into the sky. One escapee had been found and shot. Another was returned. He was hanged as morning entertainment for the inmates. They were made to watch him spasm.

At noon the November sun had height but little power. The clay ground remained frozen. That was something. Men had frostbitten toes. It would be hard to step through mud. They were released from parade.

Otto had kept the blood flowing to the tips of each of his toes. They were not frost bitten. When they needed men to clear the corpses from the parade ground, he volunteered.

The bodies were light. With two men to a stretcher it was easy work. They stripped the clothes from each dead man and replaced them with a paper shirt. The bodies were stacked in a row beside the outer fence. Otto preferred not to count them, and instead to consider each man as an individual, but the range of paper-shirted corpses was too stark not to tally. Sixty-three.

A young guard stood beside the bodies as they were stacked together.

'These were the old ones, no?' His young body was protected by a greatcoat. The deaths had shocked him. He needed to talk. 'The sick ones. Winter always takes the old and the sick.'

'They were not old and they were not sick,' Otto answered. 'They were like you.'

11
Terezín, 1943–44

This is a thin tale. Oddly, it all happens in summer because Otto did not care to imagine cold winds, snow and mud. Challenge him and he might have admitted to foolishness, but for him this scrap of story was something like a flowerbed. He tilled it, planted it, and this is what came up. You can accept your flowerbed looks bare and bleak in winter, but you don't dwell on it. Its purpose is the flowers.

He didn't bother to place the women in his family, his mother and sister and their little girl Greta, in the railway trucks that transported them from Vienna. He didn't wish to go there. Railway tracks as far as Terezín's walls were still being built, so in his mind he joined the women and their little girl when they had walked close to the town's gates. Greta had her own miniature case, between her mother and grandmother who carried two cases each.

He learned that they got to keep their own clothes inside the ghetto and nobody sheared off their hair. Otto was so glad of that. In this town guards wore uniforms while the normal folk in regular clothes wore a yellow star on their sleeves, 'Jude' written at its heart. You could pretend it was a badge of belonging.

This version of the story is selective. It's bitter enough. It's what Otto chose to bear.

Greta was nearly four. She should lodge in one of the children's wards.

The girl's fists bunched hold of her mother's blouse. When officials tried to pull her away the blouse ripped. They let her stay. Of course there were complaints, couldn't she be squeezed onto her mother's mattress instead of getting one of her own? But then one squib of a girl in a room packed so full of women hardly mattered.

And then it mattered a lot. Sometimes sadness is too much for a woman to bear. Greta was always the first to recognize such sadness. Her warm brown eyes reached you through the gloom somehow, staring and staring till you looked back and smiled. You could be up on the third row of bunks, your arm looped across your eyes to hide you away, and still this little girl would find you. Greta was a good climber. She rooted out sadness.

The women taught her songs, Czech songs and German songs, and when Greta sang the words in her sweet girl's voice it made the women tremble with memories.

Greta went out into the streets and brought back stories. She met a child, she said. And then another child. They ran on dust and then they ran on grass. She hugged a tree. Be careful, Frau Schalmik warned her, stay off the grass, don't touch the trees, they're out of bounds, but it was good she had these thrills. At school they gave her a book while others learned to read. She was already a good reader.

A famous singer, Karel Berman, came to live in the camp. Down in a cellar he pumped a harmonium with his feet and his fingers trilled tunes and crushed chords. He was a bass but he sang every other part too, even the women's, and with his fingers and feet and voices he performed an entire one-man opera. It was *The Bartered Bride*.

Frau Schalmik watched Greta watch the performance. She waited to see her little granddaughter blink. She didn't seem to. Her eyes were simply wide open all the time and her mouth hung open in astonishment. When the music was finished Greta stood in the silence, and then she cried. Frau Schalmik picked her up and held her close and carried her back to their room.

The town was filled with music, hidden away in its basements and attics and corners. Of course it was. Steal the Jews from a city such as Prague and you find the finest artists among them. The Council of Elders decided to give jobs to musicians. It helped if you smuggled your instrument in. A man dismantled his cello and wrapped the pieces and a tube of glue in a blanket. They made him a cellist.

Erna had put her violin in her suitcase instead of some clothes. It made it less heavy so she carried it with ease. The German officers at the gate pulled those aside who were struggling with the weight of their luggage. They opened cases and took away surplus for distribution. Erna they let through the gates without checking. The Elders did not allow women to be working musicians but they let her use her instrument when men had no need of it.

Erna became a baker. She rose extra early at three in the morning before the dough had need of her. A friend called Hana slipped down from her bunk and into the warm slot of Erna's bed where she held on to little Greta who always slid across from her own slim space for company.

Erna's job started at five. Until then she practised the violin in empty offices.

The kneading of the dough strengthened her arms. For weeks she rose and practised, and then an evening came when women packed into an attic. Erna made no announcement. She just tucked the violin under her chin and played Bach's Sonata in A Major. Most had never heard anything like it. 'It's like watching birds all your life,' one woman said, 'and then suddenly it's you that's flying.'

When the Bach was done and the women had settled, Greta stepped forward. Erna lifted her bow and played the melody for one verse. It was Brahms's 'Wiegenlied', his lullaby. With the tune established, Greta took over. Her voice was pure and clear, and Erna underpinned it with a little pizzicato waltz rhythm.

For a while the women let the song go silent and sat and bathed in the feeling it gave them. Frau Schalmik's cheeks were round with smiles and wet with tears. And then the women clapped. They clapped so hard.

Erna smiled, and Greta bobbed a curtsey, and then Erna picked up the violin and started again. The women thought it was to be an encore, the 'Wiegenlied' again, and indeed it was, but when Greta opened her mouth, the words that came out were in Czech. The notes were flawless, and the words all perfect.

'Your little granddaughter's an angel,' the woman beside Frau Schalmik said.

'She's a girl,' Frau Schalmik corrected, because that's all she wanted her to be, but she was pleased with the comment even so.

Erna's friend Hana likened the composer Hans Krása to a bloodhound, with that furrowed brow of his, those dark eyes, and lines that creased his mouth. She laughed when she said it, and she followed the composer about like a puppy. Some women love serious men.

Hans Krása had achieved in the world beyond the garrison's walls. His children's opera *Brundibár* received a proper performance in an orphanage. Krása missed it. He was locked up in the garrison town by then, and the authorities did not give day passes. Soon the orphanage was closed and the children and staff were transported to join Krása in Terezín.

A young man from the orphanage brought the piano score of *Brundibár* with him and gave it to Krása. The stage manager of the Czech National Theatre was on hand to design and build the sets. And children were on hand to be children. Find him someone to be the star turn of his little opera, and they would all put on a show together.

Enter a fourteen-year-old from Ward 9. At six years old Honza's parents died and he moved in with his uncle and aunt and cousins in their home in the town of Pilsen. Now they had all moved together, from Pilsen to Terezín.

Some kids have a strut, a natural swagger that says bring it on, I don't care. Honza had that. He was sweet on Lena from Room 9 and everyone was sweet on him. He could make you laugh. 'What about me?' he said to Krása, bold as you like. 'I could star in your opera.' Though fourteen the boy had the body of an imp. He had a mop of black hair. They clipped a bushy black moustache to his nose. (A toothbrush moustache would have been less subtle, and would have got them all killed.) And so Honza became Brundibár, a man who owns a barrel organ. What's not to like about such a life? He turns a handle, music resounds, and people pay him for his tunes. Hooray for the simple life.

In a loft above a boys' ward children gathered to rehearse. This is the story their little show told.

In a hovel in the town, a doctor sits by the sickbed of a woman. The woman has no husband, only a son and a daughter. She will not get better without milk to drink. The children have no money for milk. All they have are voices. They stand side by side in the market square and sing for their mother's life. Their voices are thin and vanish into open air.

The very presence of singing children outrages Brundibár the organ grinder. All money from music must be his. With adult fury on his side, he chases the children away.

Children can overcome adults, especially when a cat, a sparrow and a dog are there to give advice, and those are the creatures who enter the stage. No one hears the voices of two children, the friendly creatures say. What about the voices of twenty? Or forty?

Twenty girls and twenty boys amass into a powerful chorus. Lone voices might be snuffed out, but children who sing with one voice can beat back evil.

The children sing. Now that they give voice together they are loud enough for anyone to hear. Passers-by pour money into the boy and girl's hat.

Where's Brundibár?

Honza turns up, deep inside his starring role. He is shocked. He is furious. He stares out at the audience and flexes his nose. His moustache dips one way and then the other, like an aeroplane's wings in flight. Children in the audience had been sitting in terror. Now a sigh of relief breathes out from them. Some adults laugh. He's game, that Honza. A natural comic.

Brundibár grabs the hatful of coins and runs off. The children give chase. The organ grinder is defeated. The mother gets her milk. Children fill the stage and sing out their final song as though their lives depended on it.

The show runs and runs, as they say. Fights break out over tickets, it's such a success. The cast is occasionally broken when a child gets sick, when malnutrition bites, when one is shipped to the death camps at Auschwitz or Trostinets. And so others get their chance.

And when it seems the run is at an end, Hans Krása is commanded to deliver a full orchestral score. Bigger sets with brighter colours are built for a large outdoor stage. The Camp Commandant has visitors due. They are from the International Red Cross. They need to see what a cultured and humanized camp the Nazis are running. *Brundibár* is prepared for a gala performance.

The Red Cross inspectors must not find the camp too crowded. It was time for the old and the sick to move on. Inspectors would appreciate a more youthful crowd. Seven thousand were corralled onto trains. Mistakenly, because the old and the young are not so easily separated, a child or two from the cast were despatched in the process. They and their families chugged off on the train to concentration camps in the East. That left the director with a problem.

Rudolf Freudenfeld was twenty-two when he entered the camp, the piano score of *Brundibár* smuggled with him. His father ran the Jewish orphanage, so he knew how to steer children toward life when they have just faced death. He needed more members for his cast. And he had heard of how Erna the violinist and her little singing daughter performed Brahms's 'Wiegenlied' in gatherings around town. OK Greta was only five, but she could sing in Czech. Surely she could learn the songs and join the chorus as one of the girls?

Frau Schalmik worked in the garment shop, where she repaired clothes. She sewed a quick costume for Greta, and then they gave her time off to sit at a piano and teach Greta the songs. The girl learned them so quickly. Frau Schalmik went to watch her in rehearsal. Greta was the youngest and the tiniest yet it did not matter. She took to the stage with the other boys and girls as though she had had playmates all her life.

On stage, the children were allowed to dispense with their yellow stars. They had no need to parade as Jewish children; they were simply children. The dog, the cat and the sparrow? Well, they were like the pets that children have. In *Brundibár* children befriended animals. Carts brought ice cream for sale and milk came in bottles. Policemen were friendly. Greta sang and she danced.

Beyond the rehearsal room, work groups created playgrounds and children were assigned play duty. Rose bushes began to appear. Imagine that, rose bushes in December! Crews applied mortar to the barracks that fronted the main streets, and bright curtains appeared in their windows. With those thousands of inmates removed from the ghetto, third tiers of bunks were removed. There was room to breathe. Still more striking, shops that had been fronted by dirty windows now had proper window displays. And what's this, a bank? Suddenly they all had a bank in which to deposit their new ghetto currency.

The Red Cross inspectors were imminent; there was still so much to do. The fence was removed from the main town square. Circus tents had filled it, containing assembly lines where people worked in wartime construction. The square was now transformed into a city park, where a jazz combo spun music out of a new wooden pavilion. 'Bugle Hall Rag' they played, and 'Bei Mir Bist du Schön'. Out in the crisp air, a hundred men and women formed a choir and their voices opened out into Verdi's *Requiem*. You couldn't turn a corner without coming across an acting troupe rehearsing scenes before their own pocket audience.

Carpenters began work on the outdoor stage and the painted flats for the children's opera were hoisted into place. All was so close now. Teams washed the trim pathways along the main street, and even the street itself was swept with soapy water. Frau Schalmik stepped across the suds and climbed up to a loft. She settled in for *Brundibár*'s final off-stage rehearsal.

Yes, Frau Schalmik thought, as she sat and watched her granddaughter sing and dance and even curtsey. At last, in this fabled land of a children's opera, Greta has managed to live as a child.

The Red Cross inspectors came to the camp, they watched the children's opera, they gathered material for their report, and off they went. The authorities filmed the opera for posterity, and then the freight cars drew up beyond the gates.

Frau Schalmik, Erna, Greta and her new friends began the journey to Poland.

12
Auschwitz-Birkenau, 1944

In Terezín two wooden steps led into the freight car. At Auschwitz-Birkenau there were no steps. Just the drop to the ramp. Guards pulled open the doors. The inmates by the doors fell out. *Raus raus,* the men outside shouted. Like barking dogs. *Raus raus, raus raus.*

The guards pulled at those in front till there was room for them to jump inside and they pulled and pushed from there. Frau Schalmik sat on the edge to lever herself down. A soldier shoved her. She fell to the ramp and her legs crumpled.

The sight of her mother below on the ground ripped Erna's attention from Greta for a moment. She let go her hold. A guard picked up the girl and threw her. Greta came out of the railway car backward, her arms wide, her hands outstretched, her legs trailing.

Her body arched, and her head was set to land on concrete. Hana, who had used to sneak into Greta's mother's bed to care for the child, caught her. She swivelled the girl round, set her on her feet, and took her hand.

'Come, Greta, we must walk,' Hana said.

And Greta did walk. She didn't cry then so why did she cry out later? There are always such questions. The guards and the dogs were barking, the girl was pushed with the barrels of guns, bodies stumbled all around her, her mother and her grandmother were left behind, and yet little Greta held Hana's hand and walked beside her.

They let the new inmates keep their hair and their own clothes. Even their skin was left as it was, clear of tattoos. They were to be housed in the Theresienstadt Family Camp. If Red Cross inspectors wanted a follow-up visit after their successful day out in Terezín, then they could enter this barbed wire compound just inside the entrance gates of Auschwitz-Birkenau. Men and women were housed in separate wooden barracks, and could meet in the ground between.

And they could talk.

They had much to talk about. Flames shot out of the chimneys. Soot streaked their hair. What gives blood that smell? Is it the iron content? Trains pulled up beyond their wire fence and they watched passengers walk on down the tracks to the crematoria in the woods. This was a holding and processing station in an extermination camp.

One morning the head of their barracks shouted out news. There would be a selection. They needed able-bodied women between the ages of fifteen and forty-five to volunteer for a women's labour camp.

One basic rule for camp survival is never to volunteer, but what could be worse than what they had? This was a chance of leaving Auschwitz-Birkenau. The only chance they had.

Frau Schalmik and Erna talked. Well, Frau Schalmik talked and Erna listened. There was no counter-argument. Frau Schalmik was forty-eight. She could have lied about her age, but her hair was now white and her body was worn. The fall from the freight car sprained her ankle and she walked with a limp. She hadn't a chance in the selection.

She would stay and take care of Greta.

Erna must go. Her daughter must go.

An SS official stood with his back to the chimney in the centre of their barracks. The women took their turn to stand naked in front of him. The officer was tall and stood straight and firm. He looked Hana up and down and though she was short she held herself well and she passed. He wrote her number into his book.

Erna came next. She was strong and she was beautiful, but more than that she had bearing. Even naked in front of a Nazi selector she maintained that self-confident air. Of course she passed. The man nodded. Her number was added to the list.

The women dressed. They were to assemble outdoors and be marched off to the women's camp to await transport.

'Don't think,' Hana told Erna. 'Wipe out all your thoughts. Do this for your mother. Let your mother watch you go.'

The women and the children who would stay behind gathered in a closed group. Little Greta stood in front of her grandmother. Frau Schalmik's hands were clasped around the girl's front, but lightly. They didn't grip. They should have gripped.

The officials kept the selected women standing, checking off numbers against their lists.

'Stare straight,' Hana told Erna. It was a risk to speak but she didn't dare not to. It was a whisper without her lips moving. Erna was on her right. 'Don't look back.'

The roll call was complete. The women were ready to go.

And then Erna turned.

Just a little, not enough to get noticed by the authorities. It was just a slight adjustment of her head. She saw her mother watching her. Frau Schalmik was taking in the last sight of her daughter. And she was willing her on. Willing her daughter to safety.

And then Erna looked down from her mother to see her little Greta one more time. Erna was a mother too. She wanted one last sight of her daughter.

'Erna!' Hana whispered.

Erna snapped her look away.

The order came for the women to march. The gates were opened. The women took their first steps. It wasn't an orderly procession, the women had not been trained to march, but they were on their way.

And then that cry.

'Mutti!'

Frau Schalmik was slow. As Greta broke loose Frau Schalmik tried to grip. She stepped forward, her hand grabbed for the girl, but the move pressed weight on her bad foot. The sharp stab of pain kept her back. She grabbed at air.

Greta was too close to shoot at. A guard swiped the side of her head with the barrel of his gun.

Erna broke file. Hana watched her run back and reach the girl. Greta was alright. You know little girls. It was a blow. She was in shock. She would have recovered. Hana saw Erna's hands press hard against Greta's back. There was nothing broken. The girl was alright.

Hana saw no more. She heard shouts. The women marched away and the gates crashed shut behind them.

Hana waited for Erna to join them. Three days later transport came to move the band of working women on. Hana did not see Erna again.

You can't punish a girl for wanting her mother. That's what Hana hoped. You can't punish a mother for running to her child. They should let them stay together till the end. They should do that at least.

13
Darmstadt, 1944

A writer who includes children in a fairytale sets an ogre among the trees. Innocence has no poignancy without the presence of threat.

This thread of story starts in 1920s Darmstadt. Twenty-first century readers alive to a suffering Germany may sense what is coming. For now, the inhabitants of this medieval town expect it to endure. Ancient timbers hold its buildings together. Some lean a little, tiles ripple on roofs, but upper rooms protrude above the pathways and people walk beneath them. There is no fear that such buildings will fall.

Katja, who would grow up to study the piano and marry Dieter Birchendorf, and her brother Helmut are our two children. Usually the girl plays with girls and the boy plays with boys, and when they do each gender moves as a pack. Now they are just brother and sister out in the streets and though they think and move from separate impulses they are linked. The girl is caught by brightness in a shop window and so the boy comes to check it out. The boy rushes across the road to stare at a display of sweets and so the girl follows.

Their father has a destination. This hither thither, stop start, fast slow progress of his children is almost unbearable. When they near the library he makes them hold each other's hands. Tethered to each other they'll at least move as one. It's an absolute condition. Unless the children hold hands they will all turn around and go home at once.

Maybe that's a good idea. The children like home. The Hessian State Library has no scrap of medieval charm about it. It is vast and built of stone. School makes them sit still and try and order their minds, and this building is so much more daunting than school. It quells them. With their soft hands linked, Katja and Helmut follow their father through its doors.

At first they are tiny people inside vast spaces and follow their father because that is the only sense of direction they can have. They walk in step and their feet cross tiles and stone and wood. Ceilings vault high above them and then close in. The children pass through a door marked private and spiral down a stone staircase. Now the corridors are dark shelves that squeeze them close together.

Their father sits them down at a plain oak table and turns on a lamp. He speaks in whispers and they don't speak at all. A tall ladder leads him up through motes of dust to a high shelf. He pulls out a book to leave a gap in a wall of leather bindings and climbs down again.

They must not touch, he says. He'll turn the pages when they are ready. The book is in Latin but that doesn't mean much because even the letters are indecipherable. Pages turn and a new smell enters the children's noses. If this were a map they would decide it was a treasure map. As it's a book, they presume it is a book of spells. They are now primed for adventure.

Their father turns a new page and both children gasp out puffs of breath. The page is illuminated, their father explains, and what he says is true. Light shines from it. A lady in a halo of golden hair wears a purple gown. A thin scarlet leash trails from her hand and connects to a golden collar. The collar encircles the neck of a dragon who is three times her size. Its green is brighter than the forest through which they walk and the colour glistens in the creature's scales. Claws rake the air as the dragon lifts its front foot, a jewel of red marks the bulge of its eye, and flames flare from its mouth.

Don't touch, their father reminds them, and then reaches forward a finger to close the book. He returns the volume to the shelf, moves the ladder, and brings down another volume to show them. Its pages are a pattern of penmanship and its margins a pageant of summer. In one, a hare courses around borders, and in another two red foxes chase each other between flowers. Their father notes the stillness of his children's faces as he fingers a page to turn it. It has worked. They have glimpsed the power of books. They can guess at the purpose of his library.

Once outside, the brother and sister keep holding hands for a street or two. They talk to each other in an excited murmur.

A human life peaks in creativity and that accomplishment is then captured in books. Music too, Katja wondered, and art? Maybe, her father allowed. He was the guardian of centuries of thought and intelligence and imagination. His library held the best that humans can be and do. It was a store of understanding that passed from one generation to the next.

That day in the library, that sense of books as treasures, helped Katja explain her father's sacrifice when the time came.

Both children developed a love of reading but neither became a scholar. For Katja, music was a way to contain and yet express her wildness. Helmut developed a passion for electricity. Katja became Katja Birchendorf, a deaf pianist and the wife of the Adjutant of an internment camp and a mother. Helmut Klein became a soldier.

In April 1944 news came that Darmstadt was bombed. Katja had herself driven to the city so she could put her parents in her car and drive them back to Dachau and her home. 'Why should your home be safer than here?' her father challenged her. 'Do you think Darmstadt was bombed because it is Darmstadt? Of course it wasn't. We are a university town. Who cares to bomb such a place? Darmstadt was bombed because the clouds were low. The RAF was headed to Karlsruhe. If we lived in Karlsruhe, then maybe we would come with you. Karlsruhe has industry, there is reason to hit it, but Darmstadt?'

On September 11th 1944 the RAF returned. Two hundred and thirty-four bombers came with half a million high-explosive bombs and three hundred thousand incendiary bombs. It was a deliberate attempt to burn and blast a timbered city to the ground. Get this practice run right, and they could turn the same 'fan attack' technique on Dresden.

Katja persuaded her husband, Dieter Birchendorf, to send a car to Darmstadt even before the statistics of loss had started to come in.

Once in the town, it took a while for the two officers to make sense of their map because buildings were gone and roads were cratered. Eventually, through questioning those they encountered, they assured themselves that they were on the right street. The timbers of Katja's parents' house burned through their boots. The whole street smouldered.

If they are not at home, Katja had instructed, go to the Hessian State Library. That's where they'll be. The officers manoeuvred their car through carnage. Death seemed the norm. The bombs would be seen to have killed more than twelve thousand people. The officers were not hopeful.

When they reached the library the two men spoke about turning their vehicle around and returning direct to Dachau. The library's walls were blasted open and smoke still clouded out from what was once its roof. This whole trip was ill advised. Then the officers discussed which of them would inform the Adjutant that his wife's parents were missing, presumed dead. Birchendorf would interrogate them. That's how oral reports to the man always turned out. Give him one detail and he chased down another, and then another. Men had stepped into his office as guards at Dachau, their responses were found wanting in detail, and the men were marched out as inmates. The officers imagined their interrogation and left their car in order to supply themselves with answers.

So this was war. Five years into it and the two men now felt they knew what war looked like. It was civilians in blackened skin who stumbled where a street once held their homes. It was a couple flamed inside each other's arms. It was banks of flies and air that was choked with burned blood. And now it was this library ripped open to the skies, a place of silence in which several stones of its fabric thundered to the ground as the two men stood in the ruins of its entrance hall. This was not what war was supposed to be.

They looked around. The main staircase was destroyed.

'Do you expect men to flee upstairs in a burning building?' the young officers imagined the Adjutant asking. 'What do families do in an air raid? They head to shelters. They head to cellars. They go underground. You were searching a library. Libraries hold their collections in stacks, floor after underground floor. Surely you searched those stacks. Tell me what you found.'

And so the young men spiralled down one staircase and barked out commands for people to reveal themselves. They were standing beside a small storage room and jumped when a woman stepped out. Her hair was pulled into grey spikes and her face was grey too. They demanded to know her name. 'Frau Klein,' she said, but her voice was croaky and they made her say it again. The name tallied.

So yes, this was their miracle, they had found Frau Birchendorf's mother. This storeroom was their home now, she said. Her husband would be with his books. She directed them back upstairs and toward a rare book collection at the rear of the building.

The officers called out as they picked their way through the ruin. The man did not call back but stood and watched them approach along a corridor of charred shelves. In his hand was a leather-bound book.

'Look,' he said when they reached him, and opened the book's cover. The paper inside had no substance. His fingers passed through them as they moved to turn the pages, and text flew to the ground in flakes.

The officers had come in a car to take him back to his daughter's.

'What should I do, bring my favourite book with me?' he asked. He slid the burned book back onto its shelf. 'These are all my favourites. Some of them will be good. Some I can save. I will stay to take care of my books.'

14
A Return to Dachau, 1945

Otto Schalmik was Canadian now. He could have submitted a sworn deposition. Instead he decided to attend the Dachau War Trial in person and accepted the offer of a sea crossing from Halifax, Nova Scotia to Liverpool. Passengers complained of the quality of the food on board, but Otto recognized the vessel as a ship of plenty. As others were laid low by sickness on the Irish Sea, he loaded up. His travel pass included vouchers for food, but a voucher was no use if there was no food. He did not trust what was coming on land. Otto carried bread in his bag: two end hunks of stale rye, along with several slithers of dried meat.

Trains took him through England to Harwich, he sailed by ferry from there to Ostend, and then a sequence of rail journeys brought him to Munich. It was 1945 and Otto was back in Germany. War had ended and winter was beginning. Men haunted station platforms, dressed in grey overcoats, their faces also grey and sucked of flesh. Women were among them too, what seemed like thin and ancient women with their small faces haloed in wild hair; then as the train paused by a station platform one of these women looked directly in at him. Her eyes stared into his without engaging; they were oddly blank, and ringed in darkness like they were bruised by tiredness, and yet her hair was still black. It was the hair of someone still young. So were these not all old women? He scanned the figures on the platform, two with their arms stretched out, their fingers flattened against the train's windows. They could be in their twenties, he decided. Racked and broken.

Beyond the tracks, for mile after mile, what once were buildings now lay as rubble. Women searched beneath the rocks for wasteland salvage. These women seemed fatter, but then he saw they simply wore all the clothing they possessed. Clothes layered their bodies but their necks were scrawny.

Children without coats wore cotton clothes coloured by dust. Their heads tilted up as the train chugged past, and their hands stretched out. A woman in his carriage tugged down the window, pulled her head back at the blast of cold air from outside, dipped a hand into her basket, and took out two bread rolls. She didn't break them but threw them out of the window whole and slammed the window shut. Five children swirled in a fighting ball around the bread. Others ran, their pace just short of the trains. '*Brot Brot.*' Their cries for bread grew thinner.

Otto did not throw his bread. He kept it hidden along with his flask of water. When it was necessary to eat or drink he moved into the corridor. You get to know the people in your carriage, with their fussiness and decorum. He chose to eat among strangers. With people pressed so close, not many could watch him. He held small chunks of bread in his mouth where it grew moist and the flavour spread. He cut the meat with his nails and pressed the scraps up against his gums. Chewing was too obvious but he ground the meat between his teeth to extract all he could.

In Munich he followed his docket of information and registered into a small hotel. The following morning a car collected him to drive him to Dachau. The driver fretted about being late, but the journey was swift.

Otto looked left as they drew near the camp. It was raining. Otto noted the Birchendorf's house as he passed. Dieter now lived in a cell in the prison block and his wife and daughter were evicted, but their former home looked untroubled. It housed the American military.

Otto had known the house in summer weeks. The summer air that breezed through those rooms still blew in a chamber of his mind. The memory was a fond one. It was a shock, to look back and find a memory he cared for. He was glad for rain against the car window. He didn't need to see too clearly.

Guards checked their papers. His driver drove under the arch of the guardhouse, through the main gate, and sped across the *Appelplatz* where Otto had stood for so many hours.

The speed and comfort of this car was not a useful luxury. Some things need to be slow if they have to happen at all. He needed to walk, to feel his weight upon the ground. A body is such a suspect thing.

Otto, a man in his twenties who had crossed the Atlantic to forge a life of promise for himself, was rendered the teen-age Otto again. His heart beat fast and stretched intense pain across his chest. He could not tell what he was seeing through the rain-smeared window. His head was opened somehow; old life reassembled and tried to pack itself inside.

The driver gripped the young man's shoulder and shook. Otto's vision returned. Images were still blurred, a blast of migraine was already tucking into his left temple, but he managed to operate the door handle and climb out into the rain. A wooden board above a doorway proclaimed the building's function for those who spoke English. WAR CRIMES BRANCH – JUDGE ADVOCATES SECTOR. HQ THIRD UNITED STATES ARMY. An American officer with a clipboard stood just inside the half-open door of the entrance, prepared to process him.

You have no choice when Dachau calls, it seemed to him. None who went there went by choice. Dachau had been the model concentration camp, and now it was establishing the model of retribution. The American military had taken over this assembly hall inside the camp's fencing, and turned it into a courtroom. Men were pulled from across Germany and Austria to stand trial for crimes of war. First in the dock were those men held responsible for the horrors of Dachau itself.

It amused Otto later, when the war trial at Nuremberg had come to an end, to learn of the fate of Hermann Göring. Though at the top of the Nazi hierarchy, he remained shy of concentration camps. He had always refused to visit Dachau. Dachau brooks no such refusal.

Göring would grow to become Hitler's deputy, but as a boy he was expelled from one boarding school after another. His final act of rebellion, which propelled him out of mainstream education and into military school, was an attack as mysterious as music itself. Music is not definable, since it commands a sphere which speech only reaches in the space between words, but surely it includes a sense of communion. Music when played implies someone to listen to it. Dissonance, striding against harmony, leaves harmony empowered. We hear its absence.

So young Göring's act? His school had a fine orchestra, of which Göring was not a part. He made his way among the store of instruments, and cut the strings on all the cellos and violins. He took his knife to slash music to death.

Condemned to hang at Nuremberg, he asked to die before a firing squad. Such a death befitted his sense of honour. The request was refused. Göring bit into a cyanide capsule. The authorities ferried his body away in the night, out through Munich and beyond. They lit a fire and loaded Göring into an oven in the crematorium in Dachau. Smoke and the whiff of burning flesh rose from its chimney.

Göring's ashes were taken in a bucket and dropped into the dark waters of the Amper river. Such is a Dachau comedy.

This trial was Dachau theatre.

15
Dachau – The War Trial

Otto Schalmik sat on a wooden chair that was raised on a small carpeted platform, the audience behind him. Before him an emptiness of flooring ended with the trial judge, an American officer in full uniform. Nailed to the wall above the judge was the broad spread of the Stars and Stripes. The room was lit like a film set. Lights from overhead beat down heat and brightness.

Otto tried to remember that he was a free man who had come here by choice. It didn't work. No one comes to Dachau by choice. As his examination started, he felt accused. The prosecution counsel stood at a microphone and faced the audience.

'You knew Herr Dieter Birchendorf?'

The question came in English. Otto was fluent enough. He noted the use of 'Herr', and that they had already stripped Birchendorf of his military rank.

'Yes.'

'And this is he?'

'It is.'

Birchendorf sat in the front row of a bank of men to Otto's left. Out of uniform, in a borrowed jacket and open-necked shirt, the former adjutant seemed shrunken. A card hung from string around his neck. It identified him as prisoner number 41. His once-ginger hair, still cut close to his scalp, had turned grey and his face was gaunt.

One look at him, and Otto knew the verdict. The military tribunal had established itself in full pomp inside the perimeters of Dachau, with a showy pretence of fairness. Still, a camp was a camp and fairness had nothing to do with it. Otto had experience of such places. He could take a look at the authorities on the one side, ranged against the individual on the other, and know if that man was doomed.

Don't show fear. That was a fundamental in the camps. Show fear, perhaps flinching as a baton is drawn, or a sidelong glance at a dog's snapping jaws, and you're leapt on. They spot a weakness. You're destroyed.

Birchendorf was doing worse than showing fear. He was smiling.

It was not a broad smile, and it was not constant. His head jerked a little at any loud noise, and then a smile flicked on. He held his body like a schoolboy at prizegiving; back straight, everything of interest, pleased with himself yet unsure, ready for his moment yet daunted by unknown ritual. He wanted to do well, to be appreciated, and to go home.

When the American forces came, he had surrendered. Fleeing was the act of guilty men. He didn't feel guilty. They locked him in the prison block at night, in one of the run of tiny cells lodged behind the kitchens, but they released him during the day so that he could help with the camp's administration. He felt appreciated.

His smiles were a reminder. I'm your colleague, his smiles said. We're all civilized men.

As his translator turned the English of the courtroom into German, he nodded his head and smiled his understanding.

The smile proved he understood nothing. He was a Nazi. Nobody wants to be complicit with a Nazi. Nobody wants your clubbable smile. A smile is worse than flinching. It's ingratiating. It's wanting to be liked. A smile seeks recognition that you're a fellow human being. Such smiles are capital offences.

Otto Schalmik knew the reality of smiling in the camps. Smilers were extinguished.

Birchendorf did not smile at him, of course. Otto Schalmik was a Jew and an outsider in the court. He had no military background. Birchendorf sought no solidarity with outsiders. He had been smug too long. He couldn't believe that the sides had switched. Once a prosecutor, always a prosecutor.

Otto spoke of his selection to play the cello in Birchendorf's front room. He confirmed that the cello was a Stradivarius. Did he know the worth of such an instrument?

'I knew its value. It was exceedingly fine.'

'Did you know the provenance?'

Otto looked blank. The counsel informed the courtroom that the cello had formed part of the collection of Herr

Jakob Lasker, formerly of Vienna, present whereabouts unknown. Camp records showed that he had been processed from Dachau to Buchenwald, but from there the record was blank. 'So you, a Jew, were ordered to play an instrument appropriated from another Jew. What is your reaction to that information?'

'I have no reaction to that.'

'Did you not regard it as unusual that you were called from the camp to perform at private musical afternoons?'

'My job was to clean the floors.' He explained the nature of the cleaning.

'And then you played the cello?'

'Such an instrument needs to be played.'

'This was the main concern of the accused? He cared so much for Jakob Lasker's Stradivarius?'

'He cared for his wife. She was a musician but she had gone deaf. She was expecting a baby. He said he felt it was good for the baby to hear music, and good for his wife to feel the cello's vibrations.'

'So you played for his wife?'

'Yes.'

'He left you alone with her?'

'I had to keep my eyes closed.'

'Do you normally play with closed eyes?'

'I didn't. But it's become a habit.'

'So he forced you to keep your eyes shut?'

No, he wouldn't join in. He was a Jew stolen from internment to clean a man's floors, and then play for his amusement on a Stradivarius stolen from another Jew who Birchendorf despatched to his death. Every element of the story the counsel was forming was inflected with a savage undercurrent of meaning. Otto Schalmik, young Jewish boy, was brought from captivity to be a workhorse and plaything of the Birchendorf household. It was true, but the story cast him as a victim.

He had never played that role then, and refused to think his way into it now. Play the victim and you're playing their game. Play their game and they've won.

He was never the victim. He was a survivor.

He had opened his eyes. Katja, belly swollen, eyes round and watching, knelt on the floor before him. Birchendorf's hand swiped in to land a blow on his face. That's what they wanted to hear. When he played the Stradivarius in the Adjutant's house, he was made to close his eyes out of fear.

Who cares that that was so? You feel fear but you never show it. The slap of a man's hand was nothing. It was negligible in the account of horrors. No man should be hanged for slapping another.

Take everything from a man and one thing may be left. He retains his imagination. He has the right to choose his own tale.

Counsel had stopped speaking, leaving silence, awaiting his answer.

'I played Bach,' he said.

A fresh silence began. He explained.

'Herr Birchendorf lent me his manuscript of the Bach cello suites. I learned the music by heart. Closing my eyes kept the music inside when the manuscript was returned. I was proud to play with my eyes closed. When everything was gone the music stayed with me. Bach guided me through.'

Counsel stared at him. Otto had gone off script. To guide him back, the examination continued on a musical theme.

'You played in the camp orchestra. The players believed this to be a clandestine orchestra. Isn't that so?'

It was.

'Did Herr Birchendorf inform you that he knew of the orchestra's existence?'

'He knew I played the cello in it. That's why he selected me.'

'So the orchestra could be said to have performed under his direction?'

'Perhaps. Certainly he knew about it.'

'And the orchestral players. None of these players, and you admit that he knew about these players, were subjected to poling while the orchestra continued. They weren't strung up by their wrists, with their arms tied behind their backs?'

'Not that I knew of.'

'Was it your understanding that this was due to the protection of Herr Birchendorf?'

The suggestion was one among many in a letter from Frau Birchendorf that had reached him in Toronto.

'I have no opinion.' Counsel said nothing and waited. More seemed to be needed. 'I wasn't privy to the workings of camp command.'

'Did you not have a sense of your fellow musicians as privileged members of the camp?'

'I felt no absence of an instance of torture as any particular blessing. Camp command was not capricious. It was systematic. A day was not divisible into bad and not so bad. It was one continuous horror. If you felt any moment of relief, it was time to increase your guard, not relax it. You have brought me back to Dachau. Don't ask me to sit here and recall acts of goodness. Nobody acted out of goodness. To imagine such an act is to have hope. Invest hope in others and you will become bankrupt. Those who place hope outside of themselves become hopeless and they are taken. Nothing from outside will save you. There is no salvation. There is only this.'

Former inmates require respect. Well, counsel had shown him such respect. He had let him ramble on without interruption. However, this was a busy courtroom. The accused were stacked up, and the courtroom was filled with those eager to witness the pursuance of justice. Otto noted a change in counsel's tone. Questions became brisker. The patience allotted to him was almost spent.

'The accused states that he fed you, a Jew, in his own home.'

Otto looked blank.

'He gave you milk, fruit and sausage. With sausage to take back to the camp.'

'Oh yes. Yes, that's right. The sausage'

'Pork sausage.'

'I believed so.'

'So you, a Jew, were forced to eat pork?'

'The truly bad meat was whale. I ate the pork. I wasn't forced.'

That was enough of Dachau. The accused had scattered random instances of mitigating actions through pages of self-defence, and justice required that each should be examined. So far as the case of Otto Schalmik was concerned, one final claim needed to be resolved. It took them to Buchenwald.

Yes, the authorities at Buchenwald had received a letter for him. It informed him of the award of a scholarship to the Conservatory of Music in Toronto. No, he had not applied for such a scholarship. It came as a total surprise. Yes, it came from a connection of the Birchendorfs. He understood the professor of music in Toronto was a former teacher of Frau Birchendorf. Yes, the professor was a Jew.

'So Herr Birchendorf, spurred by his love for music and appreciation of your talent, used his association with a Jewish émigré of his acquaintance to engineer your release from protective custody. He found you passage to a country where you would be free from persecution. Is that a fair summary?'

'I can't tell what spurred him,' he said. 'That would be conjecture. But as to his actions, yes. That is a fair summary.'

'In Dachau, you hauled loads of sand in the mornings. For a short period in the afternoons you were taken to the Birchendorf household. What was the hardest thing you were ordered to do when there?'

'Play Bach,' he said.

He heard a male laugh from behind him. Laughter was not an appropriate note on which to end his investigation.

'Would you tell us, please,' counsel continued, 'of your journey from Vienna to Dachau.'

'To what purpose? I prefer not to speak of this.'

'We understand the pain of speaking of such things, Herr Schalmik. But you must understand the nature of the accusations we are examining in this court. We need to hear of the realities of mass transportation. You are one of those who survived such an experience. We need you to tell us.'

So Otto was to be the voice of those who were not there to speak. He did not want this role. But even as he sat silent, his eyes blinked and watered. The courtroom vanished a moment. In its place he saw the face of an old man, with a straggle of grey beard. It was the old man who had wandered, confused, desperate to oblige these young German soldiers who were urging him toward speed and compliance. This old man had never found need to travel beyond Vienna. From out of the press of men he wandered off across the platform of the freight terminal at Vienna Station. The train was so large and so long. What was his best way of entering it? That way? Maybe this way?

Otto felt the shock of the bullet that killed the wandering Jew. It came now, into this Dachau courtroom, as a jolt to his heart. Speak, the man seemed to be saying. Say what happened. Why did I die? I don't understand. Tell me. Explain.

And so Otto spoke. He could not tell the old man why he had to die. We die. So it is. But he was able to piece together the circumstances, this early instance of a brutal system supplanting the natural order of things. People herded, an old man exhausted and confused who strayed from the pack, a young soldier trained to distinguish Jews as disposable who shot a bullet through the old man's spine. The pack was marshalled on to board the train. Otto spoke for the courtroom to hear, he heard his words translated back into his native tongue and then lapsed into German himself, but he was not speaking for the courtroom. I watched you, old man, he was saying. And this is what I saw.

His tale jumped ahead. They had passed through Munich and were in the closed freight carriage that was transporting them to Dachau.

'And me?' A new voice punched into his head. 'I died. You were there. Why did I die?'

He recognized the voice. The man had walked beside him as they shifted themselves from one train to the next. The man stumbled. The stock of a guard's rifle slammed down onto his neck so his head bounced against the dirt. The head was bald on top, the hair was black and trimmed close, and a tidy beard edged the man's round face.

The guard ordered Otto to pick the man up, and somehow he did so. He lay the man on the floor of the freight car, his body propped against a wall and his knees hooked close to make room for others. Otto settled beside him. The man moaned and then grew silent. Otto drowsed and woke to the softness of a belly that his head was pressed against. For a moment there was comfort and then he tried to pull his head away. The belly juddered, the bowels evacuated themselves, and the body below him died. The shit ran round the carriage floor as Otto's head pressed into the dead stomach. The weight of others lodged around him made him unable to move.

Now the dead man lodged in his brain and he wanted his tale to be told. And so Otto told it.

He told more tales as they came to him. The transport from Vienna to Dachau was streaked with bleak moments, random and episodic. Counsel discovered a fresh store of patience. This was the testimony the court wished to collect.

'And that is when I first saw Herr Birchendorf,' he concluded. He had forgotten this till now, but was glad of it. His story needed a conclusion. 'He stood with a clipboard as we climbed from the train. He was marking down the dead bodies.'

'How did you see that was what he was doing?'

'I didn't,' Otto realized. 'Not precisely. I saw the man, the clipboard, and what he was watching. I saw corpses stretchered past him. He seemed displeased, and struck marks on his paper.'

'This exhibit is presented to the court,' counsel stated, and held up a paper from the table beside him. 'This is an order of April 1938 bearing the signature of Herr Birchendorf. It required that all deaths of transportees in future be fully accounted for. A change in procedure was duly effected. There is forthwith a tally in which previously unaccounted deaths equate with the increase in those stated to have been killed while trying to escape.'

The paper hung from counsel's hand, holding the court in silence for a few moments. When he placed it back on the table behind him, a new angle of examination began.

'You ask us to believe that the accused arranged your exit from Buchenwald to Toronto. You made that journey on your own? It wasn't part of a mass exodus?'

Otto had stood on the *Appelplatz* one final time, his number shouted out. The others marched and he was ordered to stand still. He looked straight ahead while the lines of men disappeared from his peripheral vision. He was marched off to the store, where a neat pile of clothes and shoes was handed to him. These were the clothes he had been wearing in Vienna. The shirt was his best white cotton, for Erna and Hugo were coming to dinner. It had been laundered, but patches of blood had set stains on the chest. The sleeves of the jacket were short, the pants did not reach down to his shoes, so it seemed he had grown, although otherwise the clothes were for someone much larger than himself.

The shoes had lost their shine. He walked down the slope and across the mud.

Yes, so far as he knew, it was only he among the inmates who stepped through the gates of Buchenwald that day.

'What made you so special, Herr Schalmik? Was yours a musical family? Did others play?'

His mother and his sister both played. His mother played the piano, and his sister Erna the violin.

'Did they play as well as you?'

'We played together.'

'But you were exceptional?'

'They had talent.'

'But you had more than talent?'

'Vienna is a musical city. Families play together. My mother was a pianist. My sister was a violinist. You ask if I was better than them? I was a teenager. I was nothing and I thought I was everything. What can I tell you?'

'So your talent did not stand out above theirs. You were all equal.'

'I was to earn my living as a musician. The family had invested in that. They believed in me.'

'What happened to your mother and your sister, Herr Schalmik?'

'My brother-in-law died. My mother moved in with my sister.'

'Your brother-in-law died?'

'He was killed. We presume Hugo was killed. We got the news in a letter my mother sent to Buchenwald. Of course she could not put much in a letter. When my father and I were taken from the home, Hugo was there and in hiding.

Home was no longer a safe place. This is what I assume. He ran a small workshop repairing bicycles. It was not official. He paid no taxes. He started sleeping with the bikes and hiding in the dark. I expect someone reported him. They came for him. He resisted arrest. The family never saw the body.'

'And your mother and sister, Herr Schalmik? What happened to them?'

'The authorities had taken the men. We thought that would be enough. We thought they would leave the women alone.'

'Do you know what happened to them?'

'They were transported to Theresienstadt.'

'And from there?'

'I'm not certain. I have found no record.'

'In all likelihood?'

'Families from Theresienstadt were shipped *en masse* to Auschwitz.'

'And there?'

Otto said nothing.

'You have no further news,' counsel interpreted.

Otto's old clothes had been set against his number. They had been cleaned and shipped on from Dachau to await his release. If he, without a chance in hell, had been released, the same could have happened to others. He had not admitted to himself that his family had been killed. He was not going to do so there.

'And your father?'

'He died in Buchenwald. He took my place in the gang to clean the sewage pits, and contracted TB within the week. My first aim on reaching Canada was to find ways to have him follow me. He was dead before the boat docked.'

'Then so far as you know, Herr Schalmik, you are the only surviving member of your family?'

He didn't speak.

'Herr Schalmik?'

He nodded.

'You're nodding. That means yes?'

He waited, and then nodded again.

'For the record, please note that Herr Schalmik nodded his assent. From Vienna to Dachau to Buchenwald. In the way that Dachau was the model for all other concentration camps, it can be argued that the pattern of rail transport to and from Dachau was a model for all transport to and from all camps. So Dachau transport provided a model for the transport from Vienna to Theresienstadt and from Theresienstadt to Auschwitz.

'From your knowledge of the accused, and your experience of mass transport, would you say that Herr Birchendorf recognized the one-way nature of all the transport he was arranging? So many freight cars stacked with human cargo kept on returning empty. Was it not a fair assumption that the only destination that holds such inexhaustible capacity is death?

'I appreciate your experience is different, Herr Schalmik, and that while the musical talents of your sister and your mother were not enough to save them, Herr Birchendorf noted special qualities in you. But how much should your solo journey to a life of music in Canada weigh when set against the journeys of so many others? Whatever his love for Johann Sebastian Bach, Herr Schalmik, do you feel the man charged with ferrying your family to their deaths holds some responsibility for those deaths?'

Otto listened to the silence, and then realized he was expected to speak.

'Some responsibility?' he repeated.

Counsel stared back at him.

'I lie awake in the night,' Otto began. The court was clearly unhappy with silence. Perhaps if he spoke he would find what to say. 'My family is gone. They are dead. I know they are dead. But sometimes I sleep. I know I sleep because my family is with me. It excites me so much that they are with me that I wake and when I wake they are gone. They are dead. In the daylight they are gone.

'Sometimes I think I see them, the way that person walks, the turn of that person's head, and I go running after strangers. Life is an illusion and my family's death is real. What is my life compared to their death? Do I feel responsible for my family's death? Of course I do. Immeasurably. If I am not responsible for their death, who is? Who else will care enough?'

The prosecutor looked to the judge.

'You are not on trial, Herr Schalmik,' the judge said.

'We considered the ways Herr Birchendorf arranged for the mass transportation of Jews,' counsel reminded him.

'Given that fact, is it fair to hold Herr Birchendorf account-able for your family's death?'

'You ask me what is fair?'

'Is it reasonable?'

'I cannot comment on what is fair and what is reasonable. I have no experience in such matters. Do I wish to blame Herr Birchendorf for my family's death? Would that do any good? A man must take on his own blame. Me, I blame myself. That is all I can do today.'

The prosecutor waited.

'Thank you, Herr Schalmik,' he then said. 'That will be all.'

Otto stood. He turned so as not to face Dieter Birchendorf and he left the court.

16
A Sea Interlude, 1948

Here's where Katja sat and what she watched.

She sat on rubble. It was comfortable enough. The sun fed warmth into her bare arms.

She watched her daughter, Uwe. Crater holes had filled with muddy water, and Uwe was inside one of these. She had made new friends and they were teaching her to swim. Well, Katja hoped they were friends and that this was a swimming lesson. A girl supported her legs and another her chest while a boy and girl sat on the crater's edge and laughed. Katja saw the children's heads tip back and their mouths open but of course she was deaf to the sound. Laughter could be free and happy and it could also be cruel.

Uwe splashed with her hands. Katja tensed, ready to stand and run and pull her daughter free. Then the girl who held the legs let go and Uwe stood. She shook the water from her face and opened her eyes. She showed shock for a moment and then laughed. Yes, Uwe was laughing. She dipped her shoulders back beneath the water and kicked with her legs and suddenly she was afloat and moving. Independently moving. Swimming. The children on the rim clapped their hands and laughed again.

Katja let herself smile and relax.

It's alright, she thought. They don't know who Uwe is. She's safe for now.

Katja and the children were in a camp for displaced persons. The rubble she sat on had once been a building. The craters came from bombs that landed on open ground. It was in a place like this that her brother Helmut died. A bomb fell on his garrison where he worked as an electrician. He survived that and went down to the boiler room to work on restoring the power supply. More bombs fell. You would hope a man in a cellar might survive such an attack.

Helmut was dead.

Her husband Dieter was dead. They hanged him.

She and Uwe walked through the ruins of her home town of Darmstadt. She had the girl question everyone they met. In time they were able to put the story together. It wasn't much of a story. Her parents were dead. That was all the story amounted to, really. Sickness was the cause, nothing more definable than that. The father died first and then the mother the following day. Officials came and took the couple away, side by side on a cart drawn by a thin horse. Nobody knew of any grave. Katja held Uwe by the hand and they walked out on the forested road beyond Darmstadt and kept on walking. At first Katja felt she had a plan. Didn't an aunt live in that town; didn't a cousin live in this village?

They reached the town and Katja found the street name fixed to a wall. House by house they drew closer to the number of her aunt's address, and then the houses were gone. Even the rubble was gone. There were houses, there was wasteland, and then the houses continued. Mother and daughter walked up and down the street a few times, and then for an hour they sat in the vacant space where her aunt's house had been. That was enough. They could call that rest. It wasn't too far to the cousin's village. If they set off at once they could be there before nightfall.

The cousin's village was intact. They could tell that from afar, its church tower solid with buildings in a cluster around it. That was hopeful. The cousin's house was on the main street. It was a small brick terrace. Gunther was Katja's age; he had left his job and gone to war, but he would be back now surely. She knocked at the door.

A woman answered. Children ran into the corridor behind and stared out before retreating. Two men stood behind the woman. Katja asked after Gunther. Was he there? When would he be back?

There was no Gunther. No one of that name had ever been near the place, they were very sure. This was their home and they should know. The men joined in. One pushed his way to the front and shouted at her to go. Beggars were one thing, they know what it's like, they help when they can, but you don't turn up and lie about dead relatives and try and claim a house as your own. Be off with you.

And so Katja recognized that she was too late. Other refugees had claimed the empty home. And Gunther was dead.

On they walked. Uwe was in her favourite red shoes. The leather cracked and turned brown and the straps broke. Holes spread through the soles and still she wore them as she kept up with her mother. Other women and children shuffled along the roads so they found paths through fields where they kept close to hedgerows. Hedgerows were good for shelter. At night they raided village gardens and ate whatever they could find.

After the first winter Uwe became light enough to carry. Katja now kept to the roads. They found soldiers there. Soldiers had rations. They were clear what they wanted in exchange. Katja led the soldiers behind hedgerows to make her trade.

They tried their way in cities. Women banded together for safety, but of course there was no safety. Katja found soldiers and did what trade she could behind the extant walls of bombed-out buildings.

Mother and daughter walked between cities. Uwe's arms hung loose around Katja's neck and her stick legs curled around her mother's chest. The rhythm of walking was a comfort and so sometimes the girl slept. Soft puffs of her daughter's breath against her skin kept Katja going.

And now they were in Rosenheim. Katja had brought Uwe full circle, close to where the girl was born. Rosenheim was once a subcamp of Dachau. Prisoners were marched out from here to work in the BMW factory. Now the war was lost and there was no work for anyone, not even slave labour. Rosenheim had become a camp for DPs, for displaced persons. That's what she and Uwe had become: displaced persons.

Katja's past was in fragments. Try as she might, no clear narrative linked the past to now. I am like a loaf of bread, she thought. The loaf doesn't know it was once a seed in the ground, a head of wheat in a summer field. It can't suspect it will be eaten or turn to mould. It is milled and stirred and baked and devoured. As with bread, so with people. So with me.

Rosenheim served as home. There was nowhere else. Months passed. And then news came. She and Uwe and a whole group of others were to be shipped from Hamburg. Australia had agreed to take them in.

Katja clutched the notification paper and watched Uwe splash about in the bomb crater. The girl was bronzed and had her own strength. She was making friends and was at play in a warzone.

Katja collected the scene as a final image of Germany.

They gave her a small suitcase so she could pack for the voyage. Katja washed her and Uwe's clothes afresh, left them in the sun to bake out the smells of their previous owners, and packed them. This was everything they owned.

They had to label the case. Without thinking, she wrote her name in large letters. FRAU K. BIRCHENDORF. It was a mistake. You don't put your true name to paper. The giddiness of having somewhere to go, the sudden release into a future, left her heedless of her past. People who guessed at it used it against her. Lies were always safer.

On the boat, she tried to be discreet. She touched an officer on the sleeve to draw him to one side. When assigning cabins, perhaps they should take care not to place former government officials and their families alongside former camp inmates? It would save friction in close confines on a long voyage.

Perhaps she spoke too loudly. Her deafness made it hard to modulate her voice. The officer shouted that she would go where the hell he sent her.

Hamburg was a jagged ridge of ruins, and then rain fell and obscured the whole country from view. Katja retreated from the railing and closed herself indoors. The North Sea heaved them around. The Jews in her cabin were sick and so was she. She was not a fool. She knew she and these Jews all shared the human condition. They just didn't know how to belong together, that was all.

In the Bay of Biscay the boat rose and fell on high waves and the crew locked all the doors that led out onto the decks. Uwe seemed unaffected. Katja could not simply keep the child among these bunks of sick women. Yes go, she said, and waved a hand. Go and play.

Out in the corridor Uwe hesitated. She kept one hand on the handle of the cabin door, for balance and to push her way back inside if needs be. Then a boy rushed past her. The boat lurched and he bounced off a wall but he ran on.

With shrieks of excitement, three more children appeared in the corridor.

'Have you seen Stefan?' they asked.

She looked right toward the running boy but he was gone already. The other children, two boys and a girl, chased after him.

Uwe followed, her hand brushing the wall of the corridor for balance. She heard the three children in the dining room. They were emerging from under the tables when she entered.

'Not here,' one shouted, and they ran out.

So they were looking for Stefan.

She decided to look herself, and did so methodically. Below a counter a black curtain shielded a storage place for bins. She had seen the bins rolling on the floor. If the bins were gone, that would make a good hiding place. She pulled back the curtain.

'Found you,' she said, and crawled inside to crouch beside the boy. She did not know the rules for hide and seek.

'You've found me,' Stefan said. 'Now it's your turn.'

She didn't want to move. The space was cramped, so when the boat rolled over a wave you fell about. Not far though. You just pressed into each other. It was fun. Soon the boy and the girl were laughing.

The next day was stormy too. Stefan had the longest eye-lashes she had seen on a boy, and Uwe told him so. They played together. The children who were not sick shared a table at lunch and because adults were too sick to eat they had a feast. Stefan and Uwe fed fruit into each other's mouths. Later the table legs became the trees of a jungle which the children crept through on their hands and knees.

The corridor was a racetrack. On the dance floor, Stefan and Uwe curled up into balls to see where the ship would roll them. It rolled them into each other.

The next morning as the ship pushed past the coast of The Gambia the storm passed. Seas grew calm and clouds peeled away from the sky. The crew unlocked the deck and adults emerged to feel the sunlight.

Stefan took Uwe to meet his family. When they saw who she was, they pulled the boy to them and walked away.

She watched them huddle together at a distance. After a few minutes, Stefan returned.

'I know what you are,' he said. 'You're a Birchendorf.'

She thought Birchendorf was just a name.

Stefan spat in her eye, and stared at her to make her walk away. Uwe wiped her face with her hand and stared back, till it was he who turned and walked away.

'You did well,' Katja said when she read the daughter's tale from her lips. 'You're my brave little girl.'

This one moment could have killed off Katja. She could have picked the tender little girl into her arms and jumped off the stern of the ship. They would have been churned in the wake like food in a mouth and then swallowed down. Nothing could get at them then. Nothing.

Instead Katja used the moment to turn her life around. She would be a Birchendorf and proud of it. In response to the boy's attack on her daughter, she chose to become ever more of who she was.

While Uwe, on the other hand, wanted nothing to do with who she was. Nothing at all.

17
Toronto, 1949

Otto Schalmik had history with Mrs Goren.

In early 1939 Otto's boat had docked in Canada and an immigration official studied him head to toe. He spoke in German. 'This form says you're Christian. That's a lie, isn't it?'

'It's a mistake,' Otto admitted, for a lie implies intent and he could not know why someone had written it. At Buchenwald he had simply signed the form that someone else had filled in.

The official detained him but only for a few hours. It was one thing to deny someone passage to Canada. It was another thing, in these political times, to deport Jews.

Otto stepped out into his new country and headed for Toronto where he made contact with the Jewish Immigration Aid Service. He needed their help in bringing his family to join him. A young woman called Mrs Goren offered translation as he worked through the forms. Things became stuck as he worked on filling in the first box, where he used miniature capital letters to squeeze in the names of his mother, of his sister, and his baby niece.

'Your sister is unmarried? Canada lets you bring in unmarried siblings.'

'She's a widow.'

'Do you have a death certificate for the husband?'

'Of course not. He was taken away and killed by the State. Do you imagine they would issue a certificate for that? I doubt they even returned the body.'

'There was no body? You have no proof?'

'My mother sent my father a letter. She asked us to say Kaddish for Hugo.'

'That's all there is? You have the letter?'

'My father has the letter.'

'In Buchenwald . . .' Mrs Goren said. They had already agreed to deal first with his female relatives.

'Greta, my niece. She is tiny. They killed her father. She is in great danger. They must let me bring in my niece.'

'Your niece is not a direct relation,' Mrs Goren explained. 'Canada's rules for the immigration of Jews are horribly clear I'm afraid. You can bring in direct relations only. Your mother. We can fill in the form for your mother.'

And so, in the end, that's what they did. Otto kept a carbon copy. And as he waited, Canada went to war.

Ten years on, Mrs Goren had grown stouter but kept on trying. 'We have found someone for you,' she told Otto. She had called him into her office at the Jewish Immigration Aid Service. 'Slečna Saudek. Slečna is Czech for Miss. She likes you to use it. Slečna Saudek was a teacher.'

'And now?'

'Now she is here. Canada doesn't need her as a teacher. Back in the German camp she retrained in needlework. We hope to find her such a job. Slečna Saudek does not speak easily of the past but she mentioned Theresienstadt. She uses its Czech name of course, Terezín, and when she said it I thought of you. I told her how you are looking for your mother, your sister and your niece. She can be caustic, I advise you not to expect too much, but when I mentioned you might meet over lunch and you would pay she agreed to meet. I recommend Switzer's. They do a fine baby beef. I shall join you. This is hardly a match-making service. It is appropriate.'

And so Otto Schalmik sat in Switzer's. Otto didn't hang out in Jewish diners as a rule. He knew these men and occasional women had lives of private sorrow and joy, but the music of their voices in one lunchtime room was cacophony. It had cadence and rhythm and volume but never silence. It was a song but it wasn't his song.

He was early, of course he was, and he tried to use the time to think.

Slečna Saudek and Mrs Goren were to come at one o'clock. As seats at his table became free, Otto put a jacket over one and his coat over the other.

It was one minute to one. They weren't coming. He knew that now.

He was angry but then he was always angry, and he was also relieved. It was stupid to think a Czech schoolteacher had come around the world to help him. Canada rejected applications from Jews and so this schoolteacher had learned how to sew and sat out the years in a camp for displaced persons. The State of Israel formed but that wouldn't do. Not for her. She wouldn't go there. She knew what she wanted. Canada at last relented and now she was here. She hadn't come around the world to help him. She was as selfish as the rest of them. She wouldn't show up.

The large clock on the wall clicked one o'clock into place, the door opened, and in she came.

Slečna Saudek was a slight thing. Her hair was thick and brushed and long and grey. Her skirt was grey, her shirt a tired white, her skin pale, her face sucked back against its bones, her eyes set in dark hollows. She moved and the folk who lined to approach the counter withdrew to make way without turning to see her. They felt her somehow.

Mrs Goren walked in her wake. Slečna Saudek spotted Otto and moved straight toward him.

'You must know a secret about this place,' she told him. 'Something not immediately obvious, to have brought us here.'

'It was my choice,' Mrs Goren stated. Her hair was the colour of raw meat and her round face shone. 'I like Switzer's. They serve the only baby beef in Toronto. Let me introduce you. Otto Schalmik, meet Slečna Saudek.'

Otto reached out a hand. Miss Saudek did not even regard it. She settled in a seat with a view toward the street and placed her hands in her lap.

'At least I can see Shopsy's from here,' she said of the delicatessen the other side of the street. 'That's somewhere I can trust.'

'Switzer's is much newer,' Otto tried. 'The corned beef here is machine cut.'

Miss Saudek suddenly faced him. Was he as simple-minded as his remark? Her look showed she was considering the question.

A waitress interrupted. Mrs Goren placed her baby beef order and then quizzed Otto and Miss Saudek about food choices and ordered for them too. The promise of food left her quiet for a moment.

Otto took his chance. 'Thank you for seeing me, Slečna Saudek,' he tried. 'Ever since I first learned that my mother and sister and my sister's baby were sent to Theresienstadt . . .'

'Terezín!' Miss Saudek snapped the word at him.

'Slečna Saudek uses the Czech name for the camp,' Mrs Goren reminded him.

'A ghetto,' Miss Saudek corrected her. 'It was termed a ghetto and not a camp. A place of transit rather than a place of extermination. Such distinctions are important.'

'Terezín,' Otto accepted. 'The ghetto at Terezín. I feel so lucky to find someone who was there. When Mrs Goren told me you . . .'

'Mrs Goren said you were troubled. A troubled young man. You don't look troubled.'

'I am worried. Worried about my family.'

'And that will do them any good?'

'I hope to find them. Bring them to Canada.'

'You hope to get what you want.'

'Mrs Goren tells me you survived Terezín. You survived Auschwitz.'

'Birkenau,' she corrected him. 'Or Auschwitz-Birkenau if you insist.'

'If you survived, then maybe my family did too. I thought you might . . .'

'Do you want the truth, young man, or do you want your own truth?'

She was in her mid-thirties, yet in that 'young man' she wielded her age like a baton. Otto had no ready answer for her question. Their food came. He snatched a bite of corned beef sandwich and swallowed it down fast.

'There's a crumb on your lip,' Miss Saudek said. 'You ate everything else. Everything else is gone. The crumb escaped. It's the same with me and Terezín and Auschwitz-Birkenau. Everyone else is gone. I'm the crumb.'

Otto licked the crumb into his mouth.

'There you go,' she said.

'My mother was Bertha Schalmik,' he began, hesitantly.

'She was Viennese?'

'Yes, that's right! You knew her?'

'It's unlikely. The Viennese kept themselves apart. They thought they were better than the rest of us.'

'Not my mother,' Otto said. 'She gets on with everybody.'

'Don't sentimentalize her, Herr Schalmik. No one gets on with everybody.'

'Her hair is brown. It has natural waves in it but she keeps it short. She makes her own clothes. Favours brown and grey and cream for the blouses. She's not tall, maybe one metre sixty, but she's big. Her arms are twice as thick as mine. We had a piano I couldn't budge but she pulled it back from the wall every week to clean behind it, so maybe you remember that. Maybe you remember her arms and her strength. She's a strong woman.'

Miss Saudek sipped a little milk from her glass. She was apparently having nothing to do with her sandwich. 'I thought you were in Dachau,' she said. 'And Buchenwald.'

Otto nodded and ate another mouthful.

'Then you know as well as I, Herr Schalmik, how fashion counts for little in such places. You remember your mother by her clothes, her hairstyle, her size, and her strength. That is good. Keep it that way.'

'My sister's name is Erna,' Otto said. Her married name eluded him for now. 'Erna looks like me, people say, but she is not so angular. She has my eyes. And she's tall for a woman. Her little girl is Greta. Bertha, Erna, Greta; a woman in her forties, one in her twenties, and a little girl, and I'm sure they kept close to one another. You'll have noticed them.'

'You've brought me to Switzer's,' Miss Saudek said. 'It's a busy place. People come, people go. Take a look around.'

Otto looked back at her and waited for more.

'I said take a look around.'

He did so. The deli was full of its late lunch crowd.

'You recognize anyone?'

'No.'

'You live near here?'

'Yes.'

'Even so there's no one you recognize. Mrs Goren, how many Jews are there in Toronto?'

Mrs Goren's knife was inserted into the last pale slice of her baby beef. 'Pardon?' she said.

Miss Saudek sighed and repeated her question.

'It's been a while since the census. At a guess? Around fifty thousand.'

'Mrs Goren guesses fifty thousand. Terezín was a town with high ramparts and trenches, a garrison town but a town nevertheless. A compact and tidy town with squares and a church and a town hall and shops and such things one expects. Seven thousand could live there in approximate comfort. It was crushed with so many maybe but the view of a mountain at the end of their streets gave them a sense of space. And then everyone who called the town home was forced to leave, the walls were guarded and sealed, and we Jews were installed in their place. We were pulled from our homes, thousands upon thousands of us. They layered us in bunks on top of each other and side-by-side, bunks filling rooms and then bunks filling attics. That's how they squeeze sixty thousand Jews into a town built for seven thousand. Close off the walls and you have your ghetto. Thousands die of illness, thousands are hauled East to the camps, thousands come and always thousands remain. Tell me, Herr Schalmik, how likely is it that I remember your mother, your sister, your niece, from among so many shifting thousands?'

'It's likely they were sent to Auschwitz-Birkenau. You were there. I understand there was a camp there. I can say camp, and use its German name? The Theresienstadt Family Camp. You got to stay together. Wear your own clothes. How many were there? Not so many. Not sixty thousand.'

Mrs Goren lay down her knife and fork. Her plate was emptied. 'Slečna Saudek was a teacher in Prague,' she said. 'She taught modern languages. At Auschwitz she . . .' She received a look and corrected herself. 'At Auschwitz-Birkenau, she was assigned to a women's work camp. There were many languages. She translated.'

'I worked.'

'She worked and translated.'

Miss Saudek took the narrative back. 'I had family of my own, Herr Schalmik. I was in Terezín and I hoped to see them. I searched. When a train came in I searched again. At Birkenau I searched. When I was released I searched. Coming along Spadina to meet you in this place, still I looked around and hoped to spot someone from my family. I know I never will. I am my family, Herr Schalmik. You are yours. That is what we have.'

She called out to stop a passing waitress and asked for a paper bag. She would take her sandwich to go.

'Thank you for the meal, Herr Schalmik,' she said, and with sip after sip finished her glass of milk. 'May you learn what you need.'

They watched her stand and go.

'At least she has her meal for tonight,' Mrs Goren said. 'Something good has come of the day.'

18
Sydney, 1962

Place a shark in an aquarium and ask it to describe the life of the little fishes it encounters there, and the shark won't account for its own impact. Similarly, Katja could not know how her shadow drove the world. When her fellow Australian citizens sensed Katja's approach, they tended to cross the street. That is one reason her portraits of the country contain no people.

'What was your maiden name?'

Katja had to think a moment. What was her name before she became Birchendorf? It was so far back.

'Klein,' she remembered.

Her daughter put her minimal English to work and wrote a translation onto the form she had taken from a resettlement officer. The German Klein became the English Little. She made the name her own. Uwe Little. She would not be a Birchendorf any more. When Katja spoke to her in German, the girl mouthed English back.

In 1951, when Uwe turned thirteen, Katja accepted that she now shared her home with an Australian teenager. When the girl dyed her hair black Katja took it to be a fashion statement. Uwe buttoned her white blouse tight around her neck and tugged her sleeves below her wrists. She wore black tights under a woollen black skirt even in summer. In a teenage world of flesh and brightness, Uwe stood out. Perhaps that's what she wanted.

Uwe went to secretarial school. She passed shorthand and typing classes with distinction. She found a job and left home. Katja did not hear from her. She waited.

In December 1962, Katja stepped out of a taxi and commanded the driver to keep the meter running. The day was mild and sunny. Katja hated the lack of a northern winter. Out on the streets she felt like a penguin in a zoo, dressed in her dark clothes and there to be laughed at.

Inside the entrance hall of the apartment block she found her daughter's name on a mailbox. Uwe had written it like a child, the nib pressed hard on the paper while she concentrated. *Uwe Little*.

Katja climbed the cement stairwell to the third floor where she pressed the bell on the black door. No one came. She hammered on the wood and shouted Uwe's name. A woman stuck her head out of the apartment next door.

'She's my daughter,' Katja snapped. 'I'm her mother.'

She banged on the door again and the neighbour retreated.

Eventually the door opened a crack. Uwe stepped back and her mother pushed her way in.

Uwe's hair was lank and unwashed and showed its brown roots. She had been sweating into a pillow. Her cheeks were drawn and her shoulders were thin yet her belly bulged out against her nightgown. She moved to her narrow bed and sat on its edge.

'Have you got money?' Katja said. 'We'll need your money. I didn't bring any and I have a taxi waiting. I am taking you home.'

Katja spotted Uwe's purse on the windowsill and walked across to fetch it. It held a few banknotes and coins. It was enough.

What a nasty little room. An electric ring, a gas boiler, a cracked enamel sink: is this what her daughter's independent life amounted to? There was a small wardrobe but it wasn't worth waiting to pack a case. Uwe wouldn't be going anywhere for a while and the taxi's meter was ticking.

A scuffed pair of shoes lay under the bed. Katja knelt and pressed Uwe's feet into them. It was a hard job because the feet were swollen, but she managed.

'There,' she said. 'Now stand up.'

The girl did as told. A light grey raincoat hung on the back of the door. When Katja held it out, Uwe fed her arms inside its sleeves.

'Come on then,' she said.

A bunch of keys hung from a nail near the door. Katja pocketed them, and steered her daughter out into the corridor.

The bathwater turned grey as Katja sponged her daughter down. She rubbed strands of hair between her hands and then checked her palms, wanting to find them black with dye.

Uwe did not have the will to feed herself, but her mouth worked when Katja fed morsels into it. She chewed and swallowed. That would do her some good.

Katja kept up a stream of speaking, in what she hoped was a soft voice. Just snippets from her life mostly. She didn't bother with any of that 'you're eating for two' nonsense. The baby was clearly sucking Uwe's life into itself. It needed no help from her.

'Your company wrote me this,' she said, and read out the letter. The company's maternity cover was considerate but it was discretionary. Employees needed to stay in touch. The secretarial pool was short staffed. Please be in touch at once.

Katja folded the letter back into its envelope.

'What happened?' she asked. 'What's happened to you?

Uwe closed her eyes. All Katja could do was wait. Watch and wait for her daughter's mouth to move.

The most figurative painting Katja had ever achieved depicted a clouded sky filled with crows. It was a portrait of her mind at rest.

She watched her daughter and inside her head a crow flashed its wings. Each crow is a memory. None lingers. Memories are the opposite of survival. Let one take root and you die.

They had shared too much, this girl and her. They had spent winters on the road. Her daughter was never raped. When Katja looked back coldly, she saw that as the main achievement of her life. Her daughter starved but she did not die of hunger. Katja saw to that. And Uwe was never raped. She saw more than a girl should ever see and who knows what she heard, but she was never raped.

If it was rape that did this to her daughter Katja did not want to know it, but if that is what she had to know then so be it.

Katja had known women who lay down. Some did so in the open and some in hollows among the rubble of war. They had hauled their bodies far enough, but they could not let go. They had a story still to tell. Their heads turned aside to look for the details. Katja became expert at lipreading from mouths that were in profile. Her act of absorbing these women's stories set them free.

Katja knew what young women on the edge of death looked like. They looked like Uwe looked now.

Uwe had a story to tell and it was Katja's job to bear witness to it. She watched her daughter's lips. That's where the story would come from.

'You remember that boy on the boat?'

The shapes of her daughter's mouth were a jolt. She was speaking German. Katja nodded and reached her fingers to lay them lightly on Uwe's throat. She felt the vibrations of speech as Uwe spoke on.

'His name was Stefan. We played and we were friends. Then he learned I was Daddy's daughter and he spat in my face. Well . . .' And she lay a hand on her belly. 'This is his.'

Her daughter's voice felt soft, like when she was six years old.

'I found him. I didn't go looking for him, well not really, but I found him. I spotted him in a kosher diner. The way he sat with his friends, the way he told stories and moved his hands, it drew me to him. I could see the boy in him. His skin had the same deep tone it had then, his face had that same angular shape, and of course there were those eyelashes. So long and dark. I waited for the friends to use his name. Stefan, one said. That's how I knew for sure. I followed them back to their workplace. It was easy to get a job there. And it was fairly simple after that to join in with the group of Stefan's friends.'

What were you doing in a kosher restaurant? Katja wanted to ask, but didn't. It was too late for challenges. Her job was to listen.

'Stefan says I planned it all. He says I'm sick. He said my black hair is the biggest lie he's ever seen. He wanted to shave my hair and push me out in the street. He says my pretending to be Jewish is like a paedophile putting on shorts and a school cap to get into a playground. That's not true is it, Mutti? I wasn't pretending. We talked about it. We killed so many Jews. Father killed so many Jews. I couldn't bring back any Jews but I could become one. That's the best I could do. Becoming a Jew was the proper Christian thing to do.'

Your father didn't kill Jews, Katja wanted to say. He wasn't a killer. And you, you were just a crazy girl with a stupid idea. You should have grown out of it. But she did not say these things.

'We went to a Torah study group together. Well, I joined the one Stefan attended. He saw how hard I was trying. I never lied. I said how my father was not Jewish but they kept him in a camp because of his association with Jews. That's what they did do to him after the war, isn't it? I said that he died in Dachau. I told how I went from place to place till I was put in Rosenheim. I worked hard at studying the Torah because I had no Jewish family left to teach me the traditional ways.'

What turned you into all this? Katja wondered. Was it the spit of that boy in your eye? Was it all that went before? Was it us?

'Stefan was preparing to go to Israel. He said he needed a new start and that was the place to go. The old ways were good but there was a new way and we could both find it. We were modern, he said. Modern and ancient both. He believed in free love. It was exciting. In Israel children would grow into the family of the kibbutz. Our children could do that.'

Katja could not grapple with the concept of a kibbutz. Jews went there to work to make themselves free. They built a camp and put up their own walls and installed their own guards. To her, a kibbutz seemed a throwback to the war.

'He took me to his home. For a Sabbath dinner. We practised beforehand. I knew when to break bread, the words to pray, and the answers to give. But not all the answers. His mother stared hard at me across the table. We finished the meal and she wiped her mouth on an edge of her napkin. "When did you first dye your hair?" she asked me. "When did you change your name? Where is your mother now? Does she pretend to be Jewish too?" I know it's important not to lie. She would not let me keep silent. Her questions pulled my story out of me. I tried to say why. Why I became a Jew. That it was the best I could do. She would not listen. She left me empty.'

Not so empty, Katja wanted to say.

'When was this?' she asked.

'In the spring.'

'Does Stefan know about the baby?'

'I never saw him after that night. He stayed at home when they asked me to leave the house. He did not come to work the next day. At the office, weeks went by and then they closed his file. They said he was leaving for Israel.'

'And you still love him,' Katja said.

Uwe did not speak. She had told enough of her tale. But for the baby inside of her, she was now empty.

At least it was not rape, Katja reflected. It was likely not that.

Katja knocked on her neighbour's door and asked her to phone for a doctor. The doctor examined Uwe and then borrowed the neighbour's phone to call an ambulance.

This wasn't an emergency, the doctor said. They just needed to keep the young woman under medical observation. They rolled her onto a stretcher, covered her with a blanket, and carried her away. Katja locked her front door, dropped her apartment's keys into her bag, and followed.

'I'm sorry, love,' the paramedic said. He dared to touch her arm but he didn't grab hold. 'You can't travel in the ambulance. It's not allowed.'

Then let them try and throw her out. She climbed in. The space on the bench at the back near the driver was wide enough for her. She would be no bother. Nobody just carried her daughter away on a stretcher. Nobody.

At the hospital, she followed as they transferred Uwe into a bed with clean sheets and fitted a plastic band to her wrist. Uwe's pulse was weak, her blood pressure low. Statistics were inked onto her chart. Katja fetched a wooden chair so she could sit nearby and wait.

There seemed to be two teams led by different doctors. One checked on Uwe's health, while the other bent over stethoscopes and listened for the health of her baby. The two teams walked away to meet out of earshot.

Katja had come to her own conclusions. Her daughter should give birth naturally. That's why, when they came back with their recommendation of a caesarean, she refused. They should wait, she insisted.

Uwe squealed at the first pain of labour. It wasn't loud. Katja could tell by the way a nurse turned her head only slowly at the sound, more like a gust of breath perhaps. Pain passed like a wave over her daughter's face, sudden and then gone.

Nurses pulled around the curtains. Katja sat outside. They insisted. They would have manhandled her out of the way if needs be, she realized. She watched the shadows of their movements upon the nylon drapes.

Uwe's body was not responding. They would have to operate.

Katja did not resist. They let her through the curtains while they went to make arrangements.

Katja took a corner of the sheet and wiped the sweat from her daughter's face. Of all the words she could have said, only four were worth saying.

'*Uwe, ich liebe dich.*' And again, because her daughter had tried so hard to become a part of this new world, she said the same four words in English. 'Uwe, I love you.'

'We're very sorry, Mrs Little,' the young doctor began.

'Birchendorf,' she corrected him.

He blinked. 'Mrs Birchendorf,' he began again. 'We did all we could. Your daughter was very weak.'

She could have slapped him for that, if the words on his slack mouth hadn't punched the strength from her body. Uwe was not weak. She was stronger than a privileged young male like him could ever guess at.

'It was heart failure. We tried to resuscitate, but the heart could not take it. Your daughter has died.'

'And the baby?'

The doctor dared to smile, as though she would let him off so easily.

'It's a baby girl,' he said. 'She is very healthy.' He paused, and then. 'Would you like to see her?' he asked.

Yes. She nodded. Katja wanted to see her. She wanted to see her daughter.

The young doctor walked away and Katja followed. He held out a hand to stop her walking through a pair of swing doors. She waited outside and he returned. A nurse came with him. Katja peered through the doors as they opened and shut.

The nurse held out a baby toward her.

'What's that?' Katja said.

'The baby,' the nurse said. 'Your daughter's baby. Your granddaughter.'

'Where is Uwe?' Katja said. 'You told me I could see Uwe. Where is my daughter? I want to see Uwe. Take me to see Uwe.'

Health visitors and social workers came to visit her in her apartment. They were checking on her suitability to parent her granddaughter.

'How will you know when the baby is crying?' one dared to ask.

'I will watch her,' Katja said. 'Like I watched my daughter.'

She filled in forms. She was as honest as she could let herself be. A blank space would do for the name of the father. For the name of the baby, she chose Rosa. Uwe once had a favourite doll she called Rosa. Perhaps that was why. And for the girl's surname, she had them write Little. She was bringing up the baby for her daughter, not stealing her away. Eventually they let her take the child home.

The baby slept in her arms while Uwe's coffin was lowered into the ground. Katja felt the heat of Rosa's body press through the black cotton of her dress and work its way toward her heart.

19
Hana's Tale:
Sydney Opera House 1972

New music was a hard sell, Otto Schalmik's agent explained to him. Yes, Sydney would stage his *Diaspora Variations*, but only if he offered them a concerto appearance as well. They could sell tickets for his world premiere as part of a two-concert package.

'Weinberg,' Schalmik said. 'If that's what they want, I'll give them Weinberg's Cello Concerto.'

They thought not. The idea was to sell tickets and who knew Weinberg? And so the New South Wales Symphony Orchestra kicked off Friday night at the concert hall of the Sydney Opera House with Wagner's Tannhäuser Overture. Schalmik then took to the stage and offered up the Dvorak Cello Concerto.

He took three curtain calls, and then showered and changed into light tan flannels and a plain white shirt. The speaker above the door of his dressing room crackled into human voice and called the orchestral players back to the platform. Schalmik was booked in for dinner with the conductor later. Before then he thought he would take an early evening walk beside the water.

A small woman was sitting on a plastic chair just inside the stage door. She wore a navy blue linen skirt and matching jacket with silver buttons. Her blouse was primrose yellow with a lacy collar. Her grey shoes, wide toes with a strap, were sturdy like a schoolgirl's. Her hair was grey and cut pageboy style to swing when she turned her head to face him. He took such people to be old at first, and then readjusted to see they were in the same age band as him.

She was moving to stand, to speak with him. He turned from her and looked ahead, ready to push his way through the door. This period when the concert played on was his private time. If she was still there when he returned, he would deal with her then.

'Mr Schalmik?' A pert young woman, plump cheeked with long ginger hair, officiated at the desk. She held out a folded piece of paper. 'I have this to deliver to you. I couldn't just up and leave the desk, now could I? But here you come. Problem solved.'

He took the note. It was dark outside so he stood in the neon glare of the stage door and read it:

Dear Mr Schalmik,

Please excuse me, but if you have the time I would like to speak with you. I knew your mother, Mrs Schalmik, and was a friend of your sister Erna. I am waiting by the stage door.

Yours sincerely,

Hana Bay (Mrs)

Schalmik turned to face the woman on the chair. She stood up.

'Mrs Bay?'

'Hana,' she said. 'Your family knew me as Hana.'

She held out her hand. The fingers were small, her grip was light. How could so frail a woman have survived?

'Otto,' Schalmik said. 'Thank you for coming. Please, let's go to the Green Room. It's empty there. We can talk.'

He nodded to the young woman behind the desk, who wrote Hana's name on a badge. They walked through the concrete basement, up a run of steps, and entered the large area shared by the artists of all the Opera House's performance spaces. A small TV monitor showed the orchestra in full action, playing their way through Dvorak's *New World Symphony*, but the Green Room was quiet.

Hana declined a drink. He led her to two armchairs by the window. Outside, boats slit furrows along the night-time Harbour.

'Your playing was wonderful,' Hana said. Her English carried Australian intonation, but he detected another accent at the root of it.

Schalmik nodded. 'I'm sorry you're missing the rest of the concert.'

'Oh, I wouldn't have come. It's a hideous programme. Why not just call it the Jackboot and the Rose and be upfront about it instead of wrapping it up as high culture? I'm surprised you agreed to take part. Who on earth dreamed of teaming Wagner with Dvorak and stopping there? The Nazis killed Czech music and here you are celebrating the fact. Dvorak, Janacek, we were already so rich and with so much to come. Prokofiev, Stravinsky, Shostakovich, we know what the Russians managed to do. But the Czechs? What happened after Janacek? Hans Krása, Victor Ullman, Pavel Haas, Gideon Klein, who knows such composers now? All killed, Mr Schalmik. All locked in Terezín and then transported to Auschwitz. Czech music was murdered in the gas chambers. I'm annoyed that I came here at all.'

'Viktor Ullman was Viennese. He studied with Schoenberg.'

'Hear yourself, Mr Schalmik. You say Viennese rather than Austrian. You're ashamed of your country yet still you're proud. Ullman was born in Moravia. He returned to Prague the year you were born. You can't have him. He's ours. And what are you now, Mr Schalmik? American?'

'Canadian.'

'Aah, Canada. So for somebody, the dream came true.'

Schalmik raised an eyebrow in query.

'A silly joke, Mr Schalmik. Excuse me. Warehouses were built at the edge of Auschwitz-Birkenau. We heard tales. These tall buildings were stacked to the rafters with precious objects. Everything of value any Jew ever brought with them was taken from them and stored there. Imagine the beauty and the wealth. It represented dreamland. We called these warehouses after the one country we most longed to move to. They represented freedom. We called them Canada.'

'The Canada I knew was not like that. It was at war.'

'While you were studying at music school. Do I have this right? You were studying the works of German musicians, no doubt, while Czech music was being murdered.'

Schalmik stiffened, prior to leaving. He did not need to face accusations.

'I'm sorry, Mr Schalmik.' The words were an apology, but her body sat rigidly erect, her jaw thrust forward. 'I will explain. I'll tell you what I have come to say. I didn't come here to berate you. But really, a programme headlining Wagner should have given you pause for thought.'

Schalmik had an intensity of stare that could turn his silence hostile. He used it for a while, and then relaxed. In its place he adopted his passive face, one that might even be viewed as smiling. He had just given his all to a cello concerto. He gave people such music, and they took it personally. Some people are sensitive about being touched like that, deep in the soul. Their response is to go on the attack. It was safest to go quiet and let it pass.

'You're humouring me, Mr Schalmik. You're waiting for me to be finished and go away. Well I will. I nearly didn't come at all. I watched you when you were playing. I listened, and I thought, "That man is full. He needs nothing you can give him, Hana." Then when you came on to take your bow that third time, something had happened. The music had left you. You looked deflated. You have your music, but when that's gone you've nowhere left to go. Isn't that right, Mr Schalmik?'

So she combined insight, empathy and arrogance. It let Schalmik label her. This Hana must be a teacher.

'You knew Erna?' he prompted.

'It's not a long tale, Mr Schalmik,' she said. 'I've rehearsed it. You think you've held things so close but then details escape. Two years I lived with Erna, from Terezín to Auschwitz. You would think I had more to tell. Perhaps you start, Mr Schalmik. Tell me all you know from the time you left. I don't want to bore you.'

Schalmik started to speak, but his mouth was dry. His tongue stuck to his palate. 'If you'll excuse me,' he said, 'I'll just fetch us both some water.'

Otto brought back a bottle and two glasses, and poured. The water was carbonated. He hated that. Why couldn't they just leave good water alone?

'I don't know my sister from that time,' he said. 'We exchanged letters but we were all aware of the censors. We wanted to sound positive. The letters ached with what was not being said.

'I never heard from them in Terezín. The last we heard they were still in Vienna. My mother vacated our family apartment and moved in with Erna. Living together saved rent, and Erna's place was more remote. I guess it seemed safer for them to be together after we men were hauled away. My mother's letters became lists of items she had sold and at what prices. She was collecting money to pay the emigration tax. Her precious things brought in nothing. Who wants to give good money to a Jew? She ended up bartering for food.

'Then Greta was born. The news in the letters was all about Greta. What can you say about a baby? Whatever you can say, they said it. The baby fed greedily and slept for no more than three hours at a stretch. That is what I remember, Hana. That is all I know. For any more, I will be grateful.'

'Not grateful. You will hate me. But so be it. You never knew Greta?'

Schalmik shook his head.

'She was a timid little thing when I first saw her. Not used to company. Back in Vienna the streets weren't safe. Erna paid for Greta's yellow star and kept it in a drawer. Why pin that on her daughter and walk those streets? You only made yourself a target. Erna kept Greta at home. So Terezín was quite a change. You know about Terezín?'

'Facts,' Schalmik said. 'I know some facts. Nothing that matters.'

'Your facts matter, Mr Schalmik. Everything matters. You're pretending. You were in Dachau. You know what matters as well as I.'

'What matters is dead,' he said. 'And here we are talking about it.'

Both held silence a while, and then reached for their glasses to sip some water. Schalmik spoke again. 'Erna is gone. I presume you can't change that fact for me?'

Hana gave a tiny, stiff shake of her head, almost a wince. 'It's not all a bad story though. Shall I just tell it?'

Schalmik stared at her, and then nodded.

'It's easier for me to speak about Greta. Shall I do that? I shall do that. Greta was our joy. Our salvation. Always remember that, Mr Schalmik. The briefest life can be so full. She just soaked in the love, did little Greta, took in all you could give her and then gave it back a hundredfold."

Schalmik didn't smile. He wasn't up to social niceties. This was not a conversation to take part in. His job was to listen. His niece was taking shape and character for him. She would never bounce on his knee or swing in his arms, she was becoming more of a fairy tale character than that, but she belonged in the tale of this woman's life and he was ready to hear it.

'Your sister, now she was a player. You're superb too, Mr Schalmik, of course you are, but what a loss we have in Erna. When she played a violin you heard a soul taking flight. I was not ignorant of music, I had sat through concerts of Bach, but when Erna played it was no longer an endurance. She took me inside Bach somehow, so I was within the music and looking out. Frau Schalmik of course was mighty talented on the piano, in a more rhythmic kind of way. She was in demand as an accompanist in rehearsals for the ghetto's concerts.'

Gradually Otto learned all he ever would learn of his niece. He heard of how Erna and her daughter Greta performed Brahms's 'Wiegenlied' for all the women who loved them.

'You knew Hans Krása, Mr Schalmik?'

He shook his head.

'Why should you? A lovely man but so serious. He was like you, Mr Schalmik. A composer. He had had success with a children's opera. *Brundibár*. Well I say success, it was performed in an orphanage. When they put it on in Terezín it was so popular. Normal folk like me could not get tickets. Then we heard the International Red Cross were coming on a visit. The SS commanders wanted to showcase how well we inmates were treated. *Brundibár* had been sung to a piano accompaniment. Now Krása was ordered to write a score for full orchestra. A new set was painted in especially bright colours, a large stage was filled, and there was room for lots of us. I got my chance. The Red Cross investigating committee needed to see a happy audience. In truth, I've never been happier in my whole life.

'Greta was still only just five. A girl had gone missing from the cast. You wouldn't think a five-year-old could fill in at short notice, a German girl singing in Czech, but that's what Greta did. I can't tell you how sweet it was. She didn't just sing the right notes, she kept up with all the others. Find the score of *Brundibár*, Mr Schalmik. You're a famous musician, you must be able to do that. Read it, and imagine a perfect five-year-old in the girl's chorus. That's the voice of your little niece. You'll hear Greta there.'

It was true. Later he did track down the score and isolated this one infant voice within it. She sang for him, pure pitched and even. This was Greta, resounding in his skull.

And of course it was not Greta at all, just some recreation of a voice detached from history. The Nazis had paraded children in song to dupe the Red Cross. Music was made an instrument of terror. You have to stay alert. Schalmik kept his compositions stoked with snares and alarms.

'In the daily life of Terezín, Mr Schalmik,' Hana continued, 'supplies were delivered around the town in hearses. That was the Nazis' own sense of theatre. They wanted us to know we lived in the shadow of death. We had no horses of course. Those hearses were pulled by children. That's the life our children knew. But in the opera the children sang and they danced. For a few vital hours they had a childhood.'

Hana picked up her glass in both hands and drank the water down. Language is civilized discourse; the reality of the ghetto is aberrant to the rational mind.

At least when survivors meet there's no questioning whether horrors really happened. They had lived them.

Schalmik saw Hana's hands clasp the glass and watched her throat gulp at the water. The act marked a shift in story. Thirst is so much more acute than hunger. Hana's drinking was a reflex action. In warding off thirst she was seeking to still panic.

'Of course, as soon as the Red Cross left, the SS had no more use for children in Terezín,' Hana said. 'They loaded them all into the freight cars soon after. Adults too. All of us.'

Schalmik drained his own water and then refilled both glasses.

'You know those freight cars,' Hana said.

It wasn't a question, but more like a reminder to herself. She was telling the particular story of Greta, and had no need to sink into the swamp of atrocity.

Schalmik nodded for her to continue. And so she did.

He heard of the life in Auschwitz-Birkenau and took in new details of the 'Family Camp'. Hana once sat next to Erna at a chamber music recital, it was Schubert's Quintet, little Rosa on Erna's lap and closing her eyes for a time as though entranced by the music while a delicate smile curved her cheeks.

'Children went to school, where they learned new songs. Singing sees people at their happiest, so why give these children less than that? Most evenings Greta would come to us with a new folk song she had learned. We'd laugh and have her sing it again and then once again. Then one late afternoon instead of a folksong she opened her mouth and out came Beethoven's "Ode to Joy". The children were learning it to sing in a concert for the camp's officers. I knew the music, of course I did, but she sang in German so I missed what made Erna choke down a sob. You'll know Schiller's text in German: '*Wir betreten feuertrunken, Himmlische', dein Heiligtum.*' The tall chimneys spewed flames and the ashes entered our lungs and the crematoria were burning us and little Greta was singing about stepping, drunk with fire, into the sanctuary of heaven. Erna hugged her tight at the close of the song but that time she didn't ask her to sing it again.'

And Otto listened on, to hear of how his sister Erna stood proud and naked and was selected to join the women who would be leaving Birkenia for the work camp. They would escape the flames. Hana was selected too. Greta would stay behind with Frau Schalmik. It might have worked. But Otto heard how Erna turned her head, how Greta cried *Mutti* and broke from Frau Schalmik's hold. The stock of a rifle felled the girl. Erna broke from the women set to leave the camp and ran to her daughter's side. 'I saw no more, Mr Schalmik,' Hana concluded. 'I heard shouts. I heard the gate crash shut behind us.'

Hana studied Otto Schalmik's face. He wasn't seeing her. The room about them was filling with orchestral players.

'It seems the *New World*'s over,' Hana said.

Schalmik's head shuddered. He blinked and looked around him.

'I think of them, Mr Schalmik. I've imagined an image that may well be true, and that is what I can bear to go back to. The crematoria with their gas chambers were built into patches of forest. The trees were mostly oaks, with some pines and birch. Families waited here when the crematoria were too full to take them. That's where I picture them, before they were made to undress. Greta is in a white dress with a pattern of apples along its hem. She wears white ankle socks and her favourite light blue shoes.'

She studied Otto. His eyes had filmed over.

'They missed you,' she told him. 'At least Otto got away, they said. I first heard of you in Terezín and then in Auschwitz-Birkenau it was still something they spoke about most every day. Otto is in Canada somewhere, they said.'

Tears smarted Otto Schalmik's eyes.

'I'll leave you, Mr Schalmik.'

Otto closed his eyes and rubbed them. When he opened them again, Hana was gone.

He left a note for the orchestra's conductor. He did not want food and he did not want company, so he made an excuse. In his hotel room Otto set a pad of music manuscript paper on the desk.

He used the hotel's courtesy pen to write; blue ink patterned one page and then the next. It took nine pages. The lyrics were in Yiddish. He could have sworn that was impossible for him to do but the words were simple and they came to him. When he finished, the sky outside was no longer dark. He stacked the pages into a neat pile. They made up Schalmik's 'Wiegenlied', a set of variations for solo violin and child soprano.

He moved from the desk to his bed. With his eyes closed, he heard the piece as thought it were being performed. So this is how Erna plays, he thought, her sound so full and lush with rubato. And just listen to Greta, that smooth flow of her Yiddish. Her five-year old voice shot from high to low like she was gulping down the notes.

Otto wrote the lullaby for his sister and his niece and they played it in his head, one variation and then the next, till he fell asleep.

20
Sydney Opera House, 1972

Rosa wanted to take a friend. That's what girls do. She was only nine.

Absolutely not, her grandmother told her. You go alone. That is the experience.

And so on the Saturday morning they stationed themselves. A dark blue broad-brimmed hat shaded the grandmother's face and matched her dress. A white headband pinned the girl's light brown curls to her scalp, and her dress was also white. They stood on a lawn of the Botanical Gardens and faced the Harbour. The sky was cloudless.

The woman, Katja Birchendorf, set up her easel. This landscape was too stark, all green and blue and white. It was impossible for painting. She needed nuance.

Still, this was not about her.

'Here,' she said. 'Your ticket. Don't lose it. Put it in your purse.'

Rosa moved her lips as she made out the words. *Diaspora Variations*. She looked up.

Katja broke the word up into plainchant. 'Di-as-po-ra.'
A family on the footpath turned and looked at her as they
passed. She had such volume. 'It means a dispersal of people
from their homeland.'

'Dispersal?'

'You have something you do not want, you give it away,
and there is so much it goes everywhere. Diaspora is when
you do that to people.'

'Like with you and my mother.'

'Ah yes.' Katja looked away from the girl's lips and toward
the sky. She only learned to speak English after she turned
deaf, and chose intonation and pronunciation that suited her
native German. 'We were dispersed. It was a great and sad
dispersal. People forget this.'

Rosa touched her grandmother's sleeve. She had another
question. Katja looked down at her lips.

'Variations. I know that's a musical term. But diaspora
variations?'

'There was a big diaspora and a little diaspora. Your mother
and I, we were the little. We were Aryans. We had ideas that
were too big for one country.'

'And the big diaspora?'

'Jews.'

The woman boomed the word. That happened randomly
whenever she spoke, words jumped out and shouted at
you, but the word 'Jews' was different. Whenever it came,
it jumped out with especial force, and ended conversation.

Rosa's purse was pink and hung from a string around her neck. She sealed the ticket inside it, alongside a coin for ice cream.

'So go,' Katja said, and pointed to the white shells of the Sydney Opera House roof. 'Come and find me when it's done.'

She watched the girl in white grow distant, and then become a speck that rose up the high range of concrete steps. And then she folded her easel, turned her back on the Opera House, and walked off into the gardens. It was useless to stand there and think about the girl. She had her own life to lead.

Rosa was used to strange sounds that fell from the sky. When she looked up to trace them, she mostly found cockatoos. She stopped on the steps and looked up now.

A man sat high above her. He straddled the white tiles at the front peak of the concert house shell. His shirt was dark green and his face so black it lost features against the white background. The long tube of a didgeridoo pointed from his mouth and straight at her. The first note he blew boomed out on the longest of breaths. It started low and roared into a wail.

The wail ended yet its absence was as strong as sound so she was still listening for it when she noticed a new note had started. This one grew too till it roared and almost screamed. Then the music became breaths, quick explosive breaths that shook Rosa back to herself.

She finished walking up the steps. Inside the glass doors of the entrance a boy tore her ticket and stuck a big green sticker to her dress.

Rosa stood still. 'I don't know where to go,' she said.

'That's the plan,' the boy replied. 'Apparently.'

He stuck a sticker on the next visitor and Rosa walked through.

People clustered into small groups. Heads turned around, and then clicked into one direction and off they went. Rosa followed and found herself in a courtyard.

Up above her a woman sat in an empty window space and dangled her legs. She was playing an accordion. It pumped breaths of loud air like the didgeridoo was doing on the roof. Then Rosa heard a single low note, which sustained and grew loud as a chord was added. It roared toward a silence and started again.

The afternoon became a hunt. Rosa found a lady in a skin-tight silver dress whose neckline dipped between her breasts, and watched the hairs in her armpits as she bowed a violin. Alone on the stage of the Concert Hall a man in a purple shirt sang in a voice that was higher than a girl's. His song had no words, just vowels, and then a rush of explosions when he spat breaths into a microphone.

To the side of the building she entered the Playhouse and found a young woman who beat padded sticks onto a kettle drum. Back in the Opera House bar a fat man sat on a barstool and streamed sounds from a clarinet.

Inside the Opera House's auditorium the walls were black and dim floodlights guided people to the rows of seats. Rosa placed herself in a pink one at the front. A spotlight dropped a small circle of light on a man on stage. He wore a white shirt, open-necked with the sleeves rolled up, and sat quite erect. On his cello he played four notes in different patterns, up and down the octaves, all with gentle strokes of the bow. His eyes stayed closed: not squeezed shut, but soft like eyes in sleep.

Suddenly Rosa found herself held inside one continuous bending note, with no beats at all any more. The cellist opened his eyes and looked up high, toward the ceiling and over to the right. Rosa turned and stared with him but found nothing to see. Music collapsed into sound. Other sounds joined in. The violinist, the accordionist, the singer, the clarinettist, the man from the roof with the didgeridoo, the drummer with a drum strung round her neck entered through different doors and walked onto the stage as they played.

The audience followed and squeezed in between the rows but no one sat. They just stood and waited inside the sound.

Rosa noticed no signal but the musicians each engaged their instrument in a peculiar dance, boosting volume and layering music on top of each other till it accumulated near the ceiling like a clouded sky, and then they became still all at once. There was no tapering off. The silence shocked her. It was like being dropped from on high and falling to the ground.

The adults stood stunned, and then they shouted and clapped their hands. The switch from that one vast and almost oppressive sound to a rage of applause was more than Rosa could take. She stood and pushed at a closed door and stepped out into the light.

She needed to leave the building, that's all she knew.

Once outside she paused. Her heart beat so fast it hurt but she was OK.

A cry shrilled across the sky. There above her cockatoos flashed white against the blue. The birds flew across the Botanical Gardens. That's where her grandmother was. She would ask questions.

Rosa was not ready for that. It was too big a reduction, to fit music into words. She needed more time.

The main stairs swept down the front of the building. She found an alternative set that led down to the lower level. To the right of an entrance door a man sat on the floor. He was young enough to have spots on his face, and dressed in a black T-shirt, jeans and big boots. He had a black straggly beard, long hair, and blue eyes that stared at her when she came near. On the floor to his left lay a hat with coins inside, and to his right a Jack Russell terrier was curled up in sleep.

The man was playing a penny whistle. She recognized the tune. It was a four-note theme, repeated through different combinations. Then he reached an endnote. He closed his eyes to keep the pressure inside them and the sound grew louder the less breath he had. The dog sat upright and tilted its head. And then the note stopped.

The man kept his eyes shut, and then opened them. Rosa was staring at him. He grinned and she grinned back.

Rosa opened her purse, took out her ice cream coin, and dropped it into the man's hat. Then she turned and ran away.

Rosa shouted once, 'Oma!'

Her grandmother was deaf, but sometimes you have to scream and shout not so someone can hear, just for the release of it.

Rosa ran across lawns and around banks of shrubs. At last she spotted her grandmother. The woman stood beside a pond and faced a palm tree. Not that you would be able to identify the scene, from the colours slashed across the canvas on her easel.

'So soon,' Katja said and waited for Rosa to regain her breath. 'So tell me, what was he like?'

'Who?'

'The cellist, of course. Otto Schalmik. The supposedly world-famous composer.'

Rosa thought. 'He was a man. A thin man with big hands.'

'Does he have much hair?'

'Quite a bit. It's long. And grey. And swept back.'

'And how does he seem?'

Musical? That's what Rosa wanted to say, but it seemed silly. 'He seemed well.'

'What do you mean, well? Did he look proud? Did he look pleased with himself?'

This was a yes or no question. Her grandmother liked clear responses. One answer would be right, the other would be wrong.

'Yes,' she tried.

'I thought so.' Katja whirled her paintbrushes inside a jar of water. The water turned dark brown with paint.

'Wipe those dry on the grass,' she told Rosa, and handed her the wooden handles of the brushes like they were a bunch of flowers. She tilted the jar to pour the paint and water into the pond. 'I believe we have both earned a glass of ice cream. Let's go to the pavilion.'

Katja read lips, which meant they could not walk and share conversation. It suited them both. The girl followed the woman across the grass, and on the path they linked hands.

21
Big Sur, California, 1994

Rosa Little tended to keep her grandmother secret. Yet when she took effort, as she had done that morning in the airport hotel bedroom, put on a dress, brushed out her hair and made up her eyes, she was sometimes shocked to find her grandmother blinking back from the mirror. Not the old Gran, grey haired and shrunken and now in fact dead. The young one of early black and white photos.

And then there was the anger. Sometimes it was her deafness that made her gran shout, but often it was anger. Rosa had that anger too but felt she knew how to bottle it up. Right now she was finding it hard. Her bottle was set to pop.

She floored the accelerator of her hire car and stormed along a largely empty highway. This was her first time in California. *Condé Nast* listed this route through Big Sur as one of the ten best stretches of coastal driving in the world. She knew of ten better in Australia alone. This road was a narrow and twisting scar across the bleak face of mountains.

Over to her left, in occasional glimpses offered by breaks in the trees, Rosa caught snatches of view where sky-blue seas crashed waves against hulks of rocks. Back home in Australia she would pull the car on to the verge, find animal tracks to follow, and scramble straight down to the beach. Here there was no stopping. The coastline was owned by forests and the rich. It was socially unsustainable.

She overshot the lane and turned back. It turned out the house had no name or number, just a PRIVATE KEEP OUT! sign with the outline of a bull-headed dog, its jaws open, fangs bared. She was driving a ridiculous upgrade, a vomit-coloured Chevy Landcruiser unwanted by others on the airport lot. Her shoulders ached from heaving it around. She pulled it off the road and drove the steep driveway down to a wooden fence.

She turned off the engine but stayed in her seat because her heart was still racing. Ostensibly she was here to get Otto Schalmik's permission to write his biography. That's the line she had spun to the publisher. She guessed she wanted to bring it off, the book would be a good career move, but in truth there was only one question she wanted to ask of the man, and that meant setting up a confrontation. And that's why she felt so angry just now. Why couldn't she just have silly secrets of her own to keep? Why wasn't she born innocent? Why let herself be stuck with all this guilt to sort out?

Rosa took off her flat driving shoes, strapped on her stilettoes, and stepped out of the car.

A side gate was built into the fence. She pushed through it and into a gravelled courtyard.

'Mr Schalmik?'

To her left was a double garage with closed doors. Sliding glass windows led into the house beyond that. Was this really Schalmik's house? Nothing gave the fact away. The yard held no scrap of clutter. Potted plants would cheer it up, even dead ones would show a bit of effort, but there was not so much as a weed. You would expect car tracks in the gravel, sweeping round to the garage doors, but all was as smooth as if raked. The place looked vacated.

'Mr Schalmik?'

The gate shut but some metal kept sounding. She stepped back. It was the move of an instant, her body reacting to danger even while she analysed it. The sound came from a chain scraping the ground. It was clipped to the studded collar around the thick neck of a dog.

Rosa was not good on dogs but she had had a run-in with this type before. Extra thick hair bristled down its spine, hair as near orange as brown. A Rhodesian Ridgeback, bred to take down lions. It had been hiding and waiting for her to close the gate. Lips were curled back across its broad face to show grey gums and bared teeth but it was soundless. The thing was stalking her. What kind of dog does that, hides behind a gate and keeps itself from barking till it can pounce? Its leg muscles tensed and its back paws pressed into the gravel.

She quickened, her instincts set to flight, but in scurrying her right foot slipped sideways in her shoes. Still she pushed back as she fell, crablike now and on her back, hands and feet both pushing.

The dog could have caught her ankle, but it was picky. It wanted her neck. She twisted sideways as it lunged. The chain caught, snatching the dog from its bite as she pulled away. The dog tried to shake its head free. Foam from its mouth hit her cheeks.

She took the chance to grab the fallen shoe and scrambled further out of reach. Even now the dog did not bark. It inched backward till the chain went slack and then it hunched down with its backside pressed against the gate.

She let the gravel cut into her foot and kept the shoe to hand as a weapon, holding it by the toe. She'd smash the stiletto into the damn thing's brain if it came for her now.

Backing all the way, watching the dog, she came to the door of the house. It was locked. She banged the heel of her hand against the glass and looked through. It was open plan inside. One glimpse took her through to a distant window and showed no one was home.

She kept backing up. A side gate sealed the courtyard from whatever lay beyond. She reached for the latch. It opened, thank God. With one swirl Rosa twisted her body around it and slammed the gate shut behind her.

This wasn't a garden, simply a sequence of slatted wooden steps with a burst of red fuchsia to either side. She pushed her foot back into its shoe (curse this footwear choice) and walked on down, ever down, like the whole property was sliding into the sea. The land soon gave up much pretence of being managed. Grass was thick, brown and wild, with just a thin dust footpath that trailed through it.

Curiously the path started to rise a little, riding one last wave of land before it dropped to the sea. Her heart was still beating fast. She paused a moment, tipped back her head to take in the sky, kicked off the damn shoes to pick up on her way back, took a few deep breaths, and continued barefoot.

The path crested between two outcrops of rock. This property was on a spur that pushed out into the Pacific. There, sitting on a boulder ten feet back from the cliff edge, was Schalmik.

She knew him from his posture. It was the same he adopted before performance, those famous still moments with his long back quite erect as he willed the audience into a starting point of silence. Now his audience was the ocean. He wore a plum-coloured shirt tucked inside jeans, his grey hair ragged over its collar.

Her heart was racing again. It was nerves. She had rehearsed their meeting, starting with a polite interchange by his front door, but those words would not work in this context.

She had a right to be here, she must just remember that. She came with her own standing. She needn't be in awe.

He turned. First his head, and then he swivelled round his whole body so as to sit and face her. Her approach became a performance for him to watch.

She took it bravely and marched toward him.

He stayed sitting.

'Mr Schalmik? I'm Rosa Little.'

'Rosa.' His eyes were grey like northern seas and stared at her a while.

She held out her right hand. He took the bait, his fingers surprisingly cool as they enveloped her own. Her hand was sweating.

'Your dog attacked me.'

'So you've met the owner of the house?'

'Had you forgotten I was coming?'

'I chained Mango up. Left the gate unlocked.'

'It came within a whisker of my throat.'

'That's a dog's job. Mango puts on a good show.'

'That dog's insane. It should be put down.'

He said nothing, as though giving her time to reconsider, and then spoke. 'Well now you're here.'

'I thought the house was empty. I thought you'd gone away.'

'But you found me.'

'That's what we biographers do,' she said. 'We find our subjects.'

They spoke about the weather, her flights, and the trip up the coastal road. He always drove slowly, he advised her. Hit a rockfall at speed and you could be thrown off the road.

The conversation was all so trivial. Smalltalk for a guest you longed to be rid of.

When she reached her shoes she leaned down and strapped them on smoothly, without comment.

'Now we'll go and make friends with Mango,' he said, and smiled.

'What do I do? Offer it my neck?'

'She's not an it. She's a she. She's a bitch.'

Too right.

'Don't worry. Mango's just a honey with her friends.'

He clicked open the gate. Rosa followed behind him. The dog stood quiet at the end of its chain and thrummed its whole body with the stub of its tail. Schalmik leaned in close so the creature could splash a lick across his face.

'Come closer,' he said.

Rosa took a few paces, and then stopped. The dog eyed her. Its tail ceased wagging.

'Not like that. You're making her nervous. Be normal. Come and say hello.'

Rosa stepped to within reaching distance.

'Hold out your hand. Let her smell the back of it.'

The cool of the dog's nostrils struck Rosa's hand as it snorted in her scent. The creature seemed to approve. Its stub of a tail started thrumming again.

'Very good.' Schalmik felt round the dog's studded collar and released the click. It bounded free, pushing Rosa aside as it raced tight circles around its master.

'She's a pack animal. Dogs make no moral judgements. They're for you or against you. Don't you feel better, having the big dog on your side?' Rosa had no ready answer so he continued. 'We'll settle you in. You're a little late, but we've waited for you. We can all have lunch together.'

Rosa collected her flat shoes and her bags. A spiral staircase led down to her room with its bed fitted into an alcove. A window let onto a pond and a cluster of dark greenery, which gave the room a subterranean feel. A bathroom was attached, with a porthole that faced the sea but looked out only onto shrubbery and trees. The towels were black and had the slight stiffness that meant they were unused.

Rosa washed her hands and checked her make-up. With gifts in hand she went upstairs.

'I've served,' he said.

He was dropping the last of the salad from a bowl onto a plate, the wooden salad servers handled neatly by his left hand, arranging them around slices of zucchini quiche.

'I thought we'd eat out on the balcony. Would you mind opening the doors?'

Mango nosed her way through the sliding doors. Schalmik set the plates down on a wooden slatted table and then made an extra visit to the kitchen, returning with a glass pitcher and a tall tin. From the tin he poured kibble into the dog's bowl.

The dog crunched and scoffed the lot, and before Schalmik sat down sent the empty bowl rattling across the decking with a few licks of her tongue. With a satisfied burp the dog collapsed to the floor.

'She's quick to satisfy.' Schalmik flipped out his own napkin and set it on his lap. 'Please, begin. Some iced tea?'

Rosa nodded. 'It's lovely out here,' she said.

And it was. This upper level let you take in the Pacific. The sun was full but gentle. The balcony was round and ringed by a low glass wall so they were sitting up among the trees, looking out beyond the branches to the ocean.

Schalmik offered a thin smile of agreement and then set to work. He held the cutlery pinched in his long fingers like a surgeon, slicing the quiche and marshalling the salad toward the prongs of his fork. His forkfuls were tiny but his manner was brisk. Soon his plate was clean. He looked up at Rosa.

She stuffed a wad of salad into her mouth and chewed while he watched. She felt like a pet rabbit.

'Do you live out here all year?' she asked when she had swallowed.

'It's not out here to me. It's home.'

'You must have a lot of people want to come and stay.'

'Who knows what people want. We don't welcome guests.'

'Well this was lovely.' She speared the last of the quiche, ate it fast, and dabbed her lips. 'I feel very welcome.'

'I know how to deal with guests. I just don't care to.'

'Don't you get lonely?'

'No.'

That was her first personal question. He had blocked it. She followed through with silence, staring him out, hoping for more.

'I suppose you have a right to be impertinent, Rosa. It's your job. But you know I don't do interviews.'

'You agreed to meet me.'

'Yes. That doesn't mean I want to be interviewed.'

'Well thank you in any case. For having me here. It's an honour.' She reached down for the shiny silver giftbag and passed it across the table. 'I brought you these.'

'You shouldn't,' he said. 'I need nothing.'

He reached inside the bag in any case, maybe glad of the distraction. He pulled out the bottles. The first was a white wine. She sensed him brighten when the tissue came off.

'Prüm. Very clever. You didn't buy this in California.'

'I brought it with me. From Berry Brothers and Rudd in London. The next one too.'

He stripped off its tissue. The bottle was thin with straight sides and a long neck, its glass clear and the liquid red. He stared at the antique script on the label. It was Zirbenz, a stone pine liqueur. His eyes watered a little.

'A taste of old Vienna,' she offered.

'Almost. Indeed. Well why not, why not. It's very thoughtful of you. You know I don't drink?'

'Oh. I'm sorry.'

'It's nothing moral. I like wine, but got bored with the snobbery. It seemed simpler to stop than to keep up. But I appreciate this. Tonight we will have a party.'

He reached into the bag for the final gift. This was a small, square box made of plywood. First Flush Darjeeling, that year's vintage and stamped with Fortnum and Mason's 'by appointment to Her Majesty the Queen' crest.

'It's from Alex,' Rosa said. She had asked the publisher for advice on what to bring.

'So why is Alex so stupid about wanting my biography? He publishes my music. That should be enough for him. Wait there, Rosa. I'll make us a pot.'

Rosa looked out towards the sea. Alex had primed her. You'll find the old man crusty, he said. Don't push him too hard. You may get few stories, but if you can just get his permission that's splendid.

Well she would see. The ice was clearly breaking. She had her hopes.

Schalmik returned with a full tray.

'See,' he said. 'I have the makings of a proper English gentleman. I even have a teacosy.'

The teacosy was old, with a musical motif of worn staves and crotchets floating on its off-white background. A sugar bowl and a small milk jug with a pink rosebud pattern matched the china teacups and saucers. A separate saucer held slices of lemon.

'I normally drink green tea. This is such a treat. How do you take yours?'

'Black,' she said. Like coffee. She hated tea.

The teapot was earthenware, round and brown and ugly. Schalmik poured through a stainless steel strainer. The tea was pale and insipid. She stirred in sugar to thicken it a little.

'Ahh,' Schalmik said. He had added nothing to his own cup. Sipping in silence while staring at her seemed to satisfy him.

'Alex said you felt we should meet before agreeing to anything,' she tried. 'That's why I'm here. I'm grateful for the opportunity. He says you've turned down others.'

'Some I turn down. Some I just ignore.'

'Why?'

'Most of them are Jews.'

Rosa raised an eyebrow. Here was a world-famous Jew speaking against Jews.

'What am I to be known as, Schalmik the musician or Schalmik the Jew? It is a big question for the *critics*.'

He gave such stress to the word that her look challenged him.

'If the critics were not Jews,' he continued, 'then they were sincere. They were all so sincere.'

'That's wrong?'

'It's not wrong. It's just so tiresome. Who cares what people think about my music?' He set down his teacup. 'This is delightful. Darjeeling of this quality gives you a special high, don't you find? It lifts the head somehow while making it wider. It makes me more receptive for a while. I hear the different notes the breeze is playing around the pine needles.'

He closed his eyes in appreciation, and then opened them to stare at the young woman.

'You'll have some more?'

What the hell. She gulped her cup down and handed it forward. He held the spout above the strainer but didn't pour. She watched and waited, then heard that he was laughing; just a little stutter of breath but it was a laugh no less.

'I'm sorry,' he said. 'I can't do it to you. You're a coffee woman. It's obvious. You're trying to be polite but it's not your strong point. You should see the face you pulled when you finished your cup. Don't worry. I have coffee. I'll show you where it is. Make some whenever you need it.'

He poured for himself and set the teacosy back on the pot.

'Be yourself, Rosa. Then we might get along.'

So be it.

'I do believe there is such a thing as Jewish music,' Rosa said.

'You think my music is Jewish?'

Why was he arguing the point? Entire tunes from the Jewish tradition were divided between solo instruments in his larger works. Critics, and not just Jewish ones, had found them. OK the tunes were scattered and drowned by orchestral volume, but know they are there and their poignancy becomes aching. He had even given his music Jewish titles. Did she think his music was Jewish?

'Sometimes,' she said.

'Ha.' He slammed his cup onto his saucer. 'Then you are wasting my time. We can have no agreement. Come, Mango.'

The dog lifted its head.

'It's time for our walk.'

'You want me to go?' Rosa asked.

'Go, come, it's all the same to me.'

'When you say we can have no agreement . . . ?'

'I live with Mango. She and I agree on everything. Still, it does me good to be disagreeable for a while. The pattern of my life is that Mango and I take a walk after lunch. If you want to write about my life, then that should be of interest to you. You're welcome to come.'

He picked up her cup and set it on the tray.

'Shall I bring in the plates?' she asked.

'Of course, of course.'

Schalmik picked up the tray and stood by the sliding doors, waiting for her to open them. As she did so, Mango nudged her way through first. Rosa pulled her legs back from contact with the dog's fur.

Schalmik paused. 'You dislike dogs,' he realized. 'You're a cat person, aren't you?'

'I shudder at the thought.'

Schalmik laughed. 'Come, Rosa,' he said. 'Let's give you some exercise. I suspect that's something else you dislike.'

22
The Cove

Rosa owned a bike. She belonged to a gym. It was a twenty-minute walk from her rented one bedroom apartment to the nearest London rail link. Schalmik's dig about exercise was quite unnecessary. She was as fit as she needed to be.

Mango was first through the gate but Rosa was second. She strode up the driveway, taking the lead to God knows where, but no way would she be seen to be dragging along on this walk.

Mango plunged through the grass away to her right. Rosa paused and looked round to check in with Schalmik.

'I take it she knows the way?' she called back.

'Mango's stupid, but what she knows she knows absolutely. She's a fundamentalist. That path leads down to the cove.'

Rosa waited for him to catch up.

'It's great to stretch my legs,' she said, 'after all those hours in planes.'

'The dog's a good excuse for me. I expect I'd sit still without her. She keeps me moving. Keeps me young.'

Schalmik was seventy-five and counting. He clearly liked the daring of calling himself young.

Mango had dashed along the path but ran back to see what was keeping them. When she saw they were talking she romped a circle through a patch of high grass.

'She's got a lot of energy,' Rosa observed.

'Mango's got two gears. Torpor and Hyper. Wait till you see her on the beach.'

'Is it far?'

'About fifteen minutes. Twenty coming back. We're normally gone for about an hour.'

The path was clear now, a dust trail between wild shrubs and undergrowth. Rosa started along it.

'Watch out for the poison oak on those bare legs.'

Poison oak. Now what the hell was that? Rosa had been ready to start a conversation, the path was wide enough to walk side by side, but now she just kept to the middle and watched her feet.

The path grew level for a stretch and opened out, with nothing but grass on either side. Schalmik took a few long steps to catch up and walk beside her.

'You've published two books,' he said. 'On Bach and Beethoven. The two greats. Since you're working through the Bs, I expected Brahms to be next. Why leap the alphabet and come to me?'

'Those books were for children.'

'Even so, why me?'

'Your music is profound. It rewards study. You have led one of the century's more significant lives. And you have the challenge of enigma. You are a recluse yet you are a celebrity. Your performances are mammoth, and electrifying. I've seen you perform three times. Once, most recently, was at the Philharmonie in Berlin. With the first stroke upon your cello I wept. Can I take something of what I heard that day and put it into words? I want to try. I believe it will make a great story.'

'Ahh,' Schalmik said. They passed a bench but he chose not to stop. He signalled her to go on ahead as the path narrowed. Slats of wood fashioned the earth into steps but the path was subsiding at its sides. Mango had gambolled down, kicking up a trail of dust.

Rosa took one step at a time, bringing both feet together before attempting the next. The steps led directly to the beach. Rosa prised off her shoes, set them to one side, scrunched her toes in the sand, and waited.

Maybe the colour of the beach did it, the sand that same off-red tone as the dog's fur, for Mango had been snatched out of physical bounds. The dog charged forward, skidding to a halt, and then bounced, leaping high to snatch at the air, again and again.

'See what I mean? She loves it down here.'

Schalmik walked toward the sea. He picked up two chunks of grey stone, and brought them back to Rosa.

'Sometimes she tries to leap up into your arms. It's unrealistic. She's not the puppy she was. If she does that to you, knock one of these rocks against her skull. It doesn't hurt her. It does her good. She comes round to her senses.'

Rosa took the stones. Schalmik sat down on one of the steps, pulled off his black lace-up brogues, placed a sock inside each one, and set them down beside her shoes. His feet were white, a bunion misshaping the right one, and all his toes were long.

'Watch out,' Schalmik suddenly cautioned. 'Get those rocks ready. Here she comes.'

Mango sprung in a circle around her, spinning a dervish dance of madness. Then, with her front paws opened wide in an insane attempt at a hug, she flung herself against Rosa's chest.

Rosa jumped back, one step, and thumped a rock onto the dog's skull.

Mango plummeted to the sand. She climbed to her feet like a cartoon dog, a spiral of dazedness around her head, limp-kneed but head erect. She looked up at Rosa's face, gathering focus, blinking.

'Brava,' Schalmik said.

'I didn't mean . . .'

'Don't apologize. Of course you meant it. You struck well. It's done her good. Tough love, it's what Mango respects. You'll be friends now. Look at those eyes. She's set to adore you.'

'Are you sure she's alright?'

'Absolutely. You're a girl after her own heart. You've both got the killer instinct.' Schalmik started to move off. 'Come on. She'll trail us for a minute or two while blood pumps back into her brain, and then she'll start exploring.'

The brown cliff walls to the side were almost vertical. The beach was flat, warmed by the sun but with the cool of compacted sand beneath its surface.

Schalmik turned to find the beach's slope. He paused in the edge of the ocean, swivelled on his toes and watched his feet sink. Rosa kept to higher ground.

'Do you swim?' she asked.

'Not down here, no. The water's too cold. Perhaps when I am old and my body needs just one more shock.'

The sea was mild, throwing waves that frothed as bubbles on the shore. Mango charged them down, stamping them into place, running deeper, snorting and shaking her demon head as saltwater sprayed from her nostrils. Schalmik rolled up the cuffs of his jeans and stepped in further. As they receded, waves plastered the hair on his shins to blackness.

The horizon between sea and sky was distinct. Schalmik could trace, just about, the curvature of the Earth along the horizon's line. The waves passed between and around his legs with different degrees of power, moving higher and lower, pulling at his sense of balance. Blood ran warm in his bulging veins but the cold in the sea was sucking at him. He would not warm the sea for long. The sea always wins.

As he stood in the ripple of waves he felt the touch of spirit in his scalp, which promptly flooded his entire body. Years ago, when an inrush of what he now knew as afterlife contact first happened, it left him shaking and weeping. Now that he understood it, he was able to accept it more easily.

Beings who he recognized as the spirits of the dead, as his lost loved ones, flowed in through his head and down the channel of his spine to reach every nerve ending where they bristled at the novelty of physical sensation. The dead had no such remnant sensory capacity and so could not feel the likes of the keen chill of seawater.

He had a living body still with its intact nervous system and so he invited them in. The girl could not know of this. For her, the dead must stay dead.

At the thought of the girl, the moment ebbed. The beings were leaving.

He was empty. The sea was cold. He shivered. As he turned back to shore his eyes were already drying.

Rosa saw the tears but did not know what they meant. Old men go rheumy sometimes. Perhaps that's all it was.

Schalmik sat on an outcrop of rock. Protecting her dress, Rosa stood nearby.

'This biography,' she started. She had a rehearsed speech.

'Let's not talk about it, Rosa.' Schalmik looked out to sea as he spoke. 'I don't care about my biography. Why should I? I'll never read it. It's nothing to do with me.'

'I've not just done dead composers,' Rosa persisted. 'I profile the living too.'

'Henze,' he said. 'And Menotti.'

She did look at him then, a moment of surprise. She didn't expect him to know about her.

'You write well, Rosa. You're good on details. And you've clearly found your secondary specialty. Male composers displaced by the late twentieth century.'

Rosa raised an eyebrow at him.

He was being arch, he supposed, but didn't know why. He didn't know what he had to gain from it. Schalmik turned aside from her stare and blew a high-pitched whistle between his teeth. Mango was shaking a shred of dried kelp between her jaws. She dropped it and came running toward them. It was time to climb their way back up the trail.

A path forked up to the right. Mango led the way with Schalmik close behind. 'If you don't mind,' he explained when they were back on the drive, 'I'll take some time to work now. It's my routine: walk, work and then a swim before evening. You're probably tired after your journey. You can take a rest. Or do what you will. I'll see you again at five thirty.'

'Do you work in this studio?' They were approaching a wooden chalet on the rim of the stockade.

'That's where I write.'

'Do you mind if I take a look inside?'

He didn't respond.

'Just a look. Nothing more. Then I'll leave you.'

Still he didn't speak. She followed him up the wooden steps. He sat down on a slice of tree trunk on the veranda and took off his shoes, peeling off the socks and dusting off sand. Rosa pulled off her shoes and wiped a hand over her feet.

Schalmik took a key from his pocket, unlocked the door, turned the knob and walked inside. He moved far enough in to leave room for Rosa to follow. It was the only invitation she was likely to get so she took it.

The dog sat on the veranda and looked in at them.

'Mango knows better than to come in here,' Schalmik said. 'Some places are private.'

The walls and ceiling were covered in plasterboard and painted white. They were bare of pictures. A day couch was set against the far wall, covered in a cotton quilt of black and red squares. To the right was a Yamaha keyboard. A trestle table was set up beneath the picture window.

Rosa looked down at the floor of pale yellow linoleum. Marks showed how the leather office chair tracked between the keyboard and the table. Two small side windows revealed the greenery of trees. The main window was the real joy of the place. The studio's height allowed a view above the house and the treetops to the Pacific.

'The view's glorious,' Rosa tried.

'I like the light at this time of day. It's rare and soft. Somehow it carries the blue inside of it.' He paused. 'It's good to work in.'

'Do you compose at the keyboard?'

'I compose wherever I happen to be . . . Wherever I am alone.'

Manuscript paper was spread across the table. Rosa peered down at it.

'You're writing for eight voices?'

'A motet.'

'Where are the words?'

'Really, Rosa, I'm in no mood for questions right now. If you don't mind.'

She nodded, smiled, took one more look around the room, and left. Schalmik clicked the door shut against her heels. Mango's tail thrummed to see her. The dog ran down the steps and then stopped, turning her head to make sure Rosa was following.

23
To the Point

Schalmik stripped off, laid his clothes out on the couch, and stepped outdoors. A boardwalk led from the steps at the far end of the veranda to the pool. He padded the route in bare feet. The routine felt different today. He was always conscious of his nudity, that was part of the point of it, but never as self-conscious as now.

He was lean to the point of scrawny yet his stomach still sagged into a slight paunch. Hairs were rooted in moles that sprouted with no obvious pattern from his skin. The body served a seventy-five-year-old well enough, but it wasn't one you would parade in front of any young woman who wasn't a nurse.

He had sent Rosa down to the house, so she was unlikely to interrupt him. Even so her presence in his home was an intrusion.

He pressed the switch and the tarpaulin cover rolled back. The water was heated. The temperature was refreshing as he climbed down the ladder and dipped his shoulders beneath the surface, but it didn't startle like the sea. Perhaps he could run it cooler.

Kicking off from the end, a mere four pulls at breaststroke brought him down the length. He reached out and turned on the motor, holding on to a chromium-plated bar with his free hand. If he failed to do that nowadays he was tumbled off his feet, his body bundled into an inglorious somersault.

He set the rate to a decorous three. Water surged against him. His physiotherapist had recommended this exercise pool and it was one of Schalmik's happier indulgences. He let go of the bar and swung out his arms in the early panic of staying afloat.

Soon he had gauged his effort against the water force and started counting strokes. Perhaps this was one of those rare days when he would hit a hundred. At thirty-seven he sensed this was unlikely. At forty-two his heart was beginning to hurt. He was being pushed backward by the water. Straining last efforts into the frogkicks of his legs he gained ground. Forty-seven, forty-eight, forty-nine, fifty and he grabbed hold of the bar. The water still roared and flipped him onto his back but he held on, flapped his free hand over the edge and hit the stop button.

That whining roar, mercy of mercies, ceased and the water grew calm. His chest heaved but that would grow still too, given time.

After a few minutes he dared to leave the side and floated on his back. It was half-hearted floating, for the pool was shallow and one heel remained on the bottom, but it was good to relieve the pressure on his spine for a while and look up. By wafting his hands he kept changing the view of sky and pine branches above him.

He gripped hold of the rail to the steps so he could pull himself out of the water with a surge. Without knowing it he had built a sequence of such dramatic gestures into his daily routine. Days could pall into a dreary sequence if you didn't wrest control.

The shower was his next trick. He had had it installed outdoors, the water running down through the wooden slats of the decking to feed the ground below. He turned the lever. The shower ran cold water only. The first burst of it made his head ache. Good. Served it right. Much good had it done him that afternoon.

Normally he moved to the edge of the platform and stood still, turning his body into the current of afternoon air as it dried him. Today he selected his oldest, most worn towel from the bottom of a pile and ran it stretched and coarse across his flesh.

At a press of a button, the tarpaulin rolled itself back across the blue of the pool. A similar thing would happen with the day, he told himself, seeking comfort. The night would roll in, the day would end, and tomorrow this young woman would be gone.

The last two hours in his studio had been bad. He had, of course, not managed a lick of work. This woman had disturbed him more than she could know. Memories came faster than he could release them. They swamped him.

He smelt the coffee. Rosa had carried it through to the balcony. Both the cafetière and her mug were now empty. She stood with her hands on the rail, looking out, and turned as he slid wide the door and stepped out to join her.

'Do you mind one more little excursion?' Schalmik asked her. 'Just down to the point?'

He handed Rosa a white tripod to carry, and picked up a leather case for himself. Dog and man led her back to the trail.

'That motet?' Schalmik said. 'The eight voices are two child sopranos, two mezzos, two sopranos, a bass and a tenor. They represent the five senses, plus growth, decay and the weather.'

'And these are lyricless voices?'

Schalmik was known for scorning words in his songs.

'If someone learned how to blow vocabulary out of an oboe, would that be progress? I don't think so. It would be banal. I wouldn't write for it. I try to write the truth. You can't write the truth and use words. People laugh, they burp, they scream, they howl, they sigh. Everybody understands such sounds. The human voice is universal. Words are not. Words are exclusive. They turn people into foreigners and restrict you to a cabal. I write for what is elemental in the human voice.'

He nodded toward the tape recorder in her hand

'You see what that tape recorder's doing to me? It's making me pompous.'

'I should have asked. Do you mind? I made notes this afternoon but I've missed so much. This lets me go back and check to get your words right.'

'I don't speak for the record. Turn it off, please.'

She did so. They walked on.

'This stretch of coast is a marine sanctuary,' Schalmik spoke as he erected the tripod. 'This sea is safe from human poisons. From human predation. That for me is something to sing about.'

The leather case contained a short blue-black spotting scope. Rosa noted the word Questar on its side as Schalmik fixed it in place.

'That motet is set at the point where we are standing.'

He looked out over the water and then bent to stare through the lens of the Questar, adjusting its focus. Whatever he had spotted made him do his breathy laugh then stood back.

'Here, take a look.'

She thought to see blue but the sea contained a kelp forest and so the surface was brown. She looked again. Among the bubbles and strands of brown a figure was moving.

'You see it?'

It made sense now. She was looking at the head of an otter. It swam on its back, its paws resting against its chest. Rosa could make out the dark pools of its eyes. Its head was tilted to one side, as if watching something.

'Shift a little to the left,' Schalmik advised. 'See them?'

'Pups?' she said.

Indeed they were, two baby otters that frisked round each other.

'The California sea otter. *Enhydra lutris nereies*. You know my *Lutrisian Sinfonie*?' Schalmik asked her.

'It's beautiful,' she offered, rather lamely, her attention still fixed on the play of the otters.

'The piece is set in that kelp forest. Kelp is anchored in the seabed but can rise two hundred feet to the surface. We see the canopy and hardly consider the whole forest that lives beneath it. My *Lutrisian* harnesses the dives of the otters and sets out to explore those depths.'

'Does such music start with an image?' Rosa asked. 'With an idea?'

'I don't know. With patience perhaps. With being unsettled. I sense something stirring and then I go still and wait for a resolution. By the time I know much more about it, it's already music.'

Rosa swivelled the Questar across to the right as he talked, and now she was barely listening. They were standing on a promontory. Below them, on the land next door, a series of low buildings were placed within lush green gardens. She watched the sheen of water glisten on the bronzed body of a woman who pulled herself out of a swimming pool. The pool was its brilliant blue and the woman's bikini a startling red.

'What's that place,' she asked.

'Esalen. It's like a New Age summer camp for adults.'

'Do you ever visit?'

'It's a camp, Rosa. With security guards. Why would I choose to step inside a camp?'

Rosa adjusted the Questar's focus. 'Is what I'm seeing real?' she asked.

'I brought you here to look at the otters.'

'There are naked people down there. Naked people on tables, and naked people standing. What is this, naked massage? Is that what they're doing?'

'I've heard it said.'

'Take a look.'

'I know what naked people look like.'

'So you've looked.'

'It's far away, Rosa. Even with the Questar everything is tiny. It's hardly spying.'

'So you have looked,' she said, and stood up. 'There's more to your life than otters. I'm glad.'

He unscrewed the Questar and zipped it into its bag. The legs of the tripod clicked together. He started the walk back toward the house. The girl was impertinent, he decided. That was the best word for her.

He paused. Nobody was following. He turned around. Rosa had just thrown a rock. It arched through the air.

Mango stood and watched for a moment, and then bounded off in pursuit.

'Mango does not play fetch!' he shouted. It was meant to be a statement of fact, but it came out like a command.

Mango picked the rock up quite delicately, lodged it in her jaws, and then raced back to the young woman. Would the dog drop the rock at her feet? Would Rosa throw it?

Such inane dramas did not belong in his life. He turned in disgust and marched back to the house.

24
Dead Chicken's Revenge

California played with Rosa's senses. The sunlight that glanced off the ocean, the distant horizon and broad sky, the waves on sand, the briny air, so much of what was here triggered thoughts of home. Rosa had bundled herself into a plane and emerged in somewhere that was like Australia, but not Australia. It was similar but different.

The smell that gusted out of the door though, she was comfortingly sure about that.

'Chicken and rosemary . . .' The rest was curiously undefined, a whole bunch of flavours stewing into each other '. . . stew. Your house seems to take care of itself, Mr Schalmik.'

When Rosa had returned from their beach outing, the table was cleared and the plates were thrumming in the dishwasher. Now, somehow, a cooked dinner greeted their return from the promontory.

Mango pushed her way indoors and climbed onto her mattress, and then sat upright so she could face the kitchen and its odours.

'You're not vegetarian?' Schalmik asked.

'I eat anything.'

'Excellent. Evie keeps chickens so I eat a lot of eggs. A hell of a lot of eggs. You've had one of her quiches already. Hopefully this bird's one of hers so that cuts into the egg supply. We won't have escaped eggs completely though. There will be a custard creation in the fridge. A trifle perhaps, or a crème brulée.'

'Evie's your cook?'

'Evie's her own woman. She brings me food and maintains some order. We communicate by written notes. She comes in the afternoon and whisks around. Leaves a meal in the oven and sets the timer if I'm to be treated to something hot. It should be ready in forty-five minutes. Would you care for a drink?'

He led her through to the living room. They decided to start with the Prüm. Schalmik placed the bottle in a clear plastic cooler and brought along two glasses as well as a tray of peanuts. He poured, they both picked up their glasses, and then Rosa put hers down again.

'I wanted to toast our book,' she said. 'I thought we'd reach an agreement this afternoon. But we haven't.'

'We can drink to our meeting.'

'Any two strangers can do that. I know this is personal for you, Mr Schalmik, it's your life story, but it's also business. You invited me here so presumably we have something to discuss, but I don't know what it is. I don't know what you want from me. From what you tell me, you've no interest in biography at all.'

'I wouldn't say that. Biography's an art form. A peculiar one, but I can find virtue in it.' Schalmik set his own glass back on the table. 'It's odd to subjugate your life to someone else's, but of course that's what most of us do. When I read biography it's to learn about the biographer. A biographer chooses the terrain of another person's life, but of course he is on a quest to discover his own.'

'Or she her own.' Rosa smiled. This wasn't so much a challenge as restating the obvious. She had taken twenty minutes in the bathroom below to freshen up. Her mirror image impressed her. Schalmik had a woman as a dinner guest. He had better not ignore the fact. 'So you think I want to find myself in you?'

He did look at her directly for a moment, a keener attention replacing that abstract gaze of his. That was something.

'That would be as vain of me as you make it sound.' He relaxed into the sofa cushions a little. She wasn't quite sure what he looked at now. It was her forehead perhaps or her hair, but not her eyes. When he looked at her eyes it was occasionally and then away, quickly away. 'A life is a passage through history in which many decisions are made. A good biography charts and examines those decisions. I have a sense of biographers floating in the present, seeking ownership of the past.'

'So you think I want to own you?'

'That's part of it, surely? You'd be known as Rosa Little, the biographer of Schalmik.'

'Big deal. And then you'd never read what I wrote.'

'It's better that way. The best subjects are dead ones. They never sue. Consider me dead.'

'But you're not.'

'I was this afternoon.'

Rosa looked at him. This needed explanation.

'My motet stopped. I couldn't hear it any more. Your coming here has pushed me back into the past. Being caught in the past like that is a definition of being dead.'

'That's stupid. I'm alive, you're alive, we're sitting here talking. This isn't history, it's not being dead, it's now.'

'I can't do this.' Schalmik reached forward and took a schluck of his wine, then leaned back into the thick cushions. 'You write biography. Go ahead. Write mine. Make of it what you will. Just don't imagine you'll capture me. You can ferret away and find facts for every month of my life but you'll still not know a thing about me. Only musicians can know me, just a few musicians, and they don't need to read a book.'

'So it's all in your music.' Rosa grabbed a mouthful of wine for herself. This was all such bullshit. She needed the taste of something sweet in her mouth to offset it. 'Your life's got nothing to do with it. You never grew up in Vienna. You had no parents and lost no parents. You've never heard music outside your own head.'

'Environment isn't biography. You want music to be self-referential? That's not music. It's tunes or it's noise. Music is a conscious denial of self. Critics don't know that. Music funnels in through their ears and they think that's important. Music's there in total, hear it or not. Strip away the listener. Strip away the writer. Music's the before and after. I shit on your biography.'

The pupils in his eyes shivered and then he looked away, out of the window.

'What about an autobiography? Is that out of the question too?' She took another glug of her wine. 'Alex and I have a back-up plan in which I am your ghost.'

Be playful, Alex had suggested. Be yourself. Schalmik's crusty. Give him space, don't let him upset you, and you might get through. She worked her cheekbones into a smile. The look he turned to her made her shiver.

Playful wouldn't do it.

'I want to put you in context. Your music engages with history like no other. It leads us into the maelstrom then out again.'

'Nonsense.'

'It's not nonsense. Your music's so brave. It stares into the blackest horror but that very act of staring is so human it's beautiful. You say music's the before and after. Well you went to a place where music should have been killed but you managed to find it. You brought it back. We can't face the abyss but we can face you, we can look into the darkened mirror that you provide. And now you're here. You're closed off in a world of sea otters and kelp. That's fine, it's lovely, it's what you've chosen, but it's not everything. There's more to you than the moment. More to you than reflecting nature. So much more.'

Schalmik stared her out.

'I can't go there,' he declared.

'That's fine. You don't have to.' Rosa picked up the bottle and recharged their glasses. 'How about this for a deal? I write your book so long as you promise never to read it.'

Schalmik gripped the stem of his glass.

'*Tjüss*,' he offered.

'*Tjüss*,' Rosa responded.

They clinked and drank.

Never look back. The motto had worked for Schalmik so far. More damn fool he to invite a biographer into his life. And now here was this young woman with her grandmother's eyes. Who knew that eyes could jump the generations like that, looking out at him now as they had done then? Let the day turn black with night and the lights stay dim and protect him.

The Prüm sent sparkles across his tongue. 'It's good,' he noted.

It played that trick of a good Riesling and blended sweetness with crispness. He checked the label. Alcohol, 9%. At that level, he might manage a glass or two without growing stupid or maudlin.

'Melon, would you say? A hint of peaches with a citrus tang?' He made a pantomime of pursing his lips and clucking his tongue against his palate. 'The garbage people get away with when they talk about wine. We should do the same with music. The ricochet of hailstones over a mountain vineyard. The tracks of a snow leopard over arctic tundra. The thrusts of crocus through cracked earth. People would love such nonsense.'

It was months since he had drunk alcohol. Drink turned him sentimental and silly and in need of more society than Mango could provide. He noted the effects and worked to hold them in check.

'They say you can taste the soil in good wine. What do you think, Rosa? Can you taste Germany? Does this wine take you back to your childhood?'

'*My* childhood? I'm Australian.'

'Don't Australians make Rieslings?' Schalmik kept watching her, as though she might yet say something interesting. 'Biographers have such personal agendas. I thought maybe you were researching your roots.'

'Not my roots. Our roots perhaps, the readers' roots. I see your story as universal. It has something to tell us all about our lives.'

'We'll see, Rosa, we'll see.' He turned away and sniffed the air. 'Time to rescue Evie's hen from the oven.'

Schalmik dropped two ladlefuls into a bowl and set it in front of Rosa. The bone of a leg stuck up from the broth like a waving arm. Pale, mottled skin had peeled away and lay on the surface, like the discarded cardigan of a drowned woman. His own bowl looked just as disgusting.

'Dead chicken's revenge,' he said. 'Still, it should be safe. The ingredients are fresh. Eat what you want and leave the rest.'

'It smells lovely.'

'Does it?' Schalmik sniffed at the air noisily. 'Of course, if the dinner looks and smells like death it's your fault. You're a biographer. You've come here sniffing out my past as though it's hidden about me somewhere but it's not. My past is burned away. I want nothing to do with it. But you, you reek of it.'

He drank from his glass, just a sip. Rosa stared at him but he didn't appear to see her. His eyes were glazed. Then he blinked and sipped again.

'I'm drunk,' he said.

'But we've barely had half a bottle.'

'Don't deny me. I need to be drunk to get through this evening. We'll talk. I'll talk. And tomorrow I'll have forgotten everything I've said. That's the way with drink. That's the way I need it. You make a start. Eat what you can and talk to me. You've seen me three times you say. When were those?'

'The first time was 1972. In Sydney.' She spooned up some of the dinner, a few white beans with shreds of cabbage. It tasted just fine. 'At the Opera House.'

'You were there?'

'The world premiere of your *Diaspora Variations*.'

'I didn't see you.'

'I was a pudgy kid, my hair frizzed in curls and dyed black. We're talking twenty-two years ago. I was nine. My grandmother took me. She waited in the Botanical Gardens and sent me in on my own.'

'Hardly an event for children.' Schalmik studied her a moment, then spooned some food into his mouth and gulped it down. 'You have a very peculiar grandmother.'

'She explained "diaspora" to me. A dispersal of a people from their homeland.'

'She used the word "dispersal" to a nine-year-old?'

'She loved the word dispersal. *Ve Vere dispersed*, she would say. *It vos a great and sad dispersal.* Her English came out loud and in a thick German accent. She was a musician who went deaf. Music no longer had value for her so she gave it to me.'

'Maybe she planned to frighten you off music for life.'

'I was walking up the steps to the Opera House when the first note sounded. I looked around, around and around, and then up. A man straddled the white tiles, a didgeridoo spouting out from his arms to aim straight down and at me, and this was the sound. The first note boomed out on the longest of breaths, starting low and roaring into a wail.'

'You heard that? As a child you heard it as a wail?'

'That's what it was. A wail that kept repeating and breaking through. And then a chugging of breaths, like trains on a track.'

'You heard trains?'

'And running, the fast breath of running, and falling, a sudden silence. Silences broken by wails, by trains, by fastness of running, by stomping of feet. All blasted and puffed out above our heads and out across Benelong Point.'

'That was Steve Murawarra. A wonderful man. He spent a night in the Gardens, talking to both the land and the Opera House, and the next morning he was ready to climb the building. "It wants to sing," he said.'

'Then I went inside. They swapped my ticket for a green sticker. I didn't know where to go.'

'That was the point. They wanted arrows directing the audience between each of the music sites. I had to grow angry to make them stop. A diaspora is not about known destinations. It's a forlorn wandering, with nowhere to return to and nowhere to go.'

'I followed other people. We went to a courtyard first. A woman sat with her legs dangling out of the building, playing an accordion.'

'They took the window out of the Greenroom to allow for that. Vera could look down on the audience, squeezed between the Concert Hall and the Opera House, or she could stare out at the waters of the Harbour.'

'Her accordion played the same music as the didgeridoo. The same, but different.'

'I wrote separately for each instrument. And included space for three cadenzas.'

'All the music notated,' Rosa took up, 'but with flexible use of multiple repeat bars. An obsession of eighth notes with a continual pull toward longer ones. Pulses that beat and also skip. Boundless combinations of a four-note theme, the same story finding different ways of expressing itself in its urgency to communicate. I know. Lately I've studied the score. Then I was a girl in rapt pursuit of strangeness. I wandered everywhere and at the end I found you. You were in a white shirt, open-necked with the sleeves rolled up, sitting quite erect. The four-note theme played around the octaves with gentle strokes of the bow. I stayed till the other musicians joined you. The Opera House filled up behind me, the music ended, and everyone applauded.'

'And we musicians applauded you the audience. You were the event. No one heard everything, but everything had been heard by someone. The experience of hearing one player was carried through to the experience of hearing the next. We each played in isolation, but as you journeyed between us our playing merged in your memory. We were separate, but we each found a home in your memory.'

'They applauded because they thought it was over.'

'That's what audiences do. You congratulate yourselves and then you get on with your lives.'

'I hated the applause. It made me run away. I went outside and got lost. Down at the bottom of the building, on the stone floor outside a minor entrance door, I found a young man with a straggly beard and blue eyes. He played a penny whistle. I recognized the tune. It was your four-note theme. I presumed he had picked it up from the didgeridoo player.'

'And you walked on?'

'Eventually. I had to meet my grandmother. But I sat and listened first. I had some money. Gran had taught me about intervals and given me some coins to buy drinks or ice cream or whatever, but there were no intervals in your show, only wanderings. The man reached an endnote, not as long as yours because he was using his breath, but it was long and then came silence. I dropped the coins in the man's hat. He opened his eyes and we smiled at each other and I ran away. And now that I've read the score I know. *Diaspora Variations* is a motet. You wrote it for eight instrumental voices, including a tin whistle.'

'I wandered the streets of Sydney searching for my players. I wrote parts for the musicians that I found. Someone told me about Ralph. He sat outside buildings he considered a blight on the landscape and played his penny whistle as an antidote. I found him and his dog outside a shopping centre in Roselands. He never told me his last name and wouldn't accept a contract. We could put money in his hat if we wanted to. If we didn't care to, that was alright too.'

'Only seven of you took the applause.'

'We were a diversion. Ralph refused to enter the building. The music never ends. It always plays. In this instance, Ralph sat outside and played on.'

'You asked your audience to walk between you, to gather you in their memories, each memory its own composition.

That's what I do. That's my job as a critic. I wander between eras, between performances and interpretations, between new works and old, and let each inform on the other.'

Schalmik looked at her a while, and then turned his attention to his plate. Spoon by spoon he finished the meal, squashing the beans against his palate before sucking them down and pausing to chew on the chicken flesh. Rosa ate too before wearying and laying her spoon to rest.

Schalmik dabbed his mouth with a paper napkin.

'I'm touched,' he confessed. 'Touched you discovered that the music plays on, and that you paused to hear it out. Thank you for the coin, and that smile.'

Rosa nodded her head, just slightly.

'Yours is a good story. It has a child and discovery in it. My story is nothing like that.'

'You've never told it. I've checked the records. Other distinguished Holocaust survivors have recorded their accounts. You've simply written short letters of refusal.'

'I watched men weep for the loss of their stories. These men had homes, families, countries, professions. Then they became numbers. They thought they had a wife and children but they couldn't be sure, because they had forgotten their names. And then they died. Such are the stories of the Holocaust. Others honour those who survive and tell their tales, it is good and impossible and right work to do, but that's not my job. I want to tell of what's left when a story is gone.'

'You tell it in music?'

'A star explodes and we inherit the static. A life story implodes and there's a similar residue. I listen out for patterns of silence and sound. Those that sound most true I seek to capture.'

'How do you know what's true? How do you source sound to a vanished life?'

'I'm a fool lost in delusions. My life's work is meaningless. What does it matter? I do what I do.'

'Me too.' Rosa pushed her plate away from her, as though clearing the way for something else. 'Your story is meaningful to me. Its absence is a hollow core at the heart of my work. Maybe I'm stupid. Maybe your story is worthless or better left unsaid. Who cares? I need it. Tell it to me.'

'I think we've both finished.' Schalmik pulled Rosa's empty bowl toward him and stacked it under his own. 'Ice cream can wait. First I must feed the dog.'

Mango had lain throughout the meal, her head resting between her paws, eyes sometimes closed and sometimes raised upward. Now she stood and started thrashing her tail side to side.

'This is a foolish game I play.' He fetched a tin and scooped kibble into Mango's bowl. 'It's called top dog. The alpha dog always eats first. In the evening I eat first and feed her second, to keep her in her place. Either that or the occasional rock to the head seems to work. She still obeys me when she chooses to.'

He set the bowl on the floor. After one brief mania of crunching, the dog whipped the empty bowl along the bottom of the cabinet with her tongue.

'Let's go outdoors,' Schalmik suggested.

'Can I bring things?' Rosa asked. 'Can I bring my recorder?'

'Bring what you will.'

25
The Frog Chorus

Thick leaves and spiked rushes formed black silhouettes against the darkness. Rosa clipped the miniature microphone to the collar of Schalmik's shirt and turned on her Sony digital Walkman. They sat on a bench beside the pond that stretched into the garden from outside her bedroom. Schalmik wouldn't speak. Instead, through minute after minute, her tape was filled by the croaking of frogs.

'Listen,' Schalmik hissed.

The frog chorus continued in full swell for thirty seconds, and then died of an instant.

'Can you hear the signal that triggers the silence?'

It seemed, for a rash moment, that he had just sought her perspective as a critic. Rosa opened her mouth to answer. Schalmik waved a hand to keep her quiet. They sat together through a further period of silence, and then with a single uniform croak the frog chorus resumed. A swathe of rhythm beat against the night, till from full swell the chorus snapped quiet once more.

'Sometimes I think I've caught it, one high note maybe, one low, a shift in rhythm, but when I look for the pattern to be repeated it's never so.'

'Such listening, the noise of frogs, does it make it into your music?'

'Music is something you hear. You train yourself into different ways of listening, and then who knows where music can come from, but it keeps on coming. I've never tried to write frog music. Maybe I will.'

'Like the way you've written otter music.' Rosa saw a chance to make her move, and played it. 'What's your first memory of sound?'

'Horses' hooves.' He went silent. Rosa hoped he was simply retrieving the memory. 'Pock pock, pock pock. The road outside my window was a traditional Viennese street. It looked like cobbles, but in fact the road was made of wood, wooden blocks covered in tar and packed in tight. As a child I lay in bed in the mornings and listened for that music of iron-shod hooves against wood. From the occasional syncopation I heard lameness, and learned to tell which of a horse's legs was in pain. And of course I could tell if it was wet or dry outside, hot or cold, for then the patterns of sound from every horse shifted together. When horses passed each other, I listened for the rhythm of their meeting. Music is loaded with story in such a way. Hooves on wood was the music of my childhood.'

'And then it changed to cars,' Rosa suggested.

'Oh there were cars even then. I'm not so old. But you're right, things changed. Vienna changed. New sounds swept in. New cries woke up. But you know this, Rosa. You've researched this. You studied in Vienna. What do you need from me?'

'Music?' Rosa suggested. 'Were you a musical family?'

'Were we musical? This was old Vienna. What are you asking?' He looked out across the pond and into the darkness. 'Was I musical? It hung in the balance. My mother played the piano, my sister played the violin, and so they needed a cellist. I played because I was told to but it was mechanical. I had no fire. In 1931 my mother bought two tickets for a recital at the *Theater an der Wien*. Already that was a treat, my mother and me at this grand theatre. This was the Vienna homecoming for Emanuel Feuermann. Applause roared out when he stepped on stage. That was magical enough, seeing a cellist as a super hero welcomed back to the city of his birth. And then he played. Do you know Feuermann? He aimed to do for the cello what Heifetz did for the violin. And he did. What a dazzle of technique he showed that night, while staring forward serenely to listen to the sounds he was making. You know *Star Wars*, with that magic sabre? I was a young teenager and that's what Feuermann's bow was like to me. It flashed inside a spotlight and conjured such power in the music. I was young of course and so I thought I could do anything and I wanted to do that. I wanted to play like Feuermann. All I had to do was practise. The next day I got up early and played my scales for two hours solid before school.'

'And so your mother got her trio.'

'We gave concerts in the living room on the first Thursday of every month, for my father in his armchair and a few family and friends.'

'What did you play?'

'Aah, all the old stuff. Beethoven. Haydn. And Mendelssohn. Here's a time from 1938. In Germany it was forbidden to play Mendelssohn because he was a Jew. In Austria Bruno Walter's contract with the Vienna Opera was renewed for a year. We were happy. A Jew, Bruno Walter, was left in charge of Vienna's music. If that was allowed then we must all be safe! That Thursday my mother, my sister and I flung open the windows and played a Mendelssohn trio for the whole street to hear.'

'Schoenberg was writing then. Berg and Webern.'

'Now you say that. Radio Vienna played for us over dinner and we didn't hear Webern, I can tell you. Something fresh from Franz Lehár perhaps – I saw him once, striding by the lake at Bad Ischl. He was the biggest but we had Oscar Strauss too, Robert Stolz, Benatsky. So many melodies. And then Haydn. It all died with Haydn.'

Rosa let the silence hold a while, but Schalmik needed prompting. He had forgotten she was there.

'When was that? When did things die?'

'You know this, Rosa. It was my birthday.'

'The 10th of March.'

'1938. I was nineteen. The radio played military marches all day. Trucks were draped in flags and workers shouted the national colours, "Red – White – Red unto Death!" Planes filled the skies and showered us with leaflets. We were voting for a "Free, German, independent, social, Christian and united Austria."'

'Christian?'

'Jews could live with that. And we were passionate Austrians.'

'And Haydn.'

'The 11th of March. We listened to the radio again. Our Chancellor Schuschnigg made a speech. Our free vote was cancelled. Hitler had threatened to invade. Sooner than fight we would all stand aside. Schuschnigg finished speaking and Haydn started. The C major quartet, The *Emperor*. It was a classic old tune. That's when the old music stopped playing.'

'The Nazis came in.'

'Of course they did. You know all this.'

'What did it sound like?'

He turned his head for a while and looked at her. Her question surprised him.

'I imagine people shouting.'

'And what do these people of your imagination shout, Rosa?'

'Slogans? "*Ein Volk, ein Reich, ein Führer*". That kind of thing.'

'That kind of thing?'

'And other things,' she tried. '"Death to the Jews".'

'*Juda verrecke.*' He paused as though recalling. '*Ju-da verr-rrecke, Ju-da verr-rrecke.*'

'I've read the Nazis pulled the Jews into the streets. Made them clean up the election slogans.'

'*Na und?*'

'This happened to you?'

'You think we were a different kind of Jew? We were exceptional?'

She let the silence hang a while. He spoke again.

'Yes, they came for us too. Two young men in brown shirts with batons. Buckets, water and brushes were provided. We got down on our knees, mother, father and me, and scrubbed. People stopped and admired us. "Hitler is good even for the Jews," a woman said. "We've done the work and they've grown rich. Now they have a job of their own." Herr Brunner watched too. He had been selling us bread all my life. His head was shaved because baking was hot work. He shot a gob of spit onto the slab by my knees. "There," he said. "That will help." They all helped. They all spat. "*Juda verrecke,*" one young man said. It was a passing comment as he spat and moved on. He was Bruno Schild, from my class way back when I was in the Gymnasium.'

The frogs went quiet. It prompted Schalmik out of the silence he had dropped into. He unclipped the microphone and handed it back to Rosa. She left her recorder running.

'Couldn't you leave?' she asked.

'Where to? Who would have us? We were not rich. Father was a government official.'

'You were a student?'

'At the Akademie. They closed it for a few days. It became barracks for the Wehrmacht. When they reopened I attended a lecture. Felix von Weingartner walked in. He was in his seventies but carried himself well, tall and erect, bald but with tidy tufts of silver hair above his ears. He conducted the Vienna Philharmonic. Imagine the power of such a man for us young musicians. He brought us lessons he had learned direct from Liszt, from Brahms and Wagner. His suit was blue, his shirt a lighter blue, his bowtie a dark silver, and his dark brown shoes were polished to a gleam. He was a civilized rather than a demonstrative man. He taught us to conduct from movements of the wrist alone.

'As he approached the lectern, two students rose and shouted at him. "*Heil Hitler!*" They each jutted their right arm forward in salute.

'Weingartner jumped. Were these men set to leap forward and pin him to the ground? Then he remembered. "*Heil Hitler*" was simply the new form of welcome, the modern "*Grüss Gott*". He lifted his hand a little in the air and mumbled. I sat near the front, close enough to study his lapel. A tiny silver swastika was pinned there.

'Weingartner was a good man. It was too late in the day for him to make much of a stab of becoming a Nazi. They forced him to retire. Our Professor Arnold Rosé went too, after being dismissed as leader of the Philharmonic. All performances with Jewish performers were cancelled.

'I had been studying Janacek. He built music onto the patterns of the human voice. That was my aim too. How could I do that now? How could I build music from the German language? Should I go back to Yiddish or Hebrew? Wittgenstein was right, meaning goes beyond the power of language to pursue it. Maybe music could fill that gap but I was young, what could I know? For now, in Vienna, music was gone and language was a barking madness. Hitler cruised the streets in his Mercedes and thousands and thousands of my townsfolk cheered.

'Come, Rosa, come. I'm tired of this and it's getting damp. Let's go in and feed you your egg custard.'

Rosa seldom ate the likes of egg custard. She avoided the calories. Oh well. This was probably a time to sacrifice dietary principle. She turned off the recorder and let Schalmik lead her back through the downstairs patio windows and into the house.

Mango poked her head down from the top of the metal spiral staircase to greet them back to her level, thrumming her tail.

26
The Admission

Schalmik dropped the chicken bones from their bowls into the bin and poured the rest down the waste disposal unit. He turned it on to roar and gurgle while he rinsed the plates and then placed them in the dishwasher. Rosa's egg custard bowl he held low to the ground for Mango's tongue to lick itself around.

'We had our aluminium bowl in the camp,' he told Rosa. 'We had to clean it in cold water after every dinner. Any trace of grease meant severe punishment. Some evenings they cooked the food in whale lard. When I noticed thick globules of white scum on top of the food pail I tucked my bowl against my chest and moved on. However hard you try, whale lard won't scrub clean in cold water. It was better to lie awake in hunger than in the fear of reprisal for a dirty bowl.

'Now I lie awake with the sound of the dishwasher, which while annoying is an improvement on both hunger and fear.'

He returned to his seat.

'So, the table is clear, the stage is set. How long does a tape last in this recorder of yours?'

'Ninety minutes if I set it on slow.'

'Set it on slow, Rosa. Slow feels increasingly good.'

And so he told of the day in 1938. It was a Friday. He had been playing the cello. His mother called him to set the table. His sister Erna was coming to dinner, along with her husband Hugo. They had such news. He told her the story.

How much did Schalmik tell her? He couldn't be sure. His words took him from his home in Vienna to the camp at Dachau, somehow.

'When we had moved from the freight car to the camp, an officer with a clipboard paid attention to the men on stretchers,' he said. 'He was tallying the men from each boxcar: some on foot, some on stretchers and living, some stretchered dead. This was a senior officer, not so tall but broad, a buzz of ginger hair above a square face. Others were still frantic, shouting us home, but he was fairly still. He seemed satisfied.'

Schalmik paused the tale and looked at Rosa.

'Birchendorf?' Rosa guessed. 'That was Dieter Birchendorf? The Adjutant at Dachau?'

He did not confirm the name but held the silence till his stare grew too uncomfortable. Rosa looked down at the recorder, ostensibly to check it was running but really to look away. He let the silence run for a few more beats and then spoke on.

'He was in charge of transport. This was a thorough job. He had despatched the guards from Dachau to collect the prisoners from Vienna, and they had succeeded. We were now in his protective custody. He could send off the train to bring back more of us. There was no need to worry about victualing it either. Enough of us had survived without food and drink. He could record the whole transport as one more triumph for the Fatherland in its battle against adversity.'

He stopped speaking.

'Thank you,' Rosa said.

'It's past. This is tiresome.' Schalmik stood. 'You'll excuse me a moment.'

Large sliding doors sealed his bedroom from the living room, and beside that was his bathroom. This is where he headed. Not so much for the toilet – the wine was wheeling round his brain like a fly and seemed to have dehydrated him – but simply to step away and regroup himself. These inner rooms looked out onto a courtyard garden. The curved ceiling-high glass wall by the sunken bathtub made the garden more like a vivarium. Schalmik turned on the outdoor light to illuminate the broad green plants and then closed the lid of the toilet and sat down. He was looking out, but also looking in.

He was being a fool. Rosa was hardly an invading agent. She had written seeking an invitation, he had considered and complied, and now he must deal with the consequences.

What had he wanted? Shifting out of his rut perhaps. Mango was four years old, with another eight or nine years in her. He expected to see her out and then die himself. It was working well enough, the dog kept him to a semblance of routine, but it was hardly stimulating.

Had he been lonely? Who gives a damn? Loneliness was as urgent as a yearning for chocolate, forgetting a name, running low on postage stamps. It's a little bud that blossoms sometimes but you don't need to stand there sniffing it, you move on.

He had presumed he was big enough to cope. That's what he'd done, and what nonsense it was. He was seventy-five years old. His emotional maturity was stunted in adolescence when it was none too bold to begin with. Even back in Vienna when life was comfortable and he had no excuses he had played out his tantrums on the cello. He pretended his refusal to speak about the past was a rational choice rather than fear. Well wake up, Otto Schalmik. You're as scared of the past as any old man alive.

Be braver. You got through it then, you can get through it now.

He stood from the toilet. Rosa was young. He could bully her. But that wasn't his intention. He must recover his intention.

She was gone when he stepped back into the stretch of the upstairs room. He heard the loo flush downstairs and stood at the top of the stairs to wait for her. It took a few minutes, for she was checking the playback on her recorder, switching tapes, changing batteries. He had kept pulling off his microphone. The sound was too poor for broadcast but then it was good enough for archival and transcription purposes. So long as she left the microphone close enough to him it would do the job.

As Rosa came up the spiral stairs She turned up her lips in a tight smile. It was gloomy below and still bright above where Schalmik was a silhouette whose head was turned down to face her. He did not back away and she did not care to finish her climb and find herself so close to him so she paused.

'This is when I move to the couch and read,' Schalmik said. 'Mango expects it of me. It's best not to disappoint her.'

He moved away. Rosa climbed into the space he had vacated and stood there herself.

A globe lamp hung from a black chain above the armchair to the right of the sofa. Schalmik turned it on and settled into the cushions beneath its glow. He sat as erect as the cushions allowed, his feet flat on the floor and his hands on his knees. The tendons in Rosa's bare feet clicked as she walked toward him. The woman stood and looked down at him. He looked up.

'I have something to tell you,' she said.

The words came out fast. She hooked a bunch of hair over her right ear and its copper locks fell loose again as she turned to stare through the window a while.

'It's an ethical thing.' She looked up toward the rafters now as she spoke. 'Writer's protocol. It's new to me. I normally write about dead composers. You're alive. It makes a difference.'

Now she looked down at him, but not into his eyes. Not yet.

'I have a declaration of interest,' she said.

She stayed silent for a while, the recorder and some papers clutched in her left hand. The fingers of her right hand had curled into a fist. She straightened them and arched the fingers back.

'Dieter Birchendorf was my grandfather.'

Her tone was assertive yet not proud. The statement came out like a dare. The inflection flicked up at the end, like she had more to say, so he waited.

'His wife was called Katja. Katja was my grandmother. She raised me.'

She pulled an old photograph from the papers in her left hand and thrust it at him. He reached up and took it.

'That's her,' she said.

It was no more than a snap. Its colours were bleached of all depth, but he was interested. The woman had grown quite stout. She sat on a wrought iron chair on a flagstone patio in the shade of a plain beach umbrella and wore a sleeveless dress of pale blue. Her arms were pale and well fleshed and a string of pearls was looped above her chest. Her hair was an arrangement of loose white curls. She stared back at the camera without smiling.

Schalmik placed the photo on his lap and looked up at Rosa.

'She died in March,' Rosa said.

'My condolences.'

'So now you know. You know who I am. We can continue our interview.'

She made no move though, but simply stared down at him. Then she moved her right hand up to her hip.

'You're very quiet, Mr Schalmik,' she said.

It was a statement. He felt no need to respond. Emotions still appeared to be bustling round her head. She wasn't finished.

She studied her recorder, turned it on, and held it out toward him.

'I have informed Mr Schalmik of my relationship with the Adjutant at Dachau,' she announced. 'Mr Schalmik, please confirm that you are happy for me to make use of the material I have already gathered and to continue this interview.'

He kept silent. She thrust the recorder closer to his mouth.

'It makes no difference,' he said.

'I'm glad you think so,' she said, enunciating every word, almost spitting them out.

'I already knew. I knew who you were.'

She stared on. The recorder quivered in her hand, and then she pulled it away and set it down on the free sofa. Its red light was still on, he noted. It was recording.

'Since when?'

'Since before you came.'

She walked away. The dog's mattress blocked the way to the window so she stopped before it and turned around. She worked to keep her voice calm.

'You should be ashamed of yourself,' she said.

He arched an eyebrow. It was response enough.

'Don't pretend, Mr Schalmik. You know what you've done. This is your home, your dog, your territory. You've got all the power. You invite me in here, feed me lunch and dinner and a preposterous egg custard you didn't even taste and I didn't even want, you make every show of old-world courtesy, and yet all the time you knew. You even spoke about my grandfather and stared at me like it was a dare. What's the point of that? Why keep your knowledge back? Is it supposed to give you a hold over me? Why would you want to do that? Frankly, your behaviour is abusive.'

He stared at her.

'Well?' she challenged.

The prompt did no good. His mind whirred a little but could find no response.

'I think I deserve an apology,' she said. 'At the very least.'

He stared a while longer, and then nodded his head toward the couch.

'Sit,' he said.

She thought a moment, and then did as he suggested. She sat on the edge of the sofa's cushion, her back upright.

'You're like her,' he offered. 'Now you're on fire, you're so like her.'

He leaned back, stretched his body and crossed his ankles.

'You make me forget I'm old. You say this is my territory. It doesn't feel like that. I don't feel at home. When I knew your grandmother, she was a woman and I was a boy. Less than a boy. I was nothing. I had no home. That's what this feels like.'

She pursed her mouth. She was waiting for an apology.

'I'm sorry,' he said.

She nodded. The photo of her grandmother lay on the table. She placed the recorder on top of it so it would catch better sound.

'You say I'm like her. Like my grandmother. Well you're wrong. My grandmother would never have come here. She hated Jews. I'm sorry but that's how it was. It was a sickness in her. An addiction. Like smoking. The world would tell her it was bad but she couldn't give it up. She'd go out onto the balcony and take another drag and feel better for it. She could be venomous. She'd speak about the Jews and her eyes turned bright. Hate kept her going.'

Schalmik drew in his knees and placed his hands back on his lap. He couldn't say where this was going so he waited.

'That's how she felt and yet she tracked your career. Now isn't that odd? A deaf old Nazi for that's what she was, no point denying it, took interest in the musical career of a young Jew.'

Rosa shook her head a little, giving the curls of her hair some bounce, and settled back into the cushions of the sofa. She put herself in storytelling mode.

'She had little money but wired me a little extra in 1981. I was studying in Vienna and she had somehow heard about this concert in Munich. The money was just enough for the train trip to Germany, two nights in a hotel, and a ticket to the concert.'

'So you have done that train journey too, from Vienna to Munich? It must have been nice, with the curtains open.'

'I went to your concert. I heard you play.'

'Thank you.'

'Clifford Curzon at the piano. Why him, I wonder? He was so formal, his fingers as precise as knitting needles.'

'Who better? He was English, but embodied the best of Vienna without all the sick permutations. He trained with Artur Schnabel in Berlin when I was just a boy. And he was a conscientious objector during the war. He came to the platform clean. It was the highest honour to play alongside him. I regret that I didn't merit it.'

'But you did. You played with your eyes shut. One movement leapt after another. You rocked on your chair like the whole sonata was a hunt and you were chasing it down. You sagged at the end and we jumped to our feet and applauded. Even Clifford Curzon jumped to his feet. The hall went wild.'

'It was a difficult night.'

'I lay on my bed afterward, wide awake. I didn't know what I'd heard. It was Beethoven but not, like you stripped out Beethoven's melodies and hacked away to come up with something raw underneath. I had to write and tell my grandmother about the evening. What was your playing like? I came up with a word, didn't like it, but could find no other so I used it. Your playing was savage.'

'Music's like that sometimes. You pick up the bow, the piece lets you in, and then you have to fight your way out again. Melody is so cloying. It can be very hard.'

'They recorded that performance. Have you ever listened to it?'

'God no.'

'*Otto Schalmik: The Last Concert* they called it. You didn't play again in public for years. You've seldom appeared in a large concert hall since. Why?'

'I choose to write instead.'

'You cancelled all performances. Venues threatened to sue. Your management company supplied doctor's evidence of a nervous breakdown.'

'A formality. The doctor was a man of fine musical sensibility. He was very obliging.'

'This was 1981, your return to a German musical platform, your first since the war. Newspapers ran with stories of Dachau. They questioned the wisdom of staging your return so close to the camp. They presumed it opened old wounds.'

'Not wounds, Rosa, not that. It was nothing. A trick of the light.'

Rosa waited for an explanation. None came.

'You saw something?' she asked.

'It can happen. Lights dim but remain. A spotlight finds you. You look out into the audience and they have been cast into grey, row after row of spectral faces turned your way. It had always been fine. That night in Munich though, it was too much. The hall was filled with visitors from the dead. All those I had known, had known in the camps and who had died there, seemed to have roused themselves and packed the hall to hear me. What has Beethoven got to say to these people? I tried to find out that night. I failed.'

'We stood and we cheered.'

'The lights came back on. You glowed in full colour. You were lying. The dead were more understanding. They left quietly.'

'And you tell me that your story has no part to play in your music . . .'

The stream of conversation had soothed the dog. Now Mango noted a silence and lifted her head. Schalmik turned toward her and she roused herself in response, lifting herself from the mattress to pad across the redwood flooring.

'Here comes my wind instrument,' Schalmik said.

Rosa smiled, that dim smile of the willing yet uncomprehending. Mango moved past, as a dim shadow cast between the woman and the coffee table. Then the dog paused.

The fart was a brief tremolo. It gusted direct into Rosa's face and then the dog completed its circuit and flopped back onto the mattress.

Schalmik giggled like a child and then opened his mouth into a full-throated laugh as Rosa turned to face him.

'Oh come,' he said, 'she didn't shit on you. It wasn't that shocking. Think what smells mean to Mango. Her farts are a gift of love. They're usually reserved for me. That rock you belted her with down on the beach clearly made an impression.'

Rosa wafted a hand in front of her face. The fart cleared from the air.

'Does she know any other tricks?' she asked. 'Like playing dead?'

The dog snored gently from her mattress. Otherwise silence resumed.

Then Schalmik reached out for the microphone and clipped it back onto his collar.

'I don't favour playing dead,' he said. 'Let's get this over with, shall we?'

And he told her about his time at Dachau. He spoke of the concerts of Herr Zipper and how he had learned Bach in the latrines.

And he told her why he learned the Bach. In her grandparents' house he swabbed floorboards. The young prisoner was introduced to a Stradivarius cello. Rosa heard how young Otto Schalmik played Bach in the German living room of her grandmother.

As she listened, Rosa stayed as silent as the womb.

27
Inside Out

'And here we are . . .' Rosa continued. The woman just couldn't let up. '. . . sitting in your home on the California coast, you famous and venerable and quasi American, but you're also that boy in Dachau. A youngster in prison drag, death and brutality ever present, trapped in the home of your tormentor. I'm sure for all the things you've done in life, for all you've achieved, you can't ever stop being that person. Thank you for telling me your story. Thanks for having the courage to go back and relive it.'

'And I thank you for your condescension, Rosa. And I wish you good night.'

Mango lifted her head from her mattress and then lay it down again. She knew the proper order of things. This was high time for deep sleep.

'Please,' Rosa said. 'You're doing great. Stop now, and I know I won't sleep. I'll worry that I slipped up on day one. Rookie biographer had the story flowing and then let it slide. I can ask more questions if it helps. Or you can just speak again and I'll listen. Don't let's stop now, Mr Schalmik. Please.'

He wandered off. 'I need the bathroom,' he said.

It wasn't a euphemism. Alcohol had completed its usual trick of desiccating him, but he did need the bathroom. He squeezed out a few drops of dark yellow that barely coloured the toilet pan, and then he shut the lid and sat on it. Locked in a house with a persistent guest, this time-out was what he needed.

Light flooded this bathroom when you let it, not just the lamps inset in the ceiling but a run of fluorescence around the mirror, glowing panels that formed a wall beside the bath, even two haloes of light burning through twin smoked-glass tiles in the floor. He turned on all the switches but one, the one which illuminated the outdoor vivarium, for he didn't want the pooled dark green of vegetation to detract from the blaze.

Bright light was cleansing. Some mornings when fog rolled in off the Pacific and refused to lift, when he couldn't bear the welter of night dragging on through such gloom, he would close himself in this bathroom, slide all the dimmer bars to maximum, and feel the light scribble away vestigial scraps of story.

Memories lurked in darkness where they grew insane.

Rosa aimed to turn his life into a book. That was like turning a mortuary slab into a picnic table. She had no idea.

He flushed the toilet so as to let her know he was returning, but he needn't have bothered. Earphones were clamped round her head as she checked in on her recordings.

'It'll do,' she said, as though he was concerned. 'The sound quality is so much better when you consent to using the microphone. Please, sit down. I'll clip it on you again.'

He obeyed. The red light popped up bright on her recorder.

'You have become one of today's top cellists,' she began.

Schalmik pursed his lips, frowned, and looked set to stand and leave her. She shouldn't have said 'one of'. She knew it at the time. He was the very best. That's what she should have said, however much she would prefer to argue the point. Flattery was an interviewer's best friend and she wasn't very good at it. She hurried on.

'You're also a great composer. That combination's unique. How does that happen? How do you make the move from interpreting a composer's work to being a composer?'

'How did you move from a love of music to writing criticism?' he threw back. 'Perhaps it's the same thing.'

'Your *Appelplatz Quintet*,' she persisted. 'It wasn't published till 1958 but your catalogue notes it as your first work.'

'I lost it for a while. I wrote down its name and pinned it to my wall. I knew it would come back.'

'You lost the manuscript?'

'I suppose so. I suppose I did. I wrote it onto paper at Dachau and of course that disappeared. What I really lost is the sheer white heat of the piece. I thought I was creating it but I wasn't. It was creating me. That quintet saved me. It made me into a composer.'

'How? How did it do that?'

Schalmik sighed, long and deep like something was escaping. 'I can't tell you,' he said. 'You have to know what it's like to be me, young and alone in the middle of the empty parade ground at Dachau. The sun is high, the guards are in their watchtowers, and I expect to die. I see this slogan on the roof of the buildings. It promises freedom and it is a lie. I counter the lie. I pick out words I can believe in. Honesty, truthfulness, freedom, love. I set them against the lie of the language till they merged and became true. Music found me. I became a composer to defeat the lie of language.'

'You chose E flat major. The same key, the same instruments, as Mozart's Quintet. That has three movements, the same as *The Appelplatz Quintet*.'

'True. But hardly pertinent at the time or even now. Mozart didn't exist when I wrote that piece. Nothing existed. I was writing against music. You take lightning and thunder and wind and rain and sunlight and make weather. That's what it's like. That's how music happens. Then you put it on paper and hand it to instrumentalists and say go on, make weather. They do their damndest, some of them, and make weather of a sort. Music turns physical, instruments send out notes that shiver into your skin, and that's the best of it. It's something vestigial though, like a memory of fire. Music takes fire in a composer's brain. The composer and the music are one. You have to combust with the music to hear it. No one else hears it truly. If they did, they would die.'

He unclipped his microphone and stood.

'I was young when I wrote the *Appelplatz*. It flared. Now, when lucky, I'm warmed by embers. Come on,' he said. 'Let me show you around. You can collect some details for your chapter on the old man and his dog.'

Rosa followed him into the kitchen area. Mango stood from her mattress and padded through too, tilting her head and wagging the stump of her tail as Schalmik lifted the lid off a trashcan.

'Kibble,' he announced, and waited till Rosa had stepped close enough to look inside. 'I buy in bulk. There's another sealed container in the garage.'

He clattered the lid back in place. Mango sat down as he opened a floor-to-ceiling door, no doubt expensive oak carpentry but with the finish and texture of a plank.

'The larder. Filled from floor to ceiling with dried goods, labelled with the date of purchase and sealed in ziplock bags to keep them safe from mice. And look at this.' He slapped a hand on the lid of a large tin left handy on a shelf at waist height. 'Powdered milk, enough to make up gallons. I stir in the water and leave the mix in a pitcher in the icebox. It makes for a passable dairy substitute. And I've a bread machine on the counter. Have you ever used one of those? Tip in the flour, the water, the yeast, set the timer, and I can wake each morning to a fresh loaf. All the daily consumables are accounted for.'

He shut the larder door and walked off. A side door led into a corridor that joined the house to the garage. Rosa took note of an old Buick, a golden brown in colour. It reflected the neon strip lighting in its polish but Schalmik was not here to show off his car. He moved to the freezer, as tall as him and double-wide.

'See!' He pulled open the freezer doors. 'I have Evie keep it full. Cooked meals in foil containers, all individual portions, beef on the top shelf, chicken below that, and then vegetarian. There's enough in here to keep me well fed for a month. Imagine that, Rosa. A month of good solid eating without ever having to leave and buy in fresh supplies. Isn't that splendid?'

He banged the doors shut and led her back to the house. Mango had returned to her mattress. She looked up as Schalmik drew wide the door to the balcony and then let herself slump into sleep once again.

Rosa walked outdoors to join him. It was almost chilly but sea mist had not rolled in. The outlines of branches were distinct against a still-darkening sky. Schalmik stood as a silhouette at the far edge of the balcony, his hands on the railing, staring out.

'I've shown you my tidy, well-provisioned life. It's a forty-mile round trip to the local store but that's not the reason I stock up like this. If the local store were opposite my driveway I would do just the same.'

'I can see that. When you've been literally starving it makes sense to want to surround yourself with food.'

'Oh, Rosa, that's true but it's not what I'm telling you. You are not so stupid. Is it just because you're young? You look at life and worry away at it till it makes sense. You can't see that what makes sense to you is just plain wrong to someone else. We think because we speak that we are able to transmit our experiences to others. That's nonsense. All people can find in another's experience is that tiniest fragment that reflects their own.'

'Empathy's got to start somewhere.'

'Empathy?'

A nearby bird cracked its wings to break from the shelter of a branch and fly against the night. Rosa wanted to break free too. There was something so forlorn about the way he spoke the word.

'Empathy brings compassion,' she tried.

'Empathy leads to compassion and compassion has the lifespan of a gnat.'

She half-thought of answers but they all dried up before she spoke them so she stood there, awkward company, until he spoke again.

'Turn your life inside out, Rosa. Then you have a chance of seeing what it's like in someone else's skin. Only then.'

'Your music turns me inside out.'

'Good. Very good.'

'Don't be so dismissive.'

'It is good, Rosa. It's death that turns you inside out and you're too young to see that but that's right. Death you think can wait until you are old but that is not my experience. It takes the children first and grabs at babies. When I see people I size them up for death which is why I stay home and stock up on food. Who needs to see death all the time?

People are born to die. I see them and that is what I see. It's not empathy, it's just true. I see people living and know they'll soon be dead. My head pulses and migraines start. There's not a soul out there I can protect, Rosa. Not one of them I can keep from death. Who needs company like mine? I keep myself to myself. It's kinder that way.'

Rosa shivered. 'We'd best get you back inside before you catch a chill,' she said.

'And then what? More questions, Rosa? Can't you see that it's better not to know?'

'No. It's never better not to know.'

'God, I'm so tired of this.'

Schalmik stepped back indoors and left her. She wondered if he was going to bed but instead he walked to the central staircase and descended, his head spiralling out of sight.

28
An Encore

The floor below was paved with natural stone. Rosa's bedroom was to the right. Light came out of a further room away to her left.

Schalmik was playing his cello. The notes were the run of a scale, D minor. Clearly she was not expected to sleep. Her eyes were smarting from the length of the day and the dryness of the flight. She went to her bathroom and took time to pop out her contact lenses and drop them into a solution, and then blinked at herself in the mirror. At least the eyes weren't bloodshot. Her make-up was still in place. She would do.

She left the bedroom light on and her door ajar. Schalmik had switched out of scales and was now playing a tune. It was J.S. Bach, one of his Suites, the opening prelude. Ah yes. The G major.

She walked barefoot to where the sliding doors were pulled full back. The six lamps flush to the ceiling were dimmed. Schalmik was barefoot like herself. His feet were flat on a rug with a design of bright interwoven circles, triangles and rectangles. His head was held as though to stare high behind her head but his eyes were closed.

He swept the bow, his fingers pincered crablike and shaking on the strings. Then the music snuck into her heart somehow and she found her eyes smarting. The tears were a surprise.

He lifted the bow to let the last note of the prelude play longer than it ought, and then snapped open his eyes.

'It's late.' Rosa wiped her cheeks dry with her hands. 'Do you always play this late?'

'*Komm.*' He pulled back his bow as though making room. 'Come here.'

She simply stood and stared at him.

'Please,' he said, and turned from her to look around the room. The only chair was the one he sat on. Bench seating, made of cement painted a glossy white, ran along one wall and he nodded toward cushions strewn along its top. 'Bring cushions. Make yourself a nest. Sit down.'

Since she hesitated he stood up, carrying the cello with him and then tucking it against his body to free his left hand. The cushions each had a separate motif of a circle, a triangle, a rectangle on backgrounds of blue, red and purple. He flung them onto the carpet.

'You sit and I'll play. If that is alright? You tire me out with your talking but I find I want to play you something. That is alright isn't it, you sit at my feet as I play? Am I wrong to suggest it?'

He took the cello back to his seat.

'Come,' he said. 'By day this Stradivarius puts up too much of a fight. She only lets me play her at night, and only then if I play Bach. But let's change all that for a moment. Let's talk about your grandmother.'

He jutted his jaw forward, stared at her, and struck a rapid series of bass chords so harsh and brisk it made Rosa jump. And then she opened her mouth and let out a yelp of laughter. 'You're right, all of that sharp growling, that's her. You caught her. How did you know?'

Schalmik bit the bow into the strings and started again. It was wild but more than he could sustain. The improvisation ended with a slumping sigh.

'Sorry, that was too much. I tried for a group of such women in conversation. It didn't work. But one German or one Austrian grandmother of a certain type, that I can do. Please, settle yourself down.'

'I don't know if she was typical. She was the only German grandmother I have known.' Rosa moved forward and bunched the cushions together. The best position she could find was leaning into a stack of them, her legs tucked to one side and her head resting on the palm of her hand.

Schalmik struck with his bow again. The cello danced on its spike as he set the bass notes grunting again, in the way that had made her laugh before.

Rosa smiled but only out of politeness. The fun had gone. Schalmik stopped.

'You're right. Music doesn't represent people, only stereotypes. I don't know what I'm scratching away at. Your grandmother was just a young woman when I knew her. Younger than you are now. With your mother just a foetus in her belly.'

'Was she beautiful?'

Schalmik had no ready answer. He stared at Rosa as though the answer lay in her face somehow. He blinked.

'I've only known her as Gran. As my Oma. She was never Katja to me. You were a boy. I'm talking about then. How you saw her. Was she beautiful?'

'Of course!' Schalmik barked his response.

Rosa had been smiling, teasing. Her face turned blank.

'What do you want me to say, Rosa? I was a boy. Shaved head. Smelly. Hungry. Thirsty. It was a hot summer. I felt near naked in my prison rags. It was a perfect house. She was radiant. She terrified me. I was like a rat to her. No not a rat. I was filthy and she wanted me out of her house but I was not a rat. More like a cat. We were both cats. I was an alley cat and she was, I don't know, a Siamese maybe. I was chained and she was free to roam but we both were trapped. We were both locked inside the house and the house was beautiful and we both wanted out. Your grandmother was beautiful and she was scary and she was scared. What do you want me to tell you? Life's not a story, Rosa. It's a mess.'

'Why was she scared? I never saw her scared.'

'You scared her. When you were little. I'm sure you did. There's nothing so scary as children. I see little ones in the street, in the park, and they terrify me. How can I keep them alive? No one can keep them alive. It's only chance.'

Rosa heard the choke in his voice. His eyes were moist. He kept them wide and unblinking, as though to dry them.

'You said you would play,' she reminded him.

He blinked.

'You played for my grandmother.'

'She sat before me. She placed her hands on the cello. She took in the sound through touch.'

'May I?' Rosa held out her hands.

He nodded. At least Rosa took it as a nod. It was a slight tick of his head, and then he closed his eyes and struck the bow across the strings. It was the opening prelude to the first Bach Suite.

Rosa touched the wood lightly. It vibrated beneath her fingertips. She lay the flesh of her palms upon the wood and felt the vibrations pass up her arms.

The cello screeched as Schalmik pulled his bow across it. He twisted his head to one side. Her hands withdrew. She rested back on her heels.

'You have me recreating the past,' Schalmik said. 'It's absurd.'

She looked at him wide-eyed still and attempted a smile.

'I think we've killed Bach for the evening.' He stood and took the cello back to its stand. 'I think we're done, Rosa.'

'You created this little scene, not me. Stay with it. What happened next?'

'Your grandmother touched my face. She opened my eyes. We exchanged our names. I kept on playing while she went to the kitchen. She came back and handed me a sausage.

Katja took hold of my cello. She curled her right hand around its neck and pressed hard so all the sound was killed.'

'What did she say?'

'My breath stank. She told me my breath stank. I should eat the sausage, get some milk and fruit from the kitchen, and go. Of course I couldn't go. I had to wait for the guards.'

'So you stayed in the room with her?'

'No I went. I left her with the cello and I walked away.'

'What did she do then?'

'I didn't look back.'

'You're a musician.' Rosa persisted. 'You play with your eyes closed. You don't need to look. What did you hear?'

'The strings. She started plucking at the strings of the cello.'

'Was it music?'

'How could I know? I'm just a musician. You're the critic. You get the right to make judgments.'

'Then show me. Do it for me. Show me the noise she made.'

'I can't. She was a mad deaf woman. It was her noise.'

'Then interpret it.' Rosa's voice hit a level of command you either strike back at or act on.

Schalmik acted. He wheeled from his chair to a kneeling position in front of the cello as though his joints didn't ache. With a finger and thumb of his right hand he pulled the G string so far out that when he let it go it struck the backboard before vibrating. That smack against wood spoiled the sound so he plucked the string again, still violent but a measured violence this time.

The string sang out.

Yes that was it. He heard it and so remembered it. As young Otto listening to the noise from the living room of her Dachau home all he heard was an attack, Katja hitting out in anger at the cello he had made his own. But this is how it was, Katja stretching the thick G string to its limit and letting go, judging the effect, adjusting, plucking at the string again.

He let the sound die down and started again. One string, a moment's attention, and then the next string while the note faded, and the next, adding speed but keeping attention, the visual of the strings face-on like this something he had never seen before, music as a vibrationary haze.

And then he was playing as she had played, he saw that now, no longer plucking but striking with the knuckles of his fingers like the knuckles were hammers sprung from a keyboard and the strings belonged to a piano. First it was note by note, one after the other, a chase to keep up the speed, but then speed was no issue and time opened out for patterns of sound to fill it. His knuckles hammered away, on and on till the music was done and he pulled them back to leave the strings shivering.

Then he leaned forward, his forehead pressing against the strings in a final muting.

Rosa withdrew.

She thought of going to her room, climbing out of her outfit, taking a shower to loosen up her hair, scrubbing off her make-up. That was her instinct. She'd towel herself dry, throw on her most casual clothes, and then seek out Schalmik to mop up the residue of the evening.

Instead she climbed the spiral of iron stairs toward the kitchen. What was it he had just done to that cello? The sound he made was monstrous, so dense and angry it made her heart ache. And then when he stopped and all the notes blended as one and he knelt forward to still them with his head it was like a prayer was answered, a prayer for silence, and what she saw there was not Schalmik, he wasn't veteran and venerable, he was just the teenage kid grown immeasurably sad.

'I've made you hot cocoa,' she said, and nodded to a steaming mug that sat opposite her at the kitchen table.

Schalmik sat down as told but did not drink straight away. He left his hands on the table. The knuckles were stained with blood.

'That was insane,' Rosa said. 'Brilliant but insane.'

'You wanted to know the sound your grandmother made.'

'And that's what you heard?'

'It came back to me.'

'You really think so?' Rosa stood, filled a saucepan with warm water, and put it on the table in front of him. 'You heard what you heard. What you played wasn't a memory. You gave me what I asked for. That was an interpretation. It's what the loss of music would sound like to a great musician who's been hammered by the twentieth century. My grandmother made a noise. She didn't make that music. She was never a genius.'

He looked at her without moving.

'Go on,' she said. 'Soak those hands.'

He looked down at the bowl, and then at his blooded fingers.

'Maybe you could sponge them clean for me?' he said. 'Then put on some ointment? And a bandaid? There's cotton wool in the bathroom cabinet.'

'There's no point going baby-eyed with me. I'm not the mothering type. Go on, soak them.'

He did as told, and made sure not to wince when his fingers stung.

'What's your memory like?' she asked. 'Could you recall what you just did? Notate it?'

'Who would play it?'

'Brash young cellists with masochistic streaks who want to make a name for themselves. Or you could devise something. Strap-on rubber knuckles for example. Or silver thimbles perhaps with amplification to get real volume. At the moment it's played fortissimo but comes out fairly quiet which is interesting in itself.'

'You thought it good?'

'It was awful. Powerfully awful.'

He started cleaning the blood from his hands by rubbing them against each other.

'You didn't hold back, Mr Schalmik. I've sensed moments like that in your works for orchestra, but those are different. In those the orchestra gangs up in its wildness to stop individual instruments sounding through. But what you improvised just now was for a solo instrument and it wouldn't be silenced. It fed on itself and just grew and grew. It was a seminal piece.'

'You heard it, Rosa. Perhaps that's enough.' He drew his hands from the water and let the fingers hang down to drip dry. 'Perhaps that's what it was meant for.'

'Tunes are meant for something, Mr Schalmik. We sing and we dance to them. Music's not meant for anything. It just is. It just does. You know that as well as anybody.' She reached back to pull a tea towel from the oven rail and pushed it across the table. 'Dab yourself dry and drink your cocoa while it's hot.'

29
One Last Swim

The noise puzzled him, a low rhythmic pulse like an engine, then he worked it out. Rosa was asleep down below and snoring. Well good for her. Schalmik could have sworn he hadn't slept, though he jolted awake from a few dreams to prove him wrong. The blush of dawn spared him staying in bed any longer.

Normal waking routine was to let out the dog, make tea, carry it out to the balcony, and listen to the morning. It gave time to think. Now he wanted no time to think. Mango pulled herself to her feet and followed him outside.

Soon the dog was bounding along the path down to the cove. This was a fun switch in routine for her. It was something fiercer for Schalmik. Perhaps it was escape. You don't think when you escape, you just act.

Down on the sand Mango began her insane bouncing routine. Schalmik reached the rocks, stripped off his clothes, and lay them down on the stone.

The sea was calm. He walked till it covered his knees and then threw himself forward. The cold shocked his lungs into standstill but he thrashed his arms and kicked his feet till his heart started pumping. He could do a passable crawl. His body stretched, his arms wheeled one after the other above his head, he turned his face from the water to catch fresh breaths, it all worked. What a break, to be out in the ocean. Why restrict himself to that old man's breaststroke in his training pool all these years?

The sun was behind him and the horizon formed a clear dark line far ahead. He would head there.

Sweep, sweep, the sea was choppier now but he cut through it. His legs began to drag. Not good enough. He kicked hard till his heels broke the surface once again.

What was that? A sharp call, something familiar. It came from the shore. He pulled himself round.

Mango was tiny. She stood so the tide caught her front paws and she barked and she barked. She faced the distant head of her master in the ocean and she yelled for his return.

Not now, Mango. I'm not coming back now.

Schalmik pulled himself round to the horizon and worked his body back to the level. Sweep sweep, he cut through the waves and brought his heels back through the surface but their weight kept pulling the legs down. Maybe change stroke.

He pushed through the water. Those years in the training pool were not wasted after all. His breaststroke was strong. He heaved the water aside with his hands to hoist his shoulders high.

Bark bark. What did that dog want? Couldn't she let him be for a moment?

He pulled himself round to face her. She stopped barking as he watched. Waves brought him high so she was in view and then they lowered him. On the next wave he looked and she was gone. He saw only her splashes as water flew into the air.

What was she doing? Damn fool dog. She had jumped into the sea and now she was swimming. He could make out that russet head of hers, her snout held high. Couldn't she be on her own for a moment?

She had no sense, that was for sure. She was stupid enough to keep swimming till she found him, keep swimming till she reached the horizon or she sank. He would get back and have to hang around for her drowned body to be swept up on the rocks.

Ah well, swimming was swimming, the direction didn't really matter. In fact, maybe it was easier this way. The tide was coming in, wasn't it? Or was it? It didn't seem any easier. His legs dropped from their crawl so he went back to frog-kicking them. That way, doing breaststroke, he could keep sight of his dog as he crested each wave. She looked like an otter, just that snout and ears and eyes above water.

With you soon, Mango, he willed, though his strokes were not cutting much distance. In fact he was making no progress at all. He was treading water.

Barely treading water.

A wave broke over his head.

You can do better than this, Otto, he told himself. Count. Count like you do in the pool. One, two, three. On the fourth stroke he was levelled out. On the count of six he was going forward again. There was his dog, a little dog a long way ahead. She was different. Her snout was gone. Ah yes, she had turned. She was heading for shore. Good dog.

Still, better to head for shore himself. Who knew what that damn dog would do next?

It was fun swimming this direction. He could look up into the sun. Not right into it, he wasn't stupid, just into the blazing blue of the sky.

A wave crossed his head and still he could look up, the sun a bright and dappled disc high beyond the sea.

He swallowed. It was a gulp for air but it brought in sea. His head broke the surface and he coughed.

Start counting, Otto. You forgot to count.

What's that noise?

That dog again, barking like crazy. There's no stopping her. He'd best pick up his breaststroke and quieten her down.

One, two, three. Where was he? Oh yes, counting his stokes. Best start again.

One, two, three.

Bark bark. That fool Mango. She never gives up.

So the tide was coming in after all. That was lucky.

The current pulled Schalmik across the bay, away from his clothes, so he reached shore near the cliff. The dog spotted him and splashed through the shallows. She never let up that damn fool barking, right in his face so the waves splashed across her. When he lifted his head he smelt her breath.

She must be standing. Maybe he could stand too? What the heck? It was worth a try. He gave it a go.

It seemed to work. He fell the first time, when a wave hit the back of his calves, but he got up again and now he was walking. The seawater dropped away from his shoulders and he picked his feet above it, splashing each one down till there was no splash left and he was treading footprints deep into sand. A little further, that would be good. Up the rise till the sand turns dry. Here is good.

He let himself drop. The sand was cool and the dog was wet. Stinky too. She lay down beside him and he clung her close, and the heat from her body reached his flesh.

His clothes scratched against the crusted salt on his skin. A bath might be good. A hot bath.

But that was back in the house. He wasn't ready for the house.

And the shower by the pool was cold water only. What sort of affectation was that?

Maybe a fire. That would help. The sun touched his skin but the sea had set a chill in much deeper than that. He had cleared scrub around his garden. There were some good dead twigs in that.

It wasn't a plan as such, it just happened piece by piece. He went to his studio for matches. They let him light the fire but the blaze was meagre. He went back for the blanket from his daybed and wrapped that around himself.

And then he saw the box, on the floor beside the day-bed. The sheets of brown paper that had wrapped it were crumpled beside it. He picked up the whole lot and carried it off to the cliff edge where his fire licked out its few flames.

The wrapping paper lay on the fire for a moment before its edges turned bright orange, and then it combusted. The ink of his name and address turned to black and curled in on itself. His hands near burned when he reached out his palms. This was getting to be a proper fire.

How many letters were in that box? Must be hundreds. They were just litter. The litter of a life. They could keep this fire burning for an hour or more.

He took out one and reached it toward the flames. Even in its envelope it was flimsy, made of blue airmail paper. The flame snatched it so fast it bit into his fingers. He pushed them into his mouth to suck out the pain. They tasted of charcoal.

Best to burn the damn things in their bundles. A bundle for every year. Thick enough to turn this into a real fire and keep it going.

Rosa had eaten her bowl of muesli, drunk her first coffee, and still there was no sign of Schalmik and his dog. Maybe they were both down on the point? She poured a fresh coffee and headed outdoors.

The crackle of fire came first, and then she smelt it. It turned her right instead of left.

Rosa called out his name. 'Mr Schalmik?'

Beyond the second gate and on the drive the taint of smoke was thicker. The crackle of fire was to her left. She headed along a narrow uphill path. The soft light of the morning was stabbed orange just ahead, and she saw a lick of flame. She drew nearer. A small bonfire was starting to blaze. Schalmik crouched beside it. He was sucking his fingers and didn't look up.

'What are you doing?' she asked.

'Getting warm.'

He reached into the box and took out a bundle of pale blue envelopes tied together in white cotton.

'What's that?'

'Litter.'

'Are they letters?'

'Litter, letters, same thing.'

He dropped the bundle onto the flames. It didn't take at once. That was good. He would get some proper heat when it burned.

'You're burning letters?' Rosa said.

She didn't think. There was no time. She simply reacted. Her foot kicked into the fire. The bundle of letters shot out onto the dusty earth of the path. She wanted to reach it, to stamp on it, to make sure it did not burn. The fire was in the way. Schalmik was in the way.

She kicked at the fire, a side scoop of a kick this time. The top layer of blazing twigs flew off and over the cliff edge. She kicked again and then one more time. The whole fire disappeared. She jumped across it and stamped on the letter bundle.

'I'm taking these,' she said. 'I'll see you back in the kitchen whenever you're ready.'

She held the charred bundle of letters in one hand, tucked the box filled with the other letters under her arm, and marched off.

You don't scatter fire. Rosa was Australian, a land of drought and dry brush. She ought to have known that.

Schalmik stood from the burnt spot of ground and turned to the plot of garden that grew up the slope behind. Mango had parked her backside on the strawberry patch. He pretended not to notice. She'd only start bouncing about if he caught her attention, and kick up more havoc. As a rule, he kept her clear of this garden. She wasn't a great one for fruit and vegetables.

He picked a young lettuce, five cherry tomatoes, and a few nasturtium flowers for their colour. That would do as a salad for lunch, along with a hard-boiled egg perhaps and a slice or two of bread and butter. Maybe melt more butter as a dip for an artichoke. And add a few slices of cold beef.

Lunch for one.

He really must make sure Rosa had quit the property by then.

'I've made you a pot of tea.' Rosa nodded across to the counter. 'You said you drank green. I found some.'

The letters were all out of the box and ranged across the kitchen table in their bundles. The empty box was tucked beneath her chair. The neatness pleased him.

'Are they all from you?' she asked.

'Probably. I've never looked.'

'The stamps change. It's like a whole history of stamps, 1949 to now. Are these the first ones, this bundle from Canada?'

She pointed to a slim bundle top left. Already they were set in chronological order.

'There was a single one from 1948. I've just burned that.'

She glared at him. Her recorder lay on the table above the letters. She reached for it and turned it on.

'Did you read it first? What did it say? Tell me now, before you forget.'

'Of course I didn't read it. Why on earth would I do that?'

She considered his answer, and then turned off her machine.

'So from 1948 to last year, you wrote to my grandmother.'

'I wrote this year too. That letter was returned. So I stopped.'

'Have you kept it?'

'Of course not.'

'You're impossible.' She gulped her coffee. 'You would have burned all these if I hadn't stopped you.'

He poured his tea and brought it to the table.

'You're shaking,' she noticed.

'I'm cold. I went for a swim. I needed to warm up. You put out my fire.'

'You swam? In the sea?'

He just looked at her.

'You're crazy,' she said. 'And mind those letters! You're spilling your tea. You'll shake yourself to death just standing there like that. Go and take a hot bath.'

He looked at her again.

'I mean it. You need to warm up. Go on, take a bath. Then we'll talk.'

Nobody ordered him around in his own house. He was set to complain. But then the words didn't come.

The tea scalded his mouth but the shiver was deep inside.

He wandered off.

He inched in his left foot first, and waited a moment before putting in his right. He looked down and saw the white feet blush red but it was bearable. Hot, but he could suffer it. He lowered himself.

At first he dared not move. Any shift of his body sent hot waves through the water. With his eyes closed, he kept still and felt the chill withdraw.

'Well, Otto Schalmik.'

The words lodged in his chest rather than in his mind. He couldn't say what language they came in, whether English or German. They slipped in like thoughts, in that space that precedes language.

Sometimes he started these conversations himself. They were with the dead, and it was his way of remembering. Only this time, the words came unbidden.

'You were a young fool, Otto, and now you are an old fool,' they said. 'What were you doing out there in that sea, swimming or dying? Do you think we dead are calling? You've dared to allow yourself a little company. That's good. We're not calling, my love. We're cheering you on.'

Who was this? Was it his mother? Was that right?

It wasn't right and it wasn't wrong. That's what it seemed. There was no mother and there was only mother.

Perhaps he dozed. The bathwater was now merely warm. Schalmik reached for the faucet with his toes. He needed longer. Hot water powered down and raised the water level above his chest toward his neck.

'Hmm,' he said. It felt good to try out his voice.

'Aah,' he tried. Its echo came back off the bathroom tiles.

He exercised his voice a little more. 'Yitgaddal veyitqaddash shemei rabba,' he began, in a low, slow murmur.

Who knows where those words came from? He tried them again and then continued: 'Be'alma di vra khiruteh.'

They were the words of the Kaddish. The prayer for the dead that froze in his heart back in Buchenwald. Further words of the prayer stayed frozen. It would take great heat to melt them.

'Yitgaddal veyitqaddash shemei rabba . . .' Here they came.

He voiced the prayer from his bath and heard it reflect off the tiles. The echo was faint but he recited louder and the echo grew stronger. He could hear it now, without saying the words. It gathered into a harmonic line that set itself against the spoken pattern of the prayer. It made him think of Hugo, and the way his brother-in-law's voice turned prayer into song. This was not a line for voice though. It was a musical line for cello to accompany a spoken voice.

He rose from the bath, wrapped a towel around his waist, and draped another across his shoulders. The girl was still at the table. Letters from the first bundle lay flattened in front of her.

'Better?' she asked.

He picked her recorder off the table and carried it downstairs.

A tiny grating showed that the machine held an internal microphone. That would have to do. He turned the recorder on and set it down on the cushions Rosa had assembled the night before.

Last night the machine had been a somewhat baffling annoyance. Now it was functional. Life took what it needed.

The Stradivarius was for night times and Bach. Instead he went to a cupboard in the corner and picked out his Gofriller. This instrument was warmer to the touch somehow, like the deep reds of its varnish, and more accommodating. Schalmik settled himself in the chair. The towel gaped as he spread his legs. So what?

His lips shaped the Kaddish. Music poured as lambent notes from his cello.

In the kitchen above, Rosa looked up from her reading. At first she troubled to analyse the music, and to place the semitones. Then she hoped the old fool had set the machine to record properly.

And then, as a theme returned in its repeated chorus and the old man sang out Hebrew in a voice both cracked and clear, her critical mind grew blank and a tear caught at the corner of her right eye.

Get a hold of yourself, Rosa, she thought.

30
The Confrontation

Schalmik came back up the stairs and into his bedroom, and reappeared wearing a rust red turtleneck, beige pants, and suede slip-ons.

'You look good,' Rosa said. 'The image of a composer at home. Was that new, the piece you just played?'

'As new as the morning.' He set her recorder down beside her. 'I recorded it. I don't know how to wipe the tape.'

'You wanted to wipe it?'

'It's in my mind now. It won't go away.'

'It was moving.'

'Moving? I didn't know that word was in a critic's vocabulary.'

'My grandmother named me a critic. It wasn't my choice. I played her a Chopin Etude once. The performance was awesome. Fast and flawless. Of course she could hear none of it. She could only watch. "You play like a critic," she told me. "A musician has something animal about her. She plays with her whole body. With you, the link is direct between brain and fingers." It hurt at the time, but it gave me much to think about, which was obviously her plan. Now when I hear what moves me, I work hard to discover why. That's my version of being a critic. You speak Hebrew?'

'I recite Hebrew.'

'What was that?'

'The Kaddish. The Jewish prayer for the dead.'

She looked up at him a while.

'It's not Jewish music though,' she said. 'I'd never be foolish enough to state that about it. Come and sit down.' She pulled some of the letters toward herself to clear space at the table. 'You swim, you build a fire, you compose, you play. At what time do you eat?'

'It's past breakfast time.'

'But you didn't eat. You got up and left the house and I didn't hear you. If you'd eaten, I would have woken. It's an elemental thing with me. I can't let someone eat alone. Sit. You've exhausted yourself. I'll make you toast.'

'I don't eat toast.'

'First you smell the toast, then you have to eat the toast. It always works for me. Sit down.'

He did as told. She took two slices out of the breadbin. There was no toaster obvious so she put them under the grill.

'Tell me about the letters.'

He sighed. 'What's there to say? I wrote to your grandmother. She wrote back. I have kept very few of hers. I presumed mine had been thrown away. In late February that box arrived. Katja said she knew she was dying and was clearing up loose ends. All my letters were inside.'

'You always wrote in English?'

'I wrote in English. On some principle I didn't understand. She answered in German.'

Rosa turned the toast. It gave her time to think.

'You say it started in 1948. Did you hear from her before that?'

'Just once. After the war.'

'Before the trial,' Rosa guessed. She buttered it and halved it. Both slices were meant for him but why resist? She put them on separate plates. And smacked them down so hard on the table they could have broken. She had been holding back long enough. This was the time to confront him. It's why she had come, after all. If not now, when?

'Why did you do it' Mr Schalmik? Why did you speak up for my grandfather at his war trial?'

He blinked at her. She wasn't making sense.

'Nazis killed your family. My grandfather was a chief among Nazis. Do you think he cared about the Jews? He didn't. Do you think he was innocent? He was complicit. He helped turn Dachau into the model for all concentration camps. He devised train transport that shuttled Jews to their deaths. You were thrown onto those trains. I've read the transcript. You're clearly in pain when you talk about that. Yet one sausage, one letter my grandfather may or not have written, a letter that let you escape to Canada, you think that mitigates evil? It doesn't, Mr Schalmik. People are mixed, yes. Maybe he loved my gran. Maybe he whistled snatches of *Winterreise* in the shower. Maybe he darned his own socks.

Gran told me he did all those things but it doesn't change a thing. It doesn't even make him interesting. My grandfather was a cruel and wicked man. Why couldn't you say that? They gave you every chance but no, you went off on a riff about your own guilt. I've watched film of the trial. You know what that lawyer who quizzed you should have done? He should have slapped you. Slapped some sense into you. Of course he couldn't, he was playing by the rules, but my grandfather? He made up the rules, he decided it was good that people should be killed for being themselves. There was no shred of decency in the man. That's what you had to say. The world's still full of people like my grandfather. People in power. If even you can't bring yourself to condemn them, what hope have we got? What can keep such beasts in check? They sniff out weakness and I'm afraid, Mr Schalmik, you were not being good when you spoke about fairness, you were being weak.'

'They hanged your grandfather.'

'I've got the photo. Him on a string. '

'So he didn't need me to condemn him.'

'You didn't have to lie. When you said it was fair to say he had fed you, saved your life, that had to be a lie.'

Schalmik paused while he chewed a bite of his toast. The thought was such a surprise.

'Lies of omission perhaps,' he conceded. 'I spoke what I thought was true. The Birchendorfs took me in, in their way. They found me the route to Canada. I was your grandmother's charity case. She fed me one meal, and wrote one letter on my behalf. I was a pre-natal blip of compassion perhaps. I wouldn't say your grandfather was complicit in her actions, but he cherished her in his way. He let her whims ride. Your grandmother wrote to me. She claimed he spoke of me often. The letter to Toronto, appealing to her former professor for my entry to the College of Music, was written in her hand but she said she had taken her husband's dictation. If such were lies, as I suspect they were, then they were her lies. She was building a case to save her husband's life. They were lies born of love.'

'Lies born of love,' Rosa voiced back to him, with derision. She swept a hand across the letters. 'So are these love letters?'

'Read them. You'll see they're nothing of the sort. They're so ordinary. The everyday nonsense of my life.'

'I checked the envelopes, going back to 1949. You wrote to post offices and then a box number.'

'Your grandmother was a displaced person. Such people had no sense of a secure address.'

'I've only ever had one family home.'

'Such is your life. It is good.'

'Yet I've never seen these letters before. They never came through our mailbox. Once a week it seems, all my life, Gran got these letters, but I never knew anything about them. That's quite a secret.'

'You left home at eighteen?'

Rosa nodded.

'And I at nineteen. What do I know about my grandparents' lives? Almost nothing. That's teenagers for you.'

Schalmik stood and went into his bedroom. Rosa heard a cupboard door open and close and he was back. He pushed the letters aside to make room and set a photograph album on the table before her. Rosa opened it toward the back.

'Who made this?' she asked.

'Your gran sent me things. I collected them in the album.'

'Gran sent you this?' The last page held just one item. 'A review of my Beethoven book, from *Music Teacher Today*? Gran would never have come across that.'

'I supplemented a little. That's via a newsclipping service.'

She flipped back a few pages. It showed a picture of herself in long straight hair, large glasses, her hands raised above the keyboard in a black and white photo from a school concert. On the opposite page was a printed cast list for her tenth grade performance of *Ruddigore*.

'It's a bit obsessive, isn't it?'

'It's a life.' He sat down opposite her, so his view of the album was upside down. 'You want me to decide what's important? Discard bits and save others? You're the biographer. This is for you.'

She turned back to the first page. It held just one image, though it was small. A woman in a pale summer dress held a baby that dangled to face the camera. Just the baby's startled face was visible with its downy hair; a trailing shawl obscured the legs and feet. A man was bent to set his face beside the woman's. The man grinned; the woman smiled. She was bareheaded in a summer park. He wore a peaked cap with its death's head insignia. His arm looped around the woman's shoulder and enfolded mother and daughter. The forked twin Ss showed clear on his upper sleeve.

Rosa barely glanced at it. She knew the picture well.

'I've seen this. I had a copy. I cut it into pieces and burned it. Why on earth should I want another?'

'They're your grandparents. And your mother as a baby. The earliest photo of her.'

'It makes me feel sick to look at it.'

'It's a nice photo.'

'Nice? It's a picture of a Nazi war criminal. Leering.'

Well yes, he supposed it was that. How beautiful Katja looked though. When the world was dark and he was still young he once played a Stradivarius. A woman pressed open his eyes, looked into him and gave him her name. This was a picture of that woman.

Schalmik turned the book to the first double page. It contained eight pictures, four per page, all black and white. All were taken outdoors, and the weather in each was sunny. They showed a girl, from the age of about eleven to her late teens.

'The next photo is of your mother,' Schalmik explained. 'Any pictures taken in wartime were lost. Perhaps there were none. Your grandfather was busy, and chemicals for film processing were in short supply. See her hair.'

It changed in length, and gained and lost its curls.

'I asked Gran about the colour of mother's hair,' Rosa said. 'It was not really blonde, she said. Definitely not ginger. Simply fair.'

Rosa was looking at the last picture in the group as she spoke. This was still her mother. Thin straps of a close-fitting floral top revealed her shoulders. Her legs were pale beneath thigh-length shorts. Her head was tilted back and she was laughing. Her hair was black.

'The man on the right?' Rosa focused. The man also wore shorts, but was bare-chested. It was a beach scene, they were on sand, and waves crested the ocean behind them. His hair was dark too, tapered at the neck and oiled back from his forehead. His nose arched down from his brows, his cheekbones were high, his lips full. He was laughing, caught in profile, as he reached an ice cream cone toward the woman's mouth.

'That's your father.'

Rosa's eyes widened.

'There's no photo of him. Gran said. He's called Steve.'

'Stefan. Yes.'

'Steve Little.'

'That's the father's name on your birth certificate?'

'That section's a blank. He died before I was born. In a car crash.'

'You've visited his grave? Seen the name there?'

'His name's on my mother's grave. Uwe Little it says. Wife of Steve Little.'

'Ha!' The sound was a real half-laugh this time. 'Katja's truth. Etched in stone.'

'Gravestones don't lie. Gran wouldn't have allowed that.'

'What was your grandmother's maiden name?' he asked.

He watched her think. Klein. Klein in German translates to Little in English. He saw the connections begin to take fire in her head.

'Stefan and your mother Uwe met on the boat from Hamburg to Sydney,' he continued. 'It was a long crossing, almost six weeks. The North Sea was rough, and the storms off the coast of France, by the Bay of Biscay, saw many of the adults keep to their bunks. For years they had kept their children alive through the hell of postwar Germany. Now they gave in for a while. They were on a boat, and they had a destination. They let the children play. Off the coast of Africa the seas grew calm. The adults emerged. They told Stefan a story about his little girlfriend. He ran up to her and spat in her eye.'

Rosa breathed in sharply.

'The boat was full of DPs. Displaced persons. Jews were displaced. Germans from the East, fleeing Russian troops, were displaced. Katja and Uwe Birchendorf were displaced too. Katja's husband, of course, was dead. Her parents too. Her brother was killed in the war and she felt they never recovered from his death. Those were desperate years. Your mother was seven when they started out on their refugee journey, and soon so starved and weak that Katja had to fold her in her arms and carry her. Their journey through Germany looped them back to a DP camp at Rosenheim, near Munich. Rosenheim was once a subcamp of Dachau. There's irony for you.

'Here we were, in a time of peace, and the camps were still filled with people waiting for countries to take them.

It was a time of survival. News came that Australia would accept another boatload. Authorities were shy of the niceties of ethnic discrimination. Camp guards and camp survivors all entered the same boat. Katja's belongings fitted into one small suitcase. The name Birchendorf was big on its label. The Schleemans saw it.'

'The Schleemans?'

'Stefan's parents. Your grandparents. They told him his little girlfriend was a Birchendorf. They spelled out exactly what that meant. Spitting in her eye was Stefan's own idea.'

'Who told you all this?'

'Your gran.'

'In a letter? Steve Little's ashes were dug into the rose garden of the local park. Roses were his favourite flowers. That's where my name comes from.'

'Your mother once had a doll called Rosa,' Schalmik told her. What trivia filled his mind! 'Stefan Schleeman emigrated to Israel. He may well still be alive. I'm sure he's not been cremated. We Jews are not cremated. At least by our own kind.'

'My father's dead.'

'You see that picture, Rosa?' Schalmik reached his forefinger to point at the couple on the beach. 'That's something to believe in. Two people at play. In love.'

'Her hair's black.'

'She dyed it. She turned up at a Torah study group at the Great Synagogue in Sydney. She saw your father there and recognized him.'

'She pretended to be Jewish?'

'A photo of your grandfather makes you sick. That same man was your mother's daddy. She sat on his shoulders and swung in his arms. They hanged him for ferrying Jews to their deaths. How does a teenager live with that?'

'That man was my grandfather. I was a teenager. I know what it's like to live with that.'

'It's more complex for you than you know, Rosa. Your grandfather was a Nazi and your father is a Jew. Your grandmother could never accept that fact. You were brought up not to know it.'

'So these are more of those lies of yours? Lies born of love?'

Rosa studied the picture a while longer, and then closed the book.

'I'm supposed to be your biographer,' she said. 'Instead, you present me with this story of my life. My nothing life.'

'It's not a nothing life.'

'I don't know what it is, to be honest. You've thrown it all up in the air. You've not told me everything, I know that much. You're holding something back. This isn't just about me. You're stuck inside this mess of a story somehow. It's about us.'

Rosa stared at him. It was a look that dared him to make the next move.

He stood up.

'I've one more photo to show you,' he said.

From between books on a bookcase Schalmik slid out a laminated photo. In black and white, the scene was of a stage set. Painted flats showed a town of medieval buildings. Lines of children filled the narrow stage. He handed it to Rosa.

'What do you think?' Schalmik stood close and pointed to a small girl toward one end of the front row. She was the smallest of those there, about four or five years old. She had bare legs, but from the quality of the photograph it was not clear whether she was wearing shorts like the boys or a skirt like the larger girls. The children's feet were hidden. Their faces were blank ovals, their eyes, noses and mouths lost in the poor focus. 'Does she look like me?'

She looks like almost anybody, Rosa thought. What did he want her to say?

'I had a niece. Her name was Greta,' he said. 'She was the same age as your mother. This picture was taken in the winter of 1943. Your mother was just turning five years old. So was Greta. I know that Greta sang in a children's opera, in the camp, in Theresienstadt. This is about the height she would have been then.'

He bent closer. It was no use. He had studied the image with a magnifying glass in bright sunlight. He had even rooted out a newsreel from when the investigating committee of the International Red Cross visited the camp. In that brief snatch of movie, the girl had stood as still as in this photographic image, her hands hanging by her side. The scene was captured onto eight-millimetre film in poor lighting. Nothing was conclusive.

'I think it's Greta,' Schalmik said.

'Tell me about Greta,' Rosa said, and turned on her recorder.

And so he did. He sat down, the photo on the table between them. He told of the evening when his sister Erna announced the pregnancy, and his brother-in-law hid while Otto emerged from a wardrobe. They heard of the birth of Greta and the death of Hugo when father and son were in Buchenwald. Greta was kept at home for years, just her and her mother and grandmother, for fear of what might happen to a little girl with a yellow star. At Terezín she made friends and sang Brahms's lullaby while her mother played the violin. She sang in the children's opera. At Auschwitz-Birkenau she called out for her mother and was struck on the head by the stock of a gun. He can imagine them there, his mother, his sister and his niece. And then his whole family was wiped out.

'I'm so sorry,' Rosa said, and stroked the back of his hand for a moment.

He let her, and then he drew his hand away and picked up the photo.

'They ask me to write for children but I tell them that's all I do.' Schalmik nodded down at the photograph of children ranged along a stage in Terezín. 'I write for these children. This photo was taken in 1943. It's now 1994. I keep writing for them. They keep growing up.'

He carried the laminated photo away and slotted it back between the books on his library shelf.

Schalmik came back to the table. He opened the album back on the page where Dieter Birchendorf smiled up from beside his wife and baby.

'You're the image of your grandmother. But you and your grandfather, you both share that little bob at the end of the nose.'

Rosa leaned closer to study it. 'I don't see it,' she said.

'That's an old photo. I remember it from life.'

'You remember that clearly?'

'Your grandfather's was a life or death face for me, Rosa. The man's moods would determine whether I lived or I died. I watched his face closely for signs.'

'A face like that belongs in nightmares. I'd work hard to forget it.'

'That photo arrived in my pigeonhole at the college in Toronto, in an envelope with no note. Your grandmother's letter came later. Look at her. She's so beautiful.'

He looked at the picture. In those moments Katja had been with him she had not smiled, and even so she had amazed him. She touched him. She knelt so he could see the roundness of her belly, the promise of life.

'You see that baby? That baby was in her womb. She pressed it against my cello as I played Bach. I remembered your grandmother's eyes. I don't remember my mother's eyes, but I remember hers. Her letter asked me to come and speak at the trial.'

'You went for my grandmother?'

'I did think I might see her there.'

'But you didn't see her.'

'Wives were kept away from the trials. News of your grandfather's hanging reached her by letter.'

'You think I believe that? A Jew travels back to Dachau to speak in defence of the Nazi who shipped his family to their deaths, because he's got the hots for the Nazi's wife?'

'You think it's unlikely?'

'It doesn't even make sense. If you want a man's wife, then you want the husband dead.'

'My testimony was never going to keep him alive. You don't put Nazis on trial in order to set men free. He'd be dead, your grandmother would be grateful.'

'She'd be grateful? To you? A Jew?' Rosa laughed.

Schalmik stared at her, and then shrugged.

'Gran hated Jews,' Rosa continued. 'She knew it was unacceptable. But I felt her shudder whenever the subject was brought up.'

'She was working on it,' Schalmik said. 'Your father was a Jew. She couldn't admit it, but she knew it. And she loved you.'

'She told you this?'

'You know the kind of thing. "Sometimes I see that Jewish glint in Rosa's eye, but I still love her." That sort of thing. I tore up some of your grandmother's letters the moment I read them. They enraged me. She wouldn't see it as Jew-baiting, but it was there.'

'And you wrote back to her. I just don't understand you. I don't understand you at all. You spoke in a Nazi's defence. You kept up a correspondence with his Nazi widow.'

'And this is so bad, Rosa? You want everything to be simple? Do you know what I felt when I pulled this photo out of its envelope?'

She stared at him, needing the answer.

'Hatred. I saw that little slip of a baby, and I hated her. It should have been her gassed to death, not my Greta. It should have been her baby body burned at Auschwitz. Her parents wouldn't be smiling then.'

He reached forward and closed the album. The photo still hurt.

'Why did I go back to Dachau? I don't know, Rosa. Sometimes we don't make the most considered of choices; we simply act. I saw a baby and I wanted her dead. I wanted her parents dead. Imagine that, Rosa. I thought I was one of the good people, then one tear of an envelope, one family snapshot, and I see I'm nothing of the sort. I'm full of murder. You can't just sit still and accept that about yourself. You have to do something.'

'We all get thoughts like that. You let them go. That's all you have to do.'

'Your mother was months old in that photo, Rosa. I looked at her, dangling in her mother's arms, and I was revolted. I saw a Nazi baby. How crazy is that? You don't judge babies. There's no such thing as a Nazi baby. A baby's a baby. And a baby needs a family. There, look.' He pointed at the photo. 'A baby with a family. Why should I judge it good or bad? It's a family. They asked me to come to Germany and speak on their behalf. I could do something, or I could do nothing. Look what happened to this baby, Rosa. Her father was hanged. The little girl grew up in guilt and died in shame.'

He looked at Rosa, tilted his head a little to the side.

'You've got your grandfather's nose, Rosa. But it's not a Nazi nose. It's your nose. It's sweet.'

One by one, in chronological order, Rosa fitted the bundles of letters back into their cardboard box.

'I'll take these away with me, if I may,' she said.

'I thought you could read them here.' Schalmik surprised himself. His salad pickings from the garden were selected as lunch for one. Now he was angling to keep the girl close. 'We'll clear this table for you, and eat out on the balcony.'

'I must be going, I'm afraid.'

'Going?'

'I have to be in LA.'

'That can wait. Now you've triggered my memories let's be done with it. Those letters won't make sense on their own. Your grandmother had a good musical training. She quizzed me on my work. Without her questions, my responses will seem random. You'll need to ask me questions.'

'I'll note down what I don't understand.'

'They're just letters. They're not written for you to understand or not understand. I think I'll burn them after all. Words are sounds. Like gasps and cries. We try them out. They belong in a moment and fade away.'

The light on Rosa's recorder still flared red. Schalmik stabbed at the off button.

'If you won't read the letters now, I'll simply burn them.'

'So you want me to stay? You don't want me to go? Is that what you're saying?'

'We're talking about the letters.'

'Of course we are.' Rosa folded the flaps of the box to close the lid. 'You should come with me. You and Mango. I'm staying with a friend who's house-sitting in LA. It's a lovely house she tells me, on 17th Street in Santa Monica. White and fancy, she says, in the style of a Spanish hacienda. The front garden is xeriscaped and there's a proper garden out the back with a lawn and an avocado tree. Mango will love it. I'm sure the area is reamed with pedigree dogs. We can take her round the streets and she can catch all their smells. Would you like that Mango?'

Mango loved to hear her name spoken. She wagged her tail.

'I've got my work,' Schalmik said.

'Me too. Tomorrow I've got an interview with John Adams. Do you know his work?'

'He's made the most of his talent. The man's done well for himself.'

'And after that I've a day planned with Lou Harrison. He and his partner have this incredible house right on the edge of Joshua Tree National Park. The *Sunday Times* has commissioned a full feature. The photographer's already been out. Do you know Lou's music?'

'It's very pleasant.'

'I'm sure the two of you would get on. It would be fun. When did you last leave here and have some fun?'

'Mango and I go for walks in the forest.'

'Wow. Real fun. You must come across slugs and everything.'

'We do in fact. Banana slugs. Very fat and long and a shiny yellow.'

'It beats me why you should ever leave here at all.' Rosa stood and picked up the box. 'You're welcome to come. Fact is, I've got to go to LA with or without you and these letters are coming with me. You want them burned, you should have got on with it and not bothered with your swim. I'm going to lock them in the car so they're safe.'

She carried the box out of the house. Mango trotted out too.

'Well,' Schalmik said.

The word came out like a sigh, for it sounded and faded and he did not know what it meant.

31
Auf Wiedersehen

A hummingbird buzzed past Rosa and Schalmik as they stood on the decking and faced the point. The bird refuelled itself from the flowers of a fuchsia but they did not watch. They simply stared forward.

'You have a beautiful place,' Rosa said. 'Thanks for having me here.'

'Your visit's changed me.' It was true, but Schalmik only recognized the fact as his words came out. 'Startled me perhaps. Here is lovely, you're right, but I might be ready to face the world again. I could start with a small West Coast tour, in some of the more intimate concert halls. Play the Bach Suites. Rent an Airstream and take Mango along with me. See how it goes.'

'Ha!'

'What I said was funny?'

'The image of you and your dog in an Airstream just struck me as comical. Don't mind me. I inherited an offbeat sense of humour. I was out by the sea with Gran once. She suddenly started laughing. It was a honk of a laugh, and she swallowed it back but it carried on as heaves in her chest before she could go still again. I asked what it was. She pointed to a group of green and red parrots that were above the path in a tree, swinging with their claws and beaks through the branches. "It was suddenly so funny," she said, "to find myself living in the same land as parrots." Now I'm staring out at the Pacific Ocean, and that's how I feel. Out of place, but it's wild and beautiful and perfect.'

It was his chance. He could say something. 'Come back soon,' he could say. 'There's no need to rush off.'

Such words floated around his head but he didn't voice them.

Rosa had been following her own thoughts. 'I've decided to believe your story about my father. Emotionally it makes no sense, I'll have to work on that. Intellectually, it solves a puzzle. All of my schooling, my travel to Vienna, my studies in the Academy, even the PhD in London, Gran said the funds came from my father's life insurance policy. It seemed way too generous, but I just accepted the story. Now you tell me there was no car crash and no death. No such father. So there was no insurance. That leaves a question. Where did the money come from? I doubt it was a benevolent fund for Nazi offspring.'

He let the silence hang.

'It *was* you, wasn't it?'

'Not directly. I pay into a trust. Just in a small way, ten percent of my earnings. The Greta Trust, in honour of my niece.'

'Does it pay for others?'

'It paid for your mother. She didn't need much, but then I didn't earn much in those days.'

'And otherwise?'

'It's a small fund. It pays scholarships for students who attend the Darmstadt International Music Festival.'

'My grandmother's family came from Darmstadt.'

'I believe they did. I see it as coincidental. The festival seeks to rebuild Germany through an appreciation of new music.'

'So besides a few scholarships to attend a festival, the main single beneficiaries of the Greta Trust, named for a girl gassed at Auschwitz, are the daughter and granddaughter of a Nazi war criminal executed for his atrocities. That's pretty ironic.'

'I hate that others live when Greta did not. We pass on hate. It brings more wars. The Greta Fund sent money where I wanted to send hate. It was just a little attempt to break the cycle.'

'When you got the news about my mother, that she died, how did you feel?'

'I wept, Rosa. I wept that a mother carried a little girl out of a war, and yet still that girl was crushed. And I sent you a teddy bear.'

'Ah,' she said. 'Well, thank you.'

She let him take hold of her bag and carry it out to the car. He waited by the trunk but she opened the passenger door instead.

'There's always something in my bag I need along the way,' she said. 'I'll stow it on the floor.'

And so he set the bag in place and she stood by the open door and was almost ready.

'I've left the LA address and phone number by the phone,' she said. 'Thank you for having me here. And for agreeing to the book. It means everything.'

'We'll see,' he said. 'Anyway, it's good to come to know you. You're quite something.'

Rosa smiled, and crouched down to the dog.

'And you're quite something too, Mango,' she said, and rubbed the dog hard behind its ears.

'She's smitten,' Schalmik said.

Rosa stood up, because there's only so much you can do with a dog. She took hold of the car door ready to slam it shut. A sudden surge made her pull back. In one bound Mango was up from the driveway and installed on the passenger seat.

'There's my girl,' Schalmik said, and laughed. 'My apologies. Get down, Mango.'

Mango turned and looked at him. Her black mouth curved up in a smile.

'You should learn from your dog. It's time for you both to get out more.' Rosa tugged at Mango's collar till the beast gave in and jumped to the ground. 'I'm sorry I laughed about the Airstream idea. It's a good one. You should get in touch with your agent. She'll be excited. And let me know the schedule. I'd like to come.'

'Oh it's just a fancy.' The moment Rosa laughed at him the idea had shrivelled. 'What shall we do about your book?'

'Our book you mean. You're happy to go ahead? I promised Alex a call after we'd met. He'll be thrilled. And we won't let your touring idea go. A mixed programme maybe, Bach alongside your new solo work. You can record both. That'll please Alex. The Airstream tour would make a great Sunday feature. I can write the pitch. They'll send out a photographer. We'll make Mango into a cover girl yet.'

Mango wagged her tail at the sound of her name.

'You'll come back?' Schalmik asked.

Rosa smiled, and kissed him on both cheeks. Air cooled the moist patches her lips left behind. Schalmik raised a hand and waved as her car disappeared up the drive.

Schalmik wondered about strolling the drive up to the road and replacing and padlocking the chain that usually blocked it, but couldn't be bothered. He walked into his house and down to the music room where he grabbed the Stradivarius by its neck and swung it off its stand. He paid it too much respect. Time for it to come out in the daylight and earn its keep.

Man, cello and dog marched to the end of the point. So he would do his tour, he now knew. He couldn't bear Rosa's biography to exist without it. Otherwise here's Schalmik for you, all nicely bound up in a dustjacket, they would say. He'll be no trouble. Ah yes, they'll agree. He's a bit of a recluse in the wilds somewhere but he does his daily stretches. On a good day he can put on his socks without sitting down. He'll reminisce for you if you're lucky, but there's no need to bother him. Just buy the book. You'll find it's all in the book.

Well he'll show them. The Bach Suites will take practice, but then everything good takes practice.

He reached the rock at the end of the point and sat and faced the ocean. Back straight, like his mother insisted. He spread his left hand and thought of Herbert Zipper. Funny that, he hadn't thought of the man in years.

Yes, Zipper had told him back in Dachau, he too had been at the Feuermann 1931 homecoming recital in Vienna. What fireworks the man produced that night. Here's the difference though. Feuermann wanted to be Heifetz. Pablo Casals only wanted to be himself. Did Otto know Casals' fingering? And Zipper took hold of young Otto's thumb and lifted it from the neck of their makeshift cello. He settled it on the string in first position, so Otto's little finger had a longer reach. From there Zipper showed the young man what Casals' technique could have him do. Rather than simply sliding up and down the single string, Otto could play the melody across all four.

He should tell Rosa that story. Audiences settle down to listen to the great Otto Schalmik, but there's no such beast. He's the sum of lots of input from lots of people, plus thousands of hours of practice that helped him put it all together.

Time to practise now.

He raised his bow. Boy, his right arm hurt. It must have been the strokes of that crazy front crawl out there in the ocean. Who was that tutor who showed him the Russian bowing technique – play with the whole arm, not just the elbow? That was important. That's what added to the big Schalmik sound.

Here goes. Let's make the sound truly big. Big enough to fill an ocean.

Acknowledgments

I'd like to give thanks to books and their writers; to places and those who care for them; and to some people.

First to books, and rather than offering up a whole library I'll mention a few that particularly informed the narrative. First comes Paul Cummins' biography of Herbert Zipper, *Dachau Song*. Zipper's was an exemplary life that guided this book from Vienna to Buchenwald, and Zipper himself alongside Maximilian and Ernst Hohenberg stepped from its pages.

For Terezín: Joža Karas's *Music in Terezín 1941–1945*; Coco Schumann's *The Ghetto Swinger*; Ruth Kluger's memoir *Landscapes of Memory* for both her childhood memories of the ghetto, and of the Theresienstadt Family Camp at Auschwitz-Birkenau.

For Vienna, Brigitte Schludermann shared family memories of the city in that period. Andrzej Panufnik's *Composing Myself* helped me hear the city and visit the Academy.

On Canada and Jewish immigration: Abella Irving and Harold Troper's *None is Too Many*.

Other historical figures from Terezín who entered the novel are Honza Treichlinger (who played the character Brundibár), Hans Krása, Rudolf Freudenfeld and Karel Berman. Honza, an orphan, was short and so suited his starring role in the children's opera. He didn't get to grow. At Auschwitz, the selection process to decide if you were man enough to work asked you to reach up and touch a taut length of string. Honza's fingertips stretched out but couldn't reach. He was sent to the gas chamber with the other children.

Bernie Glassman and his Zen Peacemakers Organization enabled my visit to Auschwitz. Visits to Dachau and Terezín were invaluable. In Sydney, my thanks to the staff of the Opera House and the Jewish Museum.

Barbara Cherish's memoir *The Auschwitz Commandant* alerted me to the quandary of considering any child 'a Nazi child'.

Conversations with Helen Bamber, in which she recalled her work in Belsen after its liberation, her role in bearing witness to the stories of survivors, and her impressions of travelling through the postwar Germany of the 1940s, quietly taught me a lot.

In terms of music, Simon Broughton's production at the Wigmore Hall of a weekend of music from Theresienstadt, and his conversations with survivors, let me hear and feel something of what was ripped out of Czech music.

The cellist Rebecca Herman and I lived on the same street but we had never met. I knocked on her door, she invited me in, and played Bach while I held on to the body of her cello.

At a masterclass, Natalie Clein's direction to students filtered back to help Otto find his way with the instrument. Jean-Guihen Queyras helped me with answers about how a cellist commits a work to memory. Queyras's recording of the Bach Suites became my touchstone, latterly joined by David Watkin's baroque performances. For me, Otto in fact played like neither. I hear him more in the temperamental fire of Daniil Shafran's performances.

Marion Hunt gave us a summer in Big Sur in 1994, and I borrowed her home and dog for Schalmik.

And readers: Martin Randall, Michael Johnstone, Peter Thornton, James Booth, Sarah Walton and Chris Rogers all gave crucial feedback. Chris Westoby and George Biggs wielded keen editorial pens and Kate Johnson delivered an earlier version into the world. James Thornton nurtured the book and me through decades of its continuing evolution.

'Berlin is brilliantly seen through the hero's eyes.'
THE SCOTSMAN

ON BENDED KNEES

MARTIN GOODMAN

If you've enjoyed *The Cellist of Dachau*, please try Martin Goodman's *On Bended Knees*.

1966, and young Tomas's England is still troubled by WW2: adults are haunted by memories of war, and buildings remain in ruins.

1975. Tomas heads to Berlin to stay with his formidable old uncle. Germany is divided with Berlin surrounded by a wall. The uncle carries scars of his Nazi past. What might we inherit from the wars of our elders, and how might we move on?

"The novel's blunt, no-frills economy is part of its charm. Goodman writes with flare and panache, and the narrative fizzes along. Goodman's novel soars." – *The Times*

"A perceptive, moving novel. Martin Goodman takes fierce delight in cutting through the easy clichés about the 'new' Europe." – Christopher Hope

"This excellent first novel's central character is so completely realised he could have walked out of one of those enigmatic Bruce Chatwin pieces about old mysterious European types." – *Time Out*

"Heralds a new dawn for British writing." – *Daily Post*

Shortlisted for the Whitbread First Novel Award – in a special 30th anniversary edition.

ISBN: 9781909954502

Printed in the USA
CPSIA information can be obtained
at www.ICGtesting.com
JSHW011831220923
49011JS00004B/5